Silken Bonds
ZARA DEVEREUX

D1439866

Ess

3013020404533 9

Silken Bonds

ZARA DEVEREUX

sphere

SPHERE

First published in Great Britain in 1998 by X Libris
Reissued in 2012 by Sphere

Copyright © 1998 by Zara Devereux

The moral right of the author has been asserted.

*All characters and events in this publication, other than those
clearly in the public domain, are fictitious and any resemblance
to real persons, living or dead, is purely coincidental.*

All rights reserved.
No part of this publication may be reproduced, stored in a
retrieval system, or transmitted, in any form or by any means, without
the prior permission in writing of the publisher, nor be otherwise circulated
in any form of binding or cover other than that in which it is published
and without a similar condition including this condition
being imposed on the subsequent purchaser.

A CIP catalogue record for this book
is available from the British Library.

ISBN 978-0-7515-5093-1

Typeset in Sabon by M Rules
Printed and bound in Great Britain by
Clays Ltd, St Ives plc

Papers used by Sphere are from well-managed forests
and other responsible sources.

MIX
Paper from
responsible sources
FSC
www.fsc.org   FSC® C104740

Sphere
An imprint of
Little, Brown Book Group
100 Victoria Embankment
London EC4Y 0DY

An Hachette UK Company
www.hachette.co.uk

www.littlebrown.co.uk

Silken Bonds

Bonds

ZARA DEVEREUX

Chapter One

'You will be there, won't you, darling? In person. Don't send one of your half-baked aides, there's a love.' Tag Padra's customary dulcet tones had a bitchy edge.

Tamzin Lawrence shifted the phone to a more comfortable position, propped between her cheek and raised shoulder, as she skimmed through a batch of photographs while listening to him.

'When is it?' she asked, playing for time, and was rewarded by an exasperated snort.

'You know damn' fine when it is. On Saturday, and I'm praying it doesn't snow. Don't want anything to stop the punters turning up.'

'Odd time for a fashion show, isn't it? I didn't think

you'd have another so soon.' Frowning slightly, she fumbled for a Biro and flipped open her day planner. A note of the event was already entered.

'It's for charity. You know, spirit of goodwill and all that? The proceeds go to the RSPCC.' He sounded agitated, touchy as a primadonna when it came to his work. 'I'm putting it on in the Knightsbridge showroom. Twenty-five quid a ticket. Booze and canapes included. Buckshee to you, of course, sweetie.'

'I don't know if I can make it,' she murmured. 'Publication date is looming. Got to get the next issue to bed before everything closes for Christmas. We're short-staffed, Kate's gone down with flu and Amanda's pregnant.'

'Done it at last, has she?' trilled Tag. 'Thank God for IVF. That cost her and Sam a packet, I know.'

She smiled, imagining him flicking back his high-lighted blond quiff, but ever so carefully so as not to disturb the Oribe cut, and said, gently reproving, 'A small price to pay for a child, if that's what you're into. Something that will never bother you.'

'Chance would be a fine thing! My designs are my babies. You *must* make it to the show. I insist. Oh, come on, Tamzin! You know how important this is to me.

Charity it may be but it's also prime publicity. You promised to do a feature in *Chimera*. I've been working my rocks off, and I haven't been well – and Ben's left me – the bastard!'

'Again?' She never took his tiffs with his lover seriously. They were always falling out and making up.

'Again. It's final this time. Over. *Finito, kaput*. Your poor old queen's on his own.'

He sounded on the verge of tears, but Tamzin was used to his histrionics. A good friend, but demanding, needing someone to listen to his catalogue of woes. Man trouble – model trouble – difficulties with manufacturers, with his work force, with the magazines. Would *Vogue* take heed of his latest creations? Would they appear in *Elle?*

He was terrifyingly talented. At that moment Tamzin was wearing one of his little numbers, a skirt no deeper than a lampshade, made of finely pleated silver lurex that displayed her slim waist, flat stomach and rounded hips to perfection.

She wondered what Tim would make of it. He'd probably get horny as hell, particularly if she wore it with stockings, a suspender belt and split-crotch knickers, but would object to her going out in public in such a skimpy thing. His possessive attitude was beginning to jar. Tamzin was not used to being told what to wear, where to go, and who to go with. She had been independent for too long, ever since her break-up with Martin. She had kept the ring but dispensed with the fiancé.

She eased her thighs against the brown leather of the executive chair that swivelled at a touch, then crossed her long legs in their black tights and low-heeled pumps. She needed no extra inches to add to her height. Tag was always urging her to prowl the catwalk at one of his spectaculars.

Now she continued to thumb through the photos spread across the rosewood surface of the desk, saying 'yes' or 'no' or 'Cottaging, was he? No!' at suitable pauses in Tag's monologue.

The extension bleeped and, 'Sorry, Tag, I've another call,' she said, thankful for the reprieve. 'I'll call you later. Bye.'

'Tim here.' A confident, masculine voice vibrated against her eardrum from the other receiver. 'I've booked a table at Momo's. Pick you up around eight. OK?'

'Fine,' she answered, riddled with guilt as she had forgotten about their date.

'See you at your place,' he said, then paused and added, 'Are you all right, darling?'

'Sure. Shouldn't I be?'

'You sound a bit off. Not starting a cold or anything? I say, I didn't exhaust you last night, did I?'

He sounded smug and had obviously come to the boringly masculine conclusion that rollicking attentions in the sack could prove too much for the little woman. Tamzin felt a yawn threatening to crack her jaw.

Stifling it, she replied a touch caustically, 'There are a few things needing sorting here pre-holiday, that's all.'

'Won't keep you then. Love you.'

'Goodbye, Tim.'

A faintly accusatory silence greeted this, but Tamzin hurriedly replaced the phone in its cradle. I can't lie and tell him I love him when I'm not sure that I do, she thought, and mourned because the timbre of his voice no longer shot straight to her core, making her clitoris throb and setting her juices flowing. This meal tonight was his idea. He wanted to celebrate the six months they had been going out together.

What a silly phrase that is. We've stayed in more than gone out – in bed most of the time. So why this discontented itch? she reflected. Is it because he's not very adventurous, likes straightforward sex with little fore-play? A quick grope at my breasts, a perfunctory touch on my clitoris and then it's in with his penis and that's that. But it was the same with other men; none have ful-filled my fantasies.

She rose and moved over to the wide window of her magnificently appointed office. It was a splendid venue for receiving clients. On the second floor of a Regency house in the heart of London's West End, it gave an uninterrupted view of the frozen bushes and bare, skele-tal trees of a grassy square surrounded by equally fine examples of architecture. Once this had been fenced in for the use of residents only. The iron railings had been taken down to aid the war-effort in 1940 and never been replaced. Now anyone could go there.

A couple of beggars huddled on one of the benches, supping cans of lager. A weary shopper rested for a moment, an assortment of carrier-bags at her feet, a festive flash of tinsel glittering in the grey light. Pigeons, in no way deterred by the biting cold, walked up to her on their turned-in toes, scrounging a few crumbs from the sandwich she had unwrapped from clingfilm.

What's wrong with me? Tamzin brooded as she continued to observe the wintry scene. Masturbation provides me with greater satisfaction than intercourse. Am I weird or perverted?

I tire of boyfriends so quickly. It's probably the side-effects of disillusion. Once upon a time I thought men were gods to be worshipped. I turned them into heroes and was woefully disappointed when I found my idols had feet of clay – or rather were just ordinary mortals after all.

Father deprivation, my shrink says, and it's true that my mother didn't let me have much to do with him after the divorce. They are both dead now and I should feel liberated, but I don't. Neither will I till I've laid the ghosts, or so I'm told.

I idolise men no longer. Time and experience have torn off the rose-coloured glasses. Jesus, listen to me! I'm talking like a cynical woman of sixty instead of someone who has just celebrated her thirtieth birthday. I'm a Libran, an autumn creature from the October country, ruled by Venus, the goddess of love – an emotion that has escaped me so far.

She returned to her desk, perched herself on the edge, feeling the coolness of polished veneer beneath her thighs, alert to the way both tights and silky knickers pressed against her crotch. A stab of heat penetrated her loins. Her clitoris stirred, needing to be played with, stroked and petted.

She slipped a hand under her skirt, fingers meeting the smooth transparency of her tights. They lingered on her mons while she wondered if she might rub herself through her underwear. She had brought herself off like this before, here in the office when there was no one about, the friction of fifteen denier and satin delicious on her labia and sensitive bud.

This sudden wave of lust shocked her, her hidden lips swelling in arousal, opening like the petals of some exotic jungle orchid. Normally she was able to control herself, but there was a restlessness within her today. A need for change, for experimental sex that carried with it no responsibility, no promises of happy-ever-after – no attempt to turn her into some-one's wife.

It had been a long hard haul getting to her present position as editor of a quality magazine, and nothing would make her relinquish that. A struggle against prejudice when she had had to prove herself equal to men every inch of the way. Even at college she had met with opposition while working on the Students' Union quarterly journal. She had always put business before pleasure, to the detriment of several failed relationships that had never really got off the starting blocks.

Men! she thought again, almost viciously.

As if conjured by her thoughts, one of that alien breed in the strikingly handsome form of her co-editor, Mike Bishop, strode through the door without knocking.

'Can I have a word?' he drawled, not asking, demanding, exuding confidence.

'Where's Diane? Didn't she tell you I'm busy?' Tamzin objected to the way in which he assumed he could interrupt her whenever he chose. Supposing she had been pleasuring herself? He would have caught her at it: excitement speared her at the thought.

'She wasn't in – not there to guard the sanctum.' He gave her a lopsided grin, the one that reduced the office-girls to jelly.

Tamzin felt a spasm of irritation, her dislike of his policies regarding *Chimera* complicated by the rampant desire he roused in her. Mike breathed out sex through his pores. Even now she could feel moisture dampening the tender opening of her sex, while her nipples chafed almost painfully against the expensive black jersey T-shirt that fitted without a wrinkle. The adrenalin rush of conflict, the challenge he presented acted like an aphro-disiac that inflamed her unbearably.

For months they had been fencing round one another. Enforced colleagues yet instant enemies, with opposing ideas regarding the magazine. Tamzin wanted a feminist angle; Mike preferred a softer approach. They clashed at every meeting, clashed and lusted and never confessed their need.

'I like this time of the year,' he vouchsafed, with a lift of his brows, his gaze shifting from her face to her breasts. 'Routine is relaxed. I expect the trusty Di's off doing a spot of Christmas shopping. It's lunchtime, after all.'

'What d'you want, Mike?' Tamzin managed to convey an aloof coolness, though she could feel her nipples puckering under his regard, becoming little crests of heat.

She motioned him to a chair on the opposite side of the desk to hers, the better to put space between them. The squashy leather enfolded her bottom as she sank into it, tights whispering as her legs touched, the seam rubbing over her secret parts.

'You've seen the photos of Yasmin?' There was some-thing vulpine about his eyes – brownish-gold, bright and alert.

Rumour had it that he could guess what one was thinking. Can you guess what's in my thoughts right now? she addressed his mind silently, projecting hard. You want to fuck me? In your wildest dreams, baby!

'I have seen them,' she answered levelly, pressing her thighs together surreptitiously under the desk.

'And?' he said, and smiled knowingly.

She could feel a flush mounting to her cheeks, a double conversation taking place, layer upon layer, as it always did when they were within spitting distance of one another. Since the day they met there had been this furtive, assessing sort of awareness flowing like a tide from one to the other.

'She's stunning.'

'I agree, but—'

Tamzin bit her lip. There was always a 'but' when Mike got involved. Concentrate, she told herself firmly. She tried another tack. 'Don't you think she's gorgeous? We've another Naomi Campbell here, but even younger, taller, more devastating.'

'She's a touch gauche.' He brought this out slowly, watching her reaction, his member stirring under his silk boxer shorts as he speculated on whether she was anything like as cool as she appeared.

In his experience such icy control usually covered a seething cauldron of passion. For ages now this notion had teased and tantalised him. He had tapped the grapevine, but no scandal had been thrown up.

Miss Lawrence was frighteningly efficient and dedicated, had a boyfriend, one Tim Herts, an award-winning architect, but lived a discreet lifestyle. No wild parties, no means of contacting her without the inestimable Tim hanging around. It was galling but intriguing. More than the actual conquest, Mike relished the chase.

They had never before been alone like this. Board-room meetings, encounters with photographers and printers, secretaries, aides, all the necessary adjuncts to running a successful enterprise had prevented intimacy. This solitude was indeed a bonus. He intended to enjoy it to the full, and slumped low on his spine, legs crossed and casually outstretched, hiding his arousal.

Tamzin had to hand it to him; he knew the fashion trade inside out. She recognised the stamp of Jean Paul Gaultier in the pin-stripe suit draping his elegant body with its lean hips and long legs. An Oxford graduate, nephew of the magazine proprietor (this had been another black mark against him in her book, smacking of nepotism and favour) he had proved to have an undeniable flair for editorship.

Wickedly handsome – that was undeniable, too, with his dark hair and finely chiselled features. He was looking at her with sherry-gold eyes under those arched brows.

Get a grip! she told herself and leaned forward, placed her elbows on the polished surface, steepled her fingers together and regarded him sternly over them. 'Isn't this precisely the quality which is so appealing? Yasmin is gamine, irresistible, the gawky teenager on the edge of discovering her sensuality and power. She'll be a hit. The TV commercial people will go mad for her.'

'You think so?' His lips quirked in a mocking smile.

'I do.' Tamzin was suddenly determined to get her way. 'She will appear on the March cover of *Chimera*. I've decided which picture to use. The one in which she's barefoot, almost crouching, wearing a gold basque and a black tulle evening coat.'

'I remember it – all legs and tits and big, big eyes. Do you respond to that, too? I did wonder about you.'

Tamzin could feel her hackles rising. Was he hinting that she viewed Yasmin as a man might, longing to touch her breasts and slip a finger inside her, testing her honey-pot, stimulating her clit?

She stirred uneasily, the image a powerful one, then got up from the desk and made an entirely unnecessary adjustment to the expensive and prestigious greeting cards festooning the ornate Adams fireplace. Everyone who was anyone courted *Chimera*. Celebrities couldn't wait to be interviewed and appear in print on those slick, gossipy, glossy pages.

'I'm speaking from a purely professional point of view,' she said over her shoulder, every word dropping from her lips as if freshly chilled.

'There's nothing more to say. I'll instruct Jeff Tate. The photos are his. Quite a coup really. He's not usually interested in fashion. Maybe Yasmin floats his boat. Will you see to the layout and typesetting?'

She heard Mike leave his chair, did not look round, concentrating on the coal-effect gas-fire purring on the wide marble hearth, a picturesque addition to central heating. The fine down rose on her limbs as she sensed his presence, nostrils flaring at the heady aroma of expensive aftershave mingled with other odours – the smell of his hair, the musky scent of his genitals.

They stayed immobile for a second, and then he

touched her averted shoulder, fragile, vulnerable under the tight T-shirt. His finger trailed over the delicate nape of her neck, bared where the honey-blonde hair was swept up and confined in a hairband.

Tamzin shivered with forbidden pleasure. She could not allow herself to enjoy the caress of this infuriating man. But though her mind censored intimate contact, her body, wilful, wanton and rebellious, pressed back against him.

He stood very still, merely moving his fingers on her neck gently, and her hips gyrated slightly, bringing her buttocks into contact with the high ridge of his turgid penis straining against the restrictive material of his trousers.

This evidence of his excitement made her feel gloriously powerful, her legs loosening, the soft moistness of her own anticipation wetting the deep cleft between. She closed her eyes, languorous and needful, ribs arching as one of his hands slid round beneath her armpit, cradling and lifting her left breast. His thumb revolved on the nipple which immediately bunched at his touch. His other hand left her neck and dipped down to lift the hem of the mini-skirt, finding the apex of her thighs, moulding his palm round her pubis.

He moved slowly, ready to stop if she asked. She didn't, hot waves spreading from the small of her back to the inside of her womb, an aching ripple of longing clenching the walls of her vagina, her clitoris throbbing hungrily.

His breath tickled her ear, warm, moist, seductive as he murmured, 'I love that perfume. I've noticed it whenever we've been in the same room. It's beautiful, tasteful, exciting – like you.' The tip of his tongue, as hard and wet as his cock, roamed round the velvety rim, reaching the lobe, tangling with the small gold earring.

What a smooth operator, she thought, while thought was at all possible, but it doesn't seem to matter. Why restrain him? I'm a free agent, despite Tim's assertions otherwise. I'll do whatever pleases me. Mike may think he's using me, but it's the other way round.

She knew he was twice divorced (so what was wrong with him if two women had found him impossible to tolerate?), had a fearsome reputation as a heart-breaker, and she had vowed never to give him the satisfaction of notching her on his bedpost. So why was she allowing this to happen? It was out of character, yet she could not stop, trembling with feverish need.

He took her by the hand and led her to the desk, swung her up as easily as if she was made of thistledown, and sat her on it.

'Mind the photos!' she cried, with prim, almost house-wifely, concern.

He chuckled deep in his throat, gathered them neatly, removed them to a side table and cleared the desk-top completely. It gleamed, bare and shiny, its surface warming rapidly in contact with Tamzin's thighs. She watched him warily, seeing each fluid movement as, his eyes still pinning hers, he unknotted his tie in a leisurely manner.

'Will you do this for me?' he asked in a low, husky tone.

'Do what?' she breathed, hardly able to speak for the drumming of her heart. She looked at the marvellously elegant lines of his body and imagined him naked, presenting her with the revelation of his sky-pointing dick.

'Wait and see.' His voice was like molten fire scalding along her nerves.

'You expect me to agree to something when I don't know what it is?' Her body had loosened, grown hot and lax, stimulated by the maleness so close to her.

'I do.'

His smile deepened as he switched off the lights. The

huge, high-ceilinged room, once a saloon where a political hostess entertained royalty, was plunged into gloom. Only the greyish twilight from the winter-bound square filtered in at the tall, brocade-draped sash windows. The gas-fire flared brighter, tiny bluish flames darting upwards, streaked with crimson, the glow reflected on Mike's face, giving it a demonic cast.

He came towards her, the tie braced between both hands. She started, drew back, a bolt of terror shooting through her. But, still smiling, he fastened it around her eyes. She was plunged into blackness, feeling him knot it loosely at the back of her head. Her breath escaped with a rush.

'I don't think I like this,' she gasped, but her protest lacked conviction.

This is insane, she thought, yet had never felt more alive, wanting something, anything, to assuage the heighted sensual consciousness that had been building since he came in.

'I'll stop any time you say,' he answered and his voice sounded deeper, more caressing. 'Just relax and leave everything to me.'

'Supposing someone comes – Diane – anyone.'

'Don't worry. I've locked the door.'

She waited tensely, centring on smell, hearing, taste and touch, these senses extraordinarily acute. She sat still as a statue. There was no sound except the hiss of the fire and the distant rumble of traffic. Then, with an abruptness that made her jump, she felt his hands on her knees, the firm pressure parting her legs, and was conscious of him bending over her, feeling the body-heat, smelling him.

She stiffened her spine as he breathed over her right breast, the nipple rising at the warm tribute. Then his mouth closed over it, sucking hard through the soft material, the sensation sharpened by the thin, stretchy barrier.

'Ah—' A moan escaped her lips.

Coolness as her breast was suddenly bereft, then scalding heat as he attended to the other one. As he did so, his fingers pinched the abandoned teat, ringed with wet jersey-cloth. Twin excitement, with a third beginning in the precious gem swelling from her unfolding labia.

Darkness, spinning, throbbing in time to the frantic surge of her blood. She squirmed on the desk, a tingle rushing through her epicentre, her secret self engorged and wet but her mouth suddenly dry.

'Hush,' he whispered, and his thumb pressed down on her cushiony lower lip.

Her tongue shot out, licking his strong, muscular fingers, tasting cigar and soap and printer's ink, his cock, too; all the things he had touched that morning, his skin impregnated with the routine actions of his life. She sucked his thumb into her mouth like a rapacious baby. When he finally drew away, his hand was slippery with her saliva.

All the while he continued to cup her breast, and now she felt the caress of his tongue across her lips. They parted almost involuntarily, and his mouth captured hers, a delicious, honeyed mouth, the pressure now hard, now feather-light. His tongue dived between her teeth, stroking her palate, using a circular motion. Her own answered, leaping to meet it, entwining, tasting, the most exquisite hot spirals spinning down to the very centre of her being – the blood-red flower of her root chakra.

She reached out and her fingers brushed the long hard baton of his sex rearing upwards, its head nearly reaching his waistband. She traced it delicately – her fingertips like eyes, almost seeing the shape, the swollen trunk, the rounded glans, registering damp heat.

After rubbing over it with rhythmic strokes, she went lower, pressing into the base, and lifting the hanging fruits of his balls. They were heavy, one slightly larger than the other, and it was possible to feel the ligament dividing them through the woollen fabric of his trousers.

He gasped against her mouth. 'Not yet. You must wait.'

He took her hands in his and placed them firmly on either side of her. Arms tensed, she gripped the desk edge, aware of the glassy smoothness of wood and of him moving in front of her. He took off her shoes, then his hands came up under her skirt, their pressure telling her to lift her bottom a little. He rolled down her tights, easing them over her thighs, the cool air stippling her skin with goose-flesh.

She swung her bare legs like a schoolgirl freed from uniform. His hands caressed her feet, each toe subjected to subtle delights, the instep fondled and massaged, then the ankles. He searched higher for her calf, subjected her knees to his administrations, and the pulse in her depths was becoming stronger. Hardly breathing, she waited for his hands to continue their climb, desperately needing them to trail over her thighs and press against the roaring furnace of her sex.

'Open your legs for me,' he whispered, and his voice had the texture of velvet as it resonated within the darkness of the blindfold, its inflection very nearly bringing her to climax.

Carefully, almost reverently, his hands coasted over her inner thighs, halting when they reached the apex, lightly brushing against the satin triangle veiling her mound. She knew it was wet, could smell the hormonal scent of her arousal, sweet and spicy, like sea-washed shells. He paused and she could hear him inhaling deeply, wildly excited to know that he, too, was savouring her fragrance.

She was burning up, hungry for orgasm, lubricious, wanting, and bit down on a moan as his index finger slid stealthily round the edge of the fabric, lingering on the mat of curling hair that concealed her treasures. His finger rubbed gently up and down, then moved across her mons, finding the succulent avenue. He parted her labia and dipped into the moisture pooling at her vulva. There he paused, and she thought she might scream with frustration.

He felt her wriggle and she heard the laughter in his voice as he said, 'Patience. It will be all the better for anticipation.'

He was on his knees between her legs in an attitude of worship and this fired her to the point of ecstasy.

Without relaxing his adoration of her sex, he continued to roll her nipples between thumb and forefinger, each receiving its share, the electric shocks connecting with her clitoris. He held off from touching it, adding to her tension.

She groaned, lifting her pelvis in an attempt to have him fondle her greedy bud. For answer, his hands left her altogether and she cried out, 'Don't! Please don't stop—'

He reached for the scrap of satin, worked it over her hips and off. She felt hands spreading her thighs wide, fingers separating the wings of her labia, pushing back the miniature foreskin, her thickened node rising from its concealing hood.

Tamzin heard someone whimpering: it was herself.

She felt his hair against her thighs, the downy brush of his beard, then his fleshy, wet tongue licking her sacred centre. Waves of pleasure engulfed her, a fluttering beginning deep in her womb, the overture to orgasm. Her blood turned to lava, boiling along her veins, her inner muscles starting to clench.

His tongue darted like a moth, pointed tip touching the achingly sensitive crown of her clitoris. Ultra-aware of her need, he plunged three fingers deep inside her while he sucked the pulsing bud hard. Wave after wave of exquisite feeling rolled through her, each one lifting her higher. She reached the peak, coming in a hot tide of release, screaming aloud, her muscles clenching round the priapic action of his fingers.

While she was still pulsating, he urged her back till she was lying on the desk. She heard the rasp of his trouser zip. The next moment he had raised her legs, holding them wide apart and resting them on his shoulders. There was chill on her skin as she was completely exposed, every private aperture on view. A moment, no more, and then she felt the impact of his massive tool as it found her slick-wet entrance and rammed into her sheath till buried to the hilt.

His movements were fast, balls tapping against her perineum with each fervent thrust and, completely satisfied, she revelled in his powerful way of taking. Harsh now, hands, teeth, prick, but this was how she wanted it. Her hips ground down on the desk, her legs spread wider, her body slid backwards and forwards till she felt him convulse, then slump across her.

She lay prone beneath him, head to one side, eyes still bound and a myriad of fragmented thoughts drifted through her consciousness. Tim – time to experience guilt later, and she knew she would. Mike – regret because she had given him a hold over her. Maybe not: wasn't she in control of him? It was not significant in that moment of satiety following the best fuck she'd ever had.

He left her, her flesh cold after his heat. He removed her blindfold and light fractured across her sight. She blinked, rubbed her eyes, remarking, 'That's fatal to a girl's mascara.'

What else to say to a man with whom she had just shared a shattering sexual encounter? He smiled, gallantly retrieved her briefs, sniffed them appeciatively, and handed them to her with an ironic bow. He was zipped up, looking suave and debonair, as if nothing had happened. Even his tie was in place.

'Too late to work any more today,' he remarked conversationally. 'May I give you a lift home?'

The phone rang as soon as she stepped into the hall. 'Hi, Tamzin. Are you coming to the party on Friday?' asked an instantly recognisable female voice.

'Hello, Janice. Which party?' Tamzin shrugged her shoulders out of her coat and kicked off her shoes, visualising her friend – voluptuous figure draped in the latest trend, kitten-shaped face topped by plum-coloured hair styled exotically.

'Dennis's, of course. Is there any other?'

Dennis Quentin, artist and illustrator. She knew him, of course. Who didn't in the somewhat incestuous circles of publishing? But she had never yet attended one of his notorious soirées.

'I've an invitation somewhere,' Tamzin murmured vaguely, feeling disoriented, part of her still with Mike as his sports car blazed a trail through the traffic. He had kissed her lightly on the cheek before she alighted at the door of her ground-floor maisonette in Kensington.

'Will you be bringing Tim?' Janice, sophisticated and worldly, designer of the most exquisite jewellery, made no secret of the fact that she considered her friend's present lover to be the biggest bore in captivity.

'He'll expect it.'

'He expects too much,' Janice said sharply. 'He doesn't own you. I've hardly seen anything of you since he hoved on the scene.'

'It's not entirely him. The magazine – so many demands on my time.' Tamzin was aware this sounded lame. 'Anyway, how is your own love-life?'

'Stunning, darling. Couldn't be better. About the

party. Ditch Tim and we'll have ourselves some fun. You're working too hard. Need a change. What are you doing for Christmas?'

'Nothing much. Tim's going to stay with his family in Scotland. He wants me to go along, but I've said no.'

'Good for you. Scotland at this time of year will be ghastly. I'm keeping a low profile during the festivities, then I've booked in at Cheveral Court for the first week in January. Why don't you join me?'

'Cheveral Court? The health farm?'

'The very same. It's an experience in a million. Do come.'

'Oh, I don't know. Can't be bothered, really. All that exercise and carrot juice and controlled eating.'

Janice chuckled. 'Sweetheart, you've got it wrong. You can do all that, if you want, but there's far, far more on offer.'

Tamzin was intrigued by the purring note that had crept into Janice's voice. 'Tell me about it,' she said.

'I'll give you the gory details later. See you.'

Tamzin was glad she had resisted the temptation to mention Mike. Janice knew she had crossed swords with him businesswise. How to explain that they had just shared the most amazing fuck, when she couldn't explain it to herself?

Sighing in perplexity, she went into the kitchen, took a carton from the fridge and poured a drink. The room was pristine clean, like the rest of the flat, leaf-green limed oak units immaculate, worktops spotless, the white Belfast sink gleaming. Her 'daily' did a first-class job. I must remember to add a generous extra to her pay, besides a seasonal gift, she thought. She looks after me like a mother.

Carrying the tumbler of orange juice, she padded across the sitting room, never tired of admiring its decor, the fabrics and furniture complementing the Victorian architecture. She knew something about this by now, thanks to Tim. He was an expert on periods and styles and had guided her when she took over the apartment, escorting her to auction sales and advising on the pieces going under the hammer. Unfortunately, his interest had not been entirely altruistic: he intended to play house with her before long.

'Don't push it,' she had warned. 'Try to cage me and I'll be off like a shot.'

Of course, he didn't believe her. He was a personable, wealthy man with the world at his feet who fully expected females to be there also, ready to pamper and admire him, fall into raptures over his athletic body, neat backside and beautiful, curving cock. That Tamzin was not ready to be slotted into this category had come as something of a shock. It had also had the reverse effect, making him even more besotted. When he proposed marriage, she had refused.

Tamzin pressed the stereo ON button and selected a CD. The dreamy, sensual notes of Delius's *Song of Summer* projected a photogravure of the countryside on the screen of her brain. Hayfields, crimson poppies and celestial corn-flowers, larks ascending against an azure sky. She longed for that, needing the sun, becoming listless if the winter lasted too long.

Maybe I'll take a spring holiday abroad, she thought as she made her way into her bedroom.

Spain, perhaps. The Easter fiesta in Seville. That drooping, tearful statue of the Madonna, the lustrous *La Macaréna,* patroness of matadors, carried through the streets by penitents. Fireworks, gypsies, and the first *corrida* of the season. Religion and death, blood and sand, passion under a blazing sun. She could almost smell the heat, the olive- and orange-groves, the hot wind blowing over from Africa. Her spirit sang with exaltation.

She pressed STOP and replaced the disc with one of traditional flamenco from Andalusia, stamping her feet to the compelling rhythm of guitars and singers, the clapping of hands. Her skirt was discarded, then tights and T-shirt. She viewed her nakedness in the pier-glass, tilting its mahogany stand to get the angle right, examining herself with that critical eye she reserved for her job.

Not bad, considering. She was lucky, she supposed, having inherited her mother's graceful figure, along with the toffee-gold hair. Slender-backed, her waist tapered to a peach-shaped bottom from which flowed slender thighs and shapely legs. And, despite her spare build, her breasts were full and crowned with large rosy nipples rising from brownish pink areolae. Firm breasts that seldom required support. She wore bras for fun, rather than as a necessity, choosing pretty, frothy, impractical ones in black or vibrant hues.

Lifting a breast in each of her hands, she remembered Mike's expert touch, and the nipples hardened. She brushed over them with the balls of her thumbs. They responded instantly, fire darting into her loins. Mike – how odd to discover such hidden depths in him after all these months. And she suspected that the afternoon's revelations had been only the tip of the iceberg.

She shuddered, and closed her eyes in an attempt to reconstruct the fear and intense pleasure she had experience when relinquishing her will to him. Bondage and the kiss of the whip had never been part of her sexual menu, but now her curiosity was roused. Mike was obviously well versed in sub/dom. What else might he teach her?

The bathwater was warm and perfumed and she relaxed in its silken embrace, indulging in sensual daydreams. She had left the door open and guitar music filtered through, evocative of tropical nights under a starspangled sky, heady with the fragrance of exotic blooms. Christmas in England seemed very far away.

She thought of Mike, musing on the possibilities of further investigation down the byways of passion. Anticipation blossomed in the magic garden between her thighs, the scented water dipping lascivious fingers into her entrance and tickling the closed nether lips and tightly secured anus. Sliding down, head resting on the rim, she allowed her legs to fall apart and the water swirled, lapping like a lover's tongue at the ever-eager head of her clitoris.

Sacred and magical little organ! Praise be to it, she thought. Temples should be built in its honour, ceremonies inaugurated. For centuries the phallus has been revered, worshipped, fashioned into icons – obelisks, standing stones, all representing the male member. But now it was time the clitoris took precedence – that febrile bundle of nerve endings designed for satisfaction.

She reached down and walked her fingers over the wet brown swathe of maidenhair forming a wedge on her pubis, pulling gently at the fronds, then parting them to expose the shining pink pearl, her excitement intensified as she continued to concentrate her thoughts on it. There was no other part of the human body fashioned exclusively for enjoyment. Only the vibrant clitoris, instantly responsive to stimulation. By comparison the penis was a dull, cloddish thing. No wonder man feared woman, and had done their best to ignore or denigrate her pleasure zone.

Giving herself up to sensation, she held her labia open with one hand and brushed lightly over the nub of her clitoris with the other. She was soapy there, divinely slippery. The enjoyment was extreme, no longer unhurried and dreamlike, urging her to rub faster and faster. The ecstasy came quickly, every muscle tensed as the spasms passed through her.

'Really, darling! Couldn't you wait for me?'

A voice shattered the afterglow. She opened her eyes to see Tim standing in the doorway, watching her, impeccably dressed in a charcoal grey suit with matching waistcoat, ready for their visit to the restaurant.

'How long have you been there?' she snapped, sitting up and clasping the sponge to her breasts like a shield, as if he was a stranger who had never seen them before.

'Long enough,' he answered, and the bulge in his trousers told its own tale. 'I didn't know you like to play with yourself.'

'There's a lot you don't know about me.' Tamzin stood up, reaching for the fluffy towel warming on the radiator. She wrapped it round her and stepped on to the tufted bath mat, water dribbling down her legs.

'Really?' One of his bushy fair eyebrows shot towards the carefully contrived lock tumbling across his forehead. 'Perhaps you'd care to tell me? There shouldn't be any secrets between couples.'

As Tamzin stood looking up at him everything became crystal-clear. Handsome he might be with that boyish charm, rich and eligible, but she did not want to spend the rest of her life having to explain things to him. In fact, she had no desire to even spend that evening with him.

'It's over, Tim,' she said firmly, and walked away into the bedroom.

The astonishment on his face was almost laughable. 'What d'you mean?' he demanded, striding after her.

'I've had enough. You're a nice man, Tim, and it's not your fault, but we're totally incompatible. Leave the key on the hall table as you leave.'

Chapter Two

The break up of a relationship is always traumatic, and
Tamzin was still fond of Tim. It was difficult not to form
an attachment to someone she had spent a lot of time
with. Christmas seemed a sad, bad moment to do it but
c'est la vie, she told herself.

As she prepared herself for Dennis Quentin's party,
she mulled over her inability to get it right. She had not
seen Mike since they acted out their fantasy in her office.
Relieved, she had also experienced disappointment, yet
felt light and free, too. No Tim. No Mike. She had
busied herself, made an offer to Jeff Tate who, after hag-
gling had accepted, phoned Yasmin with the good news,
then taken herself off to Selfridges and indulged in an
orgy of spending.

Not that she had many presents to buy. She had been an only child, so there were no siblings and their respective spouses and offspring to bother about. No cousins, no aunts, just a few friends. Cards featured high on her list. She had an enormous amount of acquaintances, mostly to do with business. Had she been different loneliness might have tempted her into delaying the split with Tim and accepting his invitation to Edinburgh. But Tamzin was a solitary who, more often than not, enjoyed her own company.

'"He travels fastest who travels alone", is a line Rudyard Kipling could have written with me in mind,' she murmured aloud, picking up her silver-backed hand mirror. 'It's great to be a free agent. Who knows what adventures I'll have tonight or in whose arms I'll wind up? It's a fascinating prospect.'

She smiled to herself and, with infinite care, traced round her full lips with a fine liner and filled it in with glossy colour. Her eyes received attention next, the lashes brushed with mascara, and enhanced by greyish pencil. She darkened her brows slightly, emphasising their wing shape. The effect was dramatic.

Unpinning her damp hair, she tipped her head to one side, admiring the picture she had painted on the canvas of her face. Should she wear it loose or swept up? It was an abundant mass of natural curls which she usually confined in a chignon.

Not tonight, she decided, giving her head a vigorous shake, then bending forward and scrunching her fingers through the tangled ringlets. She tossed her hair in a rippling mane. It gave her the look she was seeking, something out of the norm. Business associates tended to class her as cool, sleek and poised, never seeing her ruffled or hearing her give vent to strong language. Only Tag and Janice had an inkling of the truth. And now Mike, of course.

Would he be at the party? It was more than likely, and her body remembered the tie binding her eyes, the plunge into darkness, the slow burn of his hands on her craving flesh, the delicacy of his fingers and mouth, the roller-coaster ride to climax.

'No!' she said to the silent room. 'No, and no again! I won't allow myself to become obsessional about him. He hasn't changed and neither have I. We're still utterly opposed. He's a self-opinionated pig, and I'll never back down. Get on with it, girl! Find others to play with. Or if not, play with yourself.'

On this sensible thought, she fastened the narrow

black garter belt round her waist, then seated herself on the stool before the ornate, triple-mirrored antique dressing table and worked sheer black stockings carefully over her feet and up her legs.

The sight of this misty sheen contrasting with pale flesh was darkly seductive, causing a twitch in her belly. Her skin seemed extra-sensitive to the touch of her own fingers as she clipped the suspenders in place, front and back. Standing, she twisted round to make sure the seams were straight, and caught a glimpse of her tightly-clenched buttocks, two pert hillocks accentuated by the thin strips of black satin-elastic and lace.

Gentle strips, not harsh stripes. How would it feel, she wondered, if her buttocks had been reddened and marked by the opened palm of someone's hand or even a cane?

Mike would understand and satisfy her longing to take his penis in her mouth and suck it. Then he would turn her over on the desk, lift her bottom, and push his prick into the place where she was still a virgin. No one had yet penetrated the sanctity of her anus, and she was curious to know how it would feel. When he had finished buggering her, he'd punish her for flouting the taboos. How would he punish her?

She felt a trace of moisture between the lips of her sex, desire tapping a well-spring of need. Eyes closed, she pretended to be blindfolded by Mike's tie. She smoothed her hands down over her breasts, rolling and teasing her nipples then gliding across her tiny waist and concave belly, twirling her fingers in her pubic floss. Reluctantly, she put a break on the impulse to bring herself off: it was nearly time to go.

Back to reality, and she stepped into a miniscule black thong and settled it resolutely over her hips, concealing those insatiable lips which, when chafed by even the most delicate of silks, formed an instantaneous bond of excitement.

Moving to the heavily carved wardrobe, she opened the double doors and lifted out the garments she had planned to wear. A slinky, black skirt, long and concealing except when she moved – then it opened, slit to the thigh at one side. This was topped by a strapless bodice cunningly supported by bones. Both garments were examples of Tag's peerless craftsmanship. The fabric clasped Tamzin's body like a lover, embracing every curve and hollow. It added to her height and slimness – model-girl potential.

Too old, she decided sensibly, but with a satisfied little

smile. Janice was a raving beauty, but Tamzin would not be eclipsed by her that night.

The neckline was cut so low that her breasts rose above the sombre material, bare almost to the nipples. A gold choker gleamed against the softness of her throat, matching the pendant earrings that swung among the tumbled curls.

She slipped her feet into strappy, high-heeled sandals, shrugged a jacket over her shoulders, and picked up her handbag, car keys and mobile phone. After making sure the windows were locked and the burglar alarm connected, she let herself out of the door.

'Good evening, Miss Lawrence,' said the security guard, poking his head from the window of his observation post just off the hall. 'Going somewhere nice?'

'Yes, Mr Jones. Are you ready for Christmas?' It was pleasant to idle there for a moment, knowing that her property was in safe hands. It would take very determined villains indeed to get past the tough ex-paratrooper Jones.

He grinned, admiring but always respectful. 'Ready as I'll ever be. The missus sees to all that.'

'I've some sweets and presents for the children,' she said, remembering the inner glow that had warmed her when she entered the toy department of the store. For a little while she had become a child again, responding to the shimmering coloured balls and tinsel, the mock snow, the evergreen boughs, the music – catching the far-off echo of the thrilling expectation of a visit from Santa Claus. Rather shamefaced, pretending to the assistant that it was for a niece, she had bought herself a teddy bear, a Steiff copy that had cost a bomb. He was a growler with golden beige mohair fur, long arms and legs, a thin snout, and a maker's button in one ear. She had even wrapped him in shiny paper when she did up the things for the Jones kids. She would open the parcel on Christmas morning and he would be her companion. They'd sing *Jingle-bells* together.

'Thank you for thinking of them, Miss Lawrence,' Jones was saying, smiling all over his homely face. 'I suppose you'll be partying all the time.'

'Not this year, I'll be glad to put my feet up, slob out in front of the telly and catch up on my sleep.' With Teddy beside me, she thought, the only cuddly thing I want around.

Her car was parked in the converted coach-house at the rear of the building. At a signal the computer-operated doors slid silently open. It was decidedly chilly outside, and a relief to slither into the driver's seat and switch on the ignition, flooding the interior with warmth. Off came the sandals. She could never drive in heels, and she liked to drive. Most definitely. Liked all the technology that enabled her to function to maximum efficiency – mobiles, laptops, email, cars.

A thoroughly modern Milly, she concluded, smiling.

Yet, deep inside her, there was something feral, barely controlled, a Pandora's box and she dared not lift the lid a quarter inch lest—

Oxford Street and Regent Street were ablaze with lights, each emporium outdoing the next with fantastic, elaborate decorations. Sparkling fir-trees, Santa in his sleigh, the Star of Bethlehem, fairy-story and Disney characters. Night, but they were still open, hordes of shoppers wandering in and out, looking at best bemused, at worst pole-axed. Tamzin was glad that she was not involved in that exhausting, madly worrying, costly time. Her own purchases were already gift-wrapped and ready to be delivered, cards sent out with the office mail.

A brass band was playing carols in Piccadilly Circus, and charity workers, muffled in scarves, anoraks and woolly hats, were going round with collecting boxes.

The occupants of Cardboard City huddled in doorways under sleeping-bags or tatty blankets. A soup-kitchen was in operation in a side alley, doling out food.

Nine-thirty, and Dennis's studio already crowded. To avoid gatecrashers, admittance was by invitation only. Tamzin showed hers to a broken-nosed heavy on the door. He wore a tuxedo but his head was shaved, gleaming scalp tattooed with a black tarantula. She elbowed her way into the reception area, surrounded on all sides by high-pitched, excited voices, then mounted the open ironwork staircase to the bedroom set aside for coats and titivation.

This, too, was crowded, beautiful women making themselves even more lovely, eyeing each other's outfits, recognising the designers, bitching about their men or other peoples' men, bitching about rivals.

The room was redolent of perfumes costing a king's ransom, rustling with fabrics retailing at sixty pounds a metre, filled with visions of breasts large and small, waists kept doll-like by rigorous diet and workouts, montes veneris depilated or luxuriantly hirsute. It reeked of coition, recently enjoyed or hotly anticipated. A few, not many, were still naive, gazing artlessly at themselves, in love with their pretty reflections.

Wall mirrors, silver-gilt glass balls the size of melons, a sixteenth-century Spanish bride-chest, white deep pile carpet, white tiled walls, concealed lighting, a splendid, heavily fringed Mexican hammock slung on chains from a beam. How would it be to screw in it? Would it swing wildly, tipping the occupants on to the floor? It was a question Tamzin found intriguing.

'Darling! You're here!' Janice twirled round from powdering her nose, her image featured over and over, disappearing into infinity in the mirrors, along with those of the others.

'D'you think it's true that mirrors are gateways to Hades, as in the film *Black Orchid?*' Tamzin said, her mind working inwards, away from the self-obsessed, narcissistic women.

'Don't ask me! Discuss it with those frightful intellectuals downstairs. You are a funny old thing, but I'm so glad you came.' As Janice turned her head, the tiny diamonds set between spikes of mascara flashed. 'God, what a crush!' she added. 'And there are more to come. One can't possibly say that one missed a Quentin bash. Lose all possible street cred.'

Gorgeous, radiating confidence, she was acerbic yet essentially loyal to those she took under her wing.

Blessed with a magnificent figure, big-breasted but small boned, she dressed in her own inimitable, eccentric style, a showcase for the chunky jewellery she created.

A shocking pink lurex corset nipped her waist and pushed up the twin orbs of her breasts; a blue gauze tutu reached her thighs where the hem met the tops of glittery hold-up stockings. She wore turquoise patent leather ankle boots, zipped at the side and with gold six-inch spiked heels, chandelier earrings, and a massive choker. On anyone else this conglomeration could have looked a mess. On Janice it was inspired.

The stiff muslin skirt swayed, dipped and lifted, revealing tantalising glimpses of the crisp plume crowning her pubis, dyed burgundy to match her hair. Janice rarely, if ever, wore panties.

Tamzin was enveloped in a sincere embrace. 'Unlike you to be early,' she remarked with a smile, aware of the press of those lovely breasts and the pungent body scents breathing out from between them.

'It's fun to change the rules, darling. Keeps people on their toes. "Janice is always late," they say – so I make sure I'm not. It throws them. Can't have complacency setting in, can we?'

She linked her arm with Tamzin's as they strolled on

to the gallery where they could look down on the milling crowd, and added, 'Is there anybody here worth shafting? I fancy someone drop-dead gorgeous.'

'Don't you always? I've never seen you with an ugly, or even moderately plain lover. They're always spectacular.'

'But of course. Beauty is the biggest turn-on – male or female. It's necessary to my well-being to be surrounded by beauty. Speaking of which – have you decided to come to Cheveral Court?'

Tamzin lifted her shoulders in a shrug. 'Why not? I'll admit to being curious.'

'Super! I shall ring them and book in. You won't regret it, darling. I won't tell you what to expect, then it'll be a surprise, but I guarantee you'll have the time of your life.'

They leaned on the chromium rail, gazing down at the open room as big as a barn, its ceiling rearing forty feet. From the outside, Dennis's home looked unprepossessing – a hideous red-brick warehouse constructed at the turn of the century. But once one had parked one's car in the converted basement and shot upwards in the lift, one saw that it resembled the set of some futuristic movie.

Black, white, polished steel and glass predominated, while the original starkness of a strictly functional building had been retained. It was cool, astringent, yet managed to convey an air of decadence, even depravity. Dennis Quentin was definitely supremo in his particular field and could afford to indulge his every whim.

Tamzin did not like to confess that she found his work confusing. There were examples on the white-washed wall of the staircase, and those bleak representations of the human form made her uneasy. It was like being exposed to the visceral truth of her animal origins. One drawing, titled *Cunny,* was simply that, a fur-fringed oval opening, rings within rings, surmounted by a triangular blob which, she supposed, was meant to be the clitoris.

'Don't let them get to you,' Janice announced, sweeping down the stairs with enviable insouciance, people moving aside to let her pass. 'It's a load of shite anyway. He's a conman but makes a mint, his attitude being, if people are fool enough to pay vastly inflated prices for the privilege of owning examples of his crap, then that's their hard luck.'

He was suddenly there to greet them, materialising at the bottom of the stairs, a great bull of a man, shouting above the general hubbub, 'Janice. How're your parts? I'm happy now my favourite quim has arrived. Give us a kiss and a feel.'

'Hello, Dennis darling,' she gasped, as his hand disappeared under her skirt. She reached for the solid length of his rod dangling against his left thigh under cover of his trousers. 'Wonderful pictures. So gut-wrenching. They make me incredibly horny.'

'I'm glad you approve,' he said sceptically, kissing her cheek as he fingered her, then beaming at Tamzin. 'Ah, the wonderful Miss Lawrence. Glad you could make it. Any chance of a mention in *Chimera*?'

'I'll put Mike Bishop on to it,' she promised, feeling incapable of giving Dennis the rave review he obviously expected, but tingling as he bowed over her hand, kissing the air above it, not even touching. She felt his breath on her skin like the scorching blast of a sirocco.

'He's here somewhere,' Dennis waved in the direction of the heaving throng behind him.

Middle-aged, bearded and secure in his success, he was brash, noisy and magnetic in a brown cotton cardigan, beige silk sweat-shirt and cream jogging pants. An important figure in the art world, almost an emperor – and he revelled in it.

It was not the first time Tamzin had been tempted to bed him, not only because he was the father figure she unconsciously sought, but because of the superstitious feeling that making love with a famous man might have an element of magic, some of his success rubbing off.

She was aware of jealous female eyes riveting her. If looks could have killed she would have been stretched out dead at his feet. Models, stars of TV and the wide screen, celebs, sensation-seeking debs were all besotted by Dennis, drawn to him like butterflies to the pungent, insectivorous pitcher-plant that grows in steamy tropical rain forests.

He knew it, too, and grinned lewdly, grabbing Janice close, one of his large, capable hands cradling her breasts, rubbing his thumb over the pronounced nipple. The groupies were hypnotised. They drooled, each one wishing it was herself.

'There's nothing like the smell of excited woman, is there?' he remarked, craggy face flushed, bright eyes dancing as he looked across at Tamzin.

She tried not to watch him stimulating Janice, but could feel her own arousal sending messages to her clitoris and increasing the elixir already seeping from her vulva. The atmosphere was charged. An abundance of drink and other mood-altering substances had released a flow of uninhibted conversation and bursts of raucous laughter, almost drowning out the stately music of Pergolesi drifting from the thin towerblocks of Bang und Olufsen speakers.

Dennis's guests were a cosmopolitan collection, mostly wealthy or ambitious to be so, hedonistic in outlook, wearing hundreds of pounds worth of designer clothing on their backs. The time of year added to the tension. At any moment the party might tip over from a Christian celebration to a bacchanalia, as in olden days when a festival in honour of Saturn, the god of agriculture, was held mid-December.

How much more honest, Tamzin thought. Isn't that what three-quarters of the guests are here for? In search of sex, perhaps love, whatever that overworked word means. The other quarter want money, have orgasms over business deals. A few, I suppose, combine both. Mike would be one of these.

It was then that she saw Mike himself and, to her annoyance, felt her vagina spasm and her clitoris thrum. Heart-stoppingly elegant in a navy wool peacoat and light blue roll-neck pullover, he had just walked in with Yasmin on his arm.

'Bastard!' Tamzin hissed through her teeth, not sure if she was fired by envy because he had succeeded in capturing the dusky model or furious with her for having him as her escort.

'What's he done to rattle your cage?' Janice observed, brows raised.

'Don't ask!'

Janice reached out a hand adorned with gold fingernails and huge rings and patted the impressive bulge at the crotch of Dennis's loose trousers. When he pressed closer, wanting more, she smiled into his eyes and said, 'You've guests, Dennis. Remember? We'll meet up later, maybe Tamzin will turn it into a cosy threesome, but first I want to have a little talk with her.'

'He's so damn sure of himself,' Tamzin growled when Dennis had melted into the maze of slender female arms awaiting him. She fixed Mike with a baleful glare as he shepherded his companion through the mêlée towards the buffet tables at the far end of the room.

'Now then, tell me all about it. Firstly, who is that gorgeous tart with him?' Janice's violet eyes narrowed to glittering slits, feeding on Yasmin.

Every line of the model's body was displayed in an orange cheongsam, even more exciting than if she had been naked. Her pert high breasts lifted the silk, nipples jutting. It melted over her hips, the avenue between her buttocks inviting exploration. It opened over her seemingly endless thighs, affording a brief flash of a darkly plumed, deeply indented cleft.

'One of Jeff's protégées. I discovered her.'

'She's yummy. Will you introduce me?'

'If you want.'

'I do. We can have some sport, and with Mike, too.' Janice was nobody's fool, and guessed something had fazed her usually calm friend.

'Janice, there's an American buyer here interested in your jewellery,' an adronymous creature in black leather came up to her to announce, gesturing with bony white hands.

'I'm on my way,' she carolled, adding to Tamzin, 'That's my PR person. I've got to go. We'll talk about this later.'

Waiters circulated, wearing livery to match the black and white decor, offering champagne and an array of *hors d'oeuvres*. Tamzin beckoned one over and plucked a crystal flute from his silver tray. Only one glass, she reminded herself. You're driving. One was usually enough to take the edge off stress, relaxing her into enjoyment.

It was the best; Dennis never did anything by halves. It frothed over her tongue, cool as a mountain stream, yet bubbly, a wickedly expensive brew that sharpened her senses and left her mind clear. Mike: she could eat him before breakfast and spit out the bones.

'Great to see you! Doesn't that dress look divine?' Tag rushed across, arms outspread. He was followed by a wide-shouldered, sturdy youth with a grade one cropped hair-cut, a ring in his left eyebrow and a diamond stud in one nostril. 'This is Reg,' Tag added, more beautiful than any girl in his olive cotton-knit sailor top and wide wool trousers.

'Hi, Reg,' Tamzin nodded to him and he gave her an engaging grin. He was wearing a sleeveless vest and it was apparent by his over-developed pectorals and biceps that he was addicted to exercise.

'He's not exactly a candidate for a university degree,' Tag whispered confidentially. 'But he's such a kind boy, and adores me. Have you ever seen such a neat little tush?'

'Ben is obviously a thing of the past,' she replied, taking note of the aforementioned bottom tightly displayed in faded denim.

'Lost beyond recall, girl,' Tag said, as they sat on the stairs and devoured *pâté de foie gras* served on toast.

'You're over him?' She brushed crumbs from her lips.

'Absolutely. He can go screw himself.'

'Who can go screw themselves?' Janice asked, coming in at the end of the conversation. 'Not still harking on about Mike, are you, Tamzin?'

'No, we're talking about me. Much more interesting,' Tag grinned, leaping to his feet and grabbing Reg's arm. 'Let's dance. They've changed the music, thank God. Don't forget my show tomorrow, Tamzin. I'll be mortally offended if you don't turn up – probably never speak to you again.'

'I'll be there,' she promised, and he kissed his fingertips to her as Reg guided him into the fray.

'Now, what's all this about Mike?' Janice asked, taking a gold cigarette-case from her bag.

Tamzin shrugged, and crossed her legs, the black skirt slipping revealingly aside. Janice sat beside her, carved jade holder in one hand, the other caressing the bare expanse of Tamzin's thigh. She found this disconcerting, for Janice had never touched her so intimately before.

The soft fingers continued their stroking and Tamzin became attuned to their touch and the coaxing inflexions of Janice's voice, aware that she enjoyed a richly varied sex-life, as much attracted to women as men. It was an art form Tamzin herself had never tried. But now she experienced a deep, throbbing, forbidden excitement, the muscles in her lower belly spasming, the furrow of her sex growing wet. She found herself wanting to confess everything.

'Mike and I have never hit it off, but a few days ago he came to my office and ...' She hesitated, cheeks flaming.

'And?' Janice prompted, eyes bright as she leaned closer, her hand sliding a little higher, a finger easing round the top of Tamzin's silk stocking.

The noise of the party seemed to melt away. It was as if she and Janice were alone somewhere very private. Tamzin found herself wishing this were so, a tremor passing through her, a tingle that shivered from her groin to her breasts.

'He was different. Maybe it was me. I was thoroughly bored with Tim, as you know. Well, a kind of madness possessed me – both of us, I guess. I can't explain. He took off his tie and bound my eyes.'

'Did he now? How enterprising.' Janice smiled and let her hand stray upwards, finding the scrap of satin covering Tamzin's mound, exploring the thick puff of hair beneath, the line between, the erect little core. 'Go on,' she murmured, crushing out her cigarette the better to focus on this delight.

'He sat me on the desk. I couldn't see a thing, but I felt him open my legs.'

'Like this?' Janice did the same, the black satin triangle widening.

'Just like that,' Tamzin whispered, and her pubis lifted, almost involuntarily, blindly seeking the knowing friction of Janice's finger.

'What did he do next?'

Tamzin's breathing was ragged. She could feel the moist heat spreading between her legs, wetting her crotch. 'He caressed my breasts, took off my tights, fondled my feet and legs – then removed my panties. I couldn't see what he was doing – only feel his touch.'

'You found it frightening but exciting. You enjoyed his domination, wanted more. Is this the first time? Have you never experimented before?'

Tamzin shook her head, distressed but extremely aroused by reliving her awakening to new aspects of sex. 'I didn't realize – never dreamed it would be such a wonderful, powerful feeling.'

'Ah, there are things I could show you – ways and means of controlling the flesh, delaying orgasm, protracting it till, when it finally comes, the release is cataclysmic – mind-blowing. Tell me more about your master – the remarkable Mike.'

'He's not my master.'

'Oh yes, he is, my dear.'

'It only happened once.' Tamzin averred, licking over her crimson lips, wanting to stroke Janice's narrow bare shoulders, her senses zinging as she breathed in the undertones of her own sweet body incense mingled with her friend's.

Janice chuckled and lifted a hand, caressing the soft curve of Tamzin's neck and the ripe, inviting swell of her breasts. 'But you've longed for him since. Ached to have him blindfold and bind you. Isn't that true?'

'Yes, but maybe not necessarily him.'

'Now you're talking. It's not a good idea to get hung up on one person. There are plenty of other masters around – mistresses, too.' Janice's voice was beguiling. 'You've not finished telling me what he did.'

She settled on the step with Tamzin wedged between her and the wall. People passed but none seemed aware her hand was hidden beneath Tamzin's skirt. Voices from a distance, the rise and fall of conversation, the salsa music blasting from the speakers.

Tamzin's pubic hair was flattened by the thin covering of her thong. It felt silky smooth. Janice moved her fingers, sliding them backwards and forwards, but so slowly and delicately that the skirt was not disturbed.

Eyes closed, struggling to keep her excitement in check, Tamzin said, 'He made me come, there in the darkness. Then laid me across my desk. Just think, Janice – my place of work!'

'How shocking,' Janice said with a giggle, giving no quarter, the ball of her thumb brushing against the quivering stalk of Tamzin's clitoris. 'Didn't that make it even more sexy?'

'Yes – oh, yes,' she gasped, trembling on the brink of explosion, yet fearing it wouldn't happen.

'Has he a big cock?' Janice said, nuzzling her ear, tongue-tip dipping inside.

'Huge.' Tamzin remembered it with her fingers, not her eyes.

'How long? Six inches? Eight?' Janice's own juices were soaking the back of her tutu, the muslin sticking damply. She could feel the blood pounding in the closed lips of her sex beneath the plum-coloured thatch.

'I didn't see it. He'd put it away before he unfastened

my eyes. But it felt enormous. I want to see it. I want to suck it into my mouth and run my tongue up and down its thick shaft and lick off the juice.' Tamzin was burning with desire, her clitoris a throbbing point of heat, Janice's thumb continuing the slow torture, skimming over it, not pressing or giving it the rubbing it so desperately required.

'I think we should go find Dennis. His is the biggest prick I've ever had, and my experience is considerable.' Janice removed her hand and stood up, leaning a shoulder against the wall. 'Will you come with me?'

They sought him in vain, wandering through the reception room, waylaid by the cuisine laid out so temptingly between ziggurats of fruit piled around an immense centrepiece of a naked bronze woman with a man between her thighs, modelled in accord with the conventions of Art Deco, a direct and deliberate contrast to an example of Dennis's work that occupied one end of the damask-covered trestle table.

On closer inspection it was nothing more than an old-fashioned dressmaker's dummy, covered in grubby calico. Armless, headless, legless – two dark green avocado pears and a lengthy, curving cucumber had been placed at the juncture of the thighs, another set of mock genitalia stuck where a head might have been.

Tamzin studied it as she sank her teeth into a luscious, velvety-skinned peach, before turning her attention to other goodies. The most flavoursome of dainties jostled for place, a gastronomic vision enhanced by the gleam of porcelain and silver, the faceted prisms of Waterford crystal.

Which to choose? Choux pastry puffs, bursting with whipped cream and dripping with dark chocolate? Custard tartlets? Meringue garnished with maraschino sauce? Everything was craftily calculated to excite the taste buds of the most fastidious gourmet and arouse the senses to fever-pitch. Somehow, Dennis and his caterers had contrived to give every item a sexual connotation.

Massive television screens covered the walls, and guests lounged on divans watching images of couples straining in ecstasy, blown-up and exaggerated – the act performed in an amazing variety of ways. The male participants were strikingly handsome, their bodies honed and muscular. They had, without exception, giant penises and pendulous balls, rising from forests of pubic hair.

Some of the women had perfect figures, while others

flaunted unnaturally large breasts. Silicone implants, surely? Sixty inches and more. They rubbed these mammary extravaganzas with enthusiastic vigour, rolling and roiling teats the size of doorknobs. Winding their bodies round their lovers, they gave vent to excited squeals as they smothered them in those fleshy pillows.

They moaned, writhed, exploited every desire – women mounted by several men at once – cocks in mouths, rectums, vaginas. Women with women, licking one another's love-holes, men playing the hump-backed beast with their own kind. Beautiful exhibitionists – combining in a steamy saturnalia. Those watching were affected. So was Tamzin. Appetite for food was forgotten, supplanted by another, stronger one imperiously demanding satisfaction. She looked round for Janice, but she had vanished.

A space had been cleared in the centre of the dance floor, the lights dimming save for one very bright pool. The crowd gathered in a circle, watching, waiting, reserve already loosened. Dennis stepped into the spotlight, shielding his eyes against the glare.

'Ladies and gentlemen – guests – friends! I'm so happy to welcome you here tonight and wish you the compliments of the Season.'

Cheers. Shouts. Feet stamping. He held up his hand for silence and continued, 'And now – one of the hottest acts around. Give a big hand to *Feathered Friends*.'

A spattering of applause, the fanfare of trumpets, flashing lasers, then sudden blackness as they were extinguished. A woman shrieked, others laughed and murmured. In the background the video performers moaned as they climaxed, their images flickering on the wall-to-wall screens. Then these too were killed and there was abrupt silence.

A blinding ray stabbed the darkness, picking out a pair of large white feathered wings resting on the polished granite floor. A whisper of music crept over the room, softly, sensually, gently oscillating on the inner ear.

The feathers quivered, parted shyly, and the shape within them unfolded, tall, graceful, crowned by a plumed headdress. Slanting eyes glistened in a dead-white face, slashed across by a red gash of a mouth.

Then, effortlessly, almost ethereally, the bird-ballerina began to dance, the great ostrich feather fans crossing and recrossing, never revealing the form beneath. There was the exciting flash of a perfectly sculptured leg, a jewel-studded stiletto shoe, the enticing curve of an arm, a hand holding a glittering lingam-shaped object.

Silken Bonds

A subdued roar escaped the throats of the spectators. The pure white bird reclined on the stage, body partly hidden by the fans, one leg arched, the other out-stretched, every movement in harmony with the compelling drum beat underlying the sweep of strings. The shining phallus-substitute descended slowly, slowly, till the tip entered the dancer's mouth. With seductive grace, the bird suggested extreme pleasure, making love to it as if it was indeed a lover's tool.

Then, swift as flight, the creature rose, standing stork-like on one leg, raising the other and caressing the shapely limb with the dildo. The music swept upwards to a crescendo, and the crowd shouted excitedly as, spreading itself over one of the tables, the bird inserted the mock phallus between its thighs. It disappeared, lost in a flurry of feathers. Faster the dancer's movements now, and faster still as the culmination approached.

A crash of cymbals and the bird's body spasmed beneath the fans. Then the creature gathered its limbs and leapt up as cheers rocked the roof. A sudden gesture, the arms outspread, a fan in either hand. The body beneath was perfect; gilded nipples, a jewelled navel and the most exquisitely formed male genitals.

The crowd went wild.

The rest of the performance followed without a pause. Now creatures in bizarre bird masks leapt into the circle of light, gorgeous hermaphrodites – bare, upthrusting breasts, painted nipples, feathers and sequinned drapes floating open to reveal pubic areas, with dark clefts or phalluses of various shapes and sizes. These were incredible, fantastic beings of myth and legend, their virile strength, breathtaking agility and passion ravishing the senses of the audience.

No conventional ballet, within seconds the movements had become intensely sensual, gentle curves flowing and mingling with male sinews, legs locked around their partners' waists, penises plunging between slender, bejewelled thighs, breasts arching to meet lips, mouths swooping down to caress parts that were no longer private.

Their actions were echoed by the spectators. Couples joined in the spectacle. Clothes were discarded, cocks displayed through gaps in trousers, female legs opened wide, the light glittering on silvery dampness oozing between swollen sex-lips.

Tamzin, enthralled by the tableaux on every side, pushed open her skirt, edged round her panties and felt her own hidden wetness. She let her fingers glide through it, enticing her bud to emerge from its cowl, feeling it stiffen at her touch. Her breasts ached and their tips hardened. The lights were flashing, throwing a kaleidoscope of rainbow colours over the writhing throng, the party rapidly transforming into an orgy.

She felt the pressure of a man's cock rubbing against the division of her buttocks, felt his tongue caressing her ear, his voice murmuring, 'Hello, Tamzin.'

It was Mike.

As he spoke, he guided one of her hands to his companion, and her fingers encountered the springy hair covering Yasmin's mons. The girl's slender coffee-coloured fingers worked their way into Tamzin's bodice and plucked at her nipples. At the same time Mike honed in on her clitoris, subjecting it to rapid friction. She gasped with extreme pleasure, and the desire for something thick, hot and hard penetrating her vitals was undeniable.

She was very nearly there, forgetting the orgiastic crowd, blind to everything save the pressing need for release. Then, suddenly, Janice's face swam before her. Mike and Yasmin disappeared and she was being drawn up the stairs, past the writhing figures occupying every available space and into the room where the hammock swung beneath Dennis's bulk.

He was naked, his great body rippling with muscles and covered with a pelt of gingerish fur. His penis was a mighty rod, pointing to the ceiling, thick, knotted with veins like a gnarled tree-trunk, the glans purple, divided into two fat globes, a single pearly tear poised at the slit. His broad thighs supported the weight of a pair of large balls, cocooned in their hairy net, his equipment that of a mature man who has serviced many females. He was altogether magnificent, like Jupiter on Mount Olympus, ready to shower the universe with spermatic libation.

'Ah,' he rumbled, like a contented tom-cat. 'Two lovely women but I have, alas, only one cock.'

'Don't worry, Dennis,' Janice purred, caressing the side of his body, circling and then pinching the hard brown nubs of his nipples. 'We can pleasure each other, and you too, if we want.'

Tamzin imitated her, fingers tracing a line down his chest, dipping into his hairy navel, then continuing the descent to the dense thatch of his groin from which his spear of arousal soared. She fastened her palm round it and slowly eased the skin over it, watching, fascinated, as the blunt head quivered and wept milky tears.

Janice had unhooked her basque, the material falling away, breasts bared, the nipples puckered and dark as cob-nuts. Next her skirt dropped to the ground and she was naked except for her glittery stockings and high-heeled boots. Dennis gritted his teeth as he reached out to stroke her plum-hued pubes.

'That's gorgeous,' he panted, bearded face alight with lust, eyes bright. 'Dyed pussy-feathers! I love it! I want to paint you—'

His prick was jerking under Tamzin's attentions. 'Hold back a bit,' Janice advised. 'We don't want him coming yet.'

Standing by the hammock, she spread her legs, those outrageous shoes making the calf muscles clench and thighs bunch, while he dipped a finger into the scented pool of her entrance. Wriggling the digit, making her squirm with need, he withdrew it and inhaled her fragrance.

He slipped a hand between Tamzin's thigh and she could feel him following the petals of her labia through the thin silk, his thumb seeking out her clit. It was ready, having never subsided from Mike's stimulation, and she wanted him to go on and on.

Janice came round to her side of the hammock and undressed her. Soon she was wearing nothing but suspender belt and stockings. Dennis feasted his eyes on the lovely women, so different in their beauty, each perfect in her way. He explored their wet avenues, caressed the stalks of their love-buds, felt both of them opening for him, pulsating and eager. A connoisseur of erotic stimulation, applying his artist's imagination, the party had been his idea, and the presence of these twin paramours was the high spot.

Their eyes met across his recumbent body, and they reached out to touch each other's breasts, lids narrowed with the exquisite pleasure it evoked. They drew closer, climbing into the hammock. It stabilised, no longer rocking, controlled by a brake. Tamzin need have no fear of it collapsing.

'She's so beautiful', Dennis said, kissing Janice. 'The first time she's played in a trio, you say? Thank you for bringing her.'

Tamzin felt his hands on her breasts, then Janice's, and their combined caressing motions gliding past the garterbelt to the triangle between. She was lost in a sublimely sensual web, trapped by the fingers circling her nipples and the echoing pulse in her clitoris, melting heat gathering to sweep her towards orgasm.

She needed a tongue on that sensitive nub, licking and tasting, sucking her to completion. Dennis lifted her in his strong arms and laid her flat on her back down the length of his body. She felt the solid bulk of his chest and belly along her spine, then the press of his uplifted shaft as he eased her over it. With one sharp thrust he penetrated deep inside her.

She was wide open, her head resting against his shoulder, and she could feel his cock within her, stretching her to capacity, throbbing its need. Dennis held it tightly leashed, unwilling to let go yet. Her senses swam, roused beyond endurance by the fingers plucking music from her pebble-hard nipples, her clit so ripe and randy that the slightest flick of a fingertip would have sent her spinning over the edge.

Janice settled herself astride Dennis's face, and he tongued her wet pink cleft, licking in the juices and taking the enlarged bud between his fleshy lips. From where she lay, Tamzin was almost enveloped in Janice's thighs, smelling the ripe, sensual odour seeping from her. Janice bounced up and down in a frenzy, screaming when she came. Straightaway she abandoned her pose, and positioned herself between Tamzin's legs, nuzzling the damp bush and circling her pleasure point.

Tamzin had never been more tumid and full, hot and needful. Janice's tongue flickered like fire on the delicate tissues, then her lips closed over the inflamed organ and she settled into a steady sucking rhythm. Raising her head, she blew gently over it to prolong the sensation. Tamzin cried out impatiently, the blood thickening her membranes, that ache in her loins demanding release.

Smiling, Janice wetted her fingers from the honey-dew glistening at Tamzin's vulva, spreading it over the plump, rose-red petals of the labia and the area each side. With every stroke she advanced a little closer, till a finger skimmed over the exposed clit-head.

Tamzin gasped, the first spasms of orgasm flaming through her. Janice caressed her firmly now, moving her finger up and down, then from side to side. Dennis drove into her from beneath, lifting her body with the force of his thrusts. She felt his cock-head penetrating deeply, felt the energy rushing to meet Janice's finger, and her body convulsed again with the intensity of the climax that roared through her.

Chapter Three

'Come on, Kev! What a dork! I'll get there long before you!' the girl shouted, teasing the stocky young man who was plodding up the slope some distance behind her.

'I gave you a head start,' he grumbled in his slow Hampshire drawl. 'And anyway, I've got a stinking hangover.'

She laughed and crunched over the frosty glade in her black DMs, coming to rest near a tree-trunk and dropping her tote-bag beneath its leafless, rime encrusted branches.

Mocking hazel eyes under thick fair lashes assessed her panting companion. 'Shouldn't spend your nights in the bar of the King's Arms, should you?' she said scathingly. 'If that's where you were. I've a hunch you might have been giving the landlady a right seeing-to out the back.'

'Don't be daft, Maria.' He stumped up to her, and leaned a broad shoulder against the lichenous bark, a solid figure in blue jeans and red tartan lumber-jacket.

'I'm not daft, though you like to kid yourself I am,' she retorted, sticking out the tip of her wet tongue, then circling her coral lips suggestively. 'You're a dirty sod – always shoving your dick where you're not supposed to, digging other men's potatoes. The landlady's married and old enough to be your mother.'

He scowled, half annoyed, half amused, and lunged for her. She dodged out of his reach, though every inch of her wanted to be in his arms. Men, however, needed to be shown their place every so often, Kevlin included, even though she was more than a little in love with his handsome, roughly-hewn face, unruly hair, well-muscled body and the fat pink snake that nestled between his thighs. Her favourite plaything – his too, and not only with her.

He chased her round the snowy dell in the pale January sunshine, and she shrieked in mock terror, blood rushing, heart pounding, looking forward to the outcome. He liked to be rough sometimes, and she knew that when he finally caught her, he would be fully roused, wanting to get out his big, one-eyed serpent and plunge it into her.

They were well matched – barely twenty, at their peak of fitness and animal energy, and everyone thereabouts looked upon them as an item. Even the owners of Cheveral Court, though they expected them to entertain the guests, if required, as part of their duties. Maria Banting was a maid and Kevlin Scully worked about the place as an odd-job man. But there were times when they were called upon to adopt other roles, participating in activities Maria would not have dared mention to her mother, and which even Kevlin baulked at discussing when out on a binge with his mates.

He caught her in a bear-hug and brought her crashing to the ground, their clothing powdered with snow. Gripping her wrists and holding her arms outspread, he knelt over her, glaring down into her face with feigned rage. She could feel the heat of his thighs penetrating his Levi's and her black woollen leggings. The snow was melting under her anorak, the hood falling back from her mass of tousled peroxide blonde hair, and one of her boots had sprung a leak, slush soaking through the sole.

'Let me go, you bugger!' she shouted. 'I've got to get those things to the cottage.'

He sat back on his heels without releasing her, grinning. 'Say sorry first.'

'Get lost!' She wriggled ineffectively between his spread thighs, pressing upwards against the fullness restricted by the denim strained across his crotch.

For answer, he released one hand, bending back to avoid the slap she aimed at him and diving for the zip that fastened her mauve waterproof. It ran down easily, and with unerring aim he reached in and squeezed the plump mounds hidden by a hand-knitted jumper. It was the work of a second to push it up and expose the ample breasts spilling over the lacy top of her bra.

'That's better,' he crooned, feasting his eyes on those magnificent globes, firm and taut despite their size, Maria's major asset. 'Jesus! Look at your tits! They're all over goose-pimples.'

'Your balls would be goose-pimply too, if I was to get 'em out. It's brass-monkey weather,' she rejoined, though her voice was breathy as he pinched a nipple as hard and juicy as a cherry.

'Unbutton me, then. I want you to,' he growled, his

deep voice sending shivers down her spine and connecting directly with her sex.

His work-roughened hand pushed aside the white lace and cotton of Marks & Spencer's best, and lifted out one breast. Then he lowered his head and took the ardent teat into his mouth, sucking strongly. Maria squirmed and moaned. The dark stubble on his chin was as harsh as sandpaper but this abrasive quality added to her arousal. She could feel her sap wetting the gusset between her thighs, the walls of her vagina pulsating with want.

Maria's instincts and expectations were basic, Kevlin her ideal mate, but even she could be piqued if he strayed, as he often did, a stud with a roving eye, over-blessed with testosterone.

'Why d'you do it?' she demanded, moving her head from side to side to avoid his darting tongue, knowing she would be lost once that fleshy organ penetrated her mouth.

'Do what?' Kevlin expressed injured innocence, working his way past the elasticated waist of her leggings, finding the top of her white cotton briefs, creeping underneath to bury his fingers in the wiry brown bush covering her mons.

'Screw around,' she went on, though overwhelmed with pleasure as he fingered her labia majora, parting the pink lips and finding the hard nub of flesh he knew so well. He'd been finding it for years now, ever since they were in the fifth-form at secondary school.

He continued that lubricious, enticing stroking, and she knew he was diverting her attention from his other women but could not help responding. In a perverse way her jealousy was a turn-on, as she imagined him driving that lively prick of his into someone else's cuzzy.

'You don't say nothing when we do it up at the house,' he objected sulkily, tweaking her nipple.

A fiery dart shot down into her already palpitating clit. 'That's different,' she managed to say. 'That's work, though I don't much go on you fucking Inga when I'm not there to watch, just 'cause she's bored, run out of batteries for her vibrator or just fancies a bit of rough.'

There was a wealth of resentment in her tone. Inga Steadson was enough to rouse the envy of any red-blooded female – so willowy and beautifully groomed, with wardrobes stuffed full of clothes and naturally white-blonde hair, as against Maria's Scandinavian Gold colouring kit purchased from the Winchester branch of Boots.

'No need for you to be jealous of her. You've always given me everything I want. Reckon I don't need no one else if I've got a girl like you with the biggest tits this side of Southampton. I get hard just thinking about squeezing my cock between 'em.' Kevlin knew that smutty talk added to her excitement. He could tell by the succulent honeydew smearing his fingers.

'I'm quite enough for you. That's what I'm always telling you, stupid!' Vainly she tried to keep a grip on her indignation, but was rapidly losing control.

She knew he meant what he said while he was saying it, unable to think of anything except that inflamed dick and aching testicles heavy with the need to ejaculate. Maria, young though she was, had few illusions. Men would promise anything in order to shoot their load.

Faithful to him in her own fashion, she was not above having sex with anyone who took her fancy if Kevlin annoyed her too much with his dalliances. She would avenge herself by sleeping around, and making sure he found out about it. But they always came back together in the end, hard young phallus to tight-muscled girlish vagina, like two homing pigeons.

'Stop talking. I need to fuck you,' Kevlin groaned, and his finger began a more rapid action, stimulating her

clitoris, her inner lips swelling round that busily working digit.

Maria fidgeted, the exposure, the cold, distracting her
from reaching the ultimate sensation. 'Can't we go
somewhere? I don't want you to do it like this,' she complained, though partly to torment him. 'It's too
uncomfortable. Get your hand out my knickers.'

'Fussy all of a sudden,' he said, then smiled into her
eyes as he raised his wet fingers to his nose and sniffed
her juices. 'I know just the place. Come on.' He leapt up
and reached down a hand for her.

'Where're we going?' She trudged along at his side,
bag hefted over one shoulder, aware of the dampness
soaking through her cotton briefs and into her leggings.

Her cheeks were rosy, eyes sparkling, warmed to the
core by Kevlin's caresses and the heady anticipation of
completion. He never let her down, an enthusiastic lover,
proud of the number of times he was able to bring her
off. Her pleasure-nub meant almost as much to him as
his prick.

The layer of snow was thin, grass underfoot stiff and
rustling. 'There'll be more afore the day's out,' Kevlin
proclaimed, a countryman to the bone, born in a small
rural hospital within sight of the South Downs.

Maria knew where they were heading now, glistening gables showing through the trees. Smoke twirled lazily from a chimney pot, rising to the milky-blue sky.

Kevlin stopped and hauled her up against him, crushing her lips with his, tongue plunging in, meeting hers. She relaxed in his arms, reminded of why, no matter what he did, she always forgave him. It was worth it to keep a man who made her feel so randy.

Arms entwined, they walked the rest of the way, through the wicket gate, up the crooked path to the porch sheltering the front door. Both had keys and this was, in all events, a perfectly legitimate visit.

'I got the fire going earlier and checked the Aga. The radiators and water are piping hot,' Kevlin remarked as they stood in the hall, shelling off their padded jackets and unlacing their boots. 'Someone important's expected later today.'

'Who is it? A pop star? Think I can get an autograph?'

'Dunno. She didn't say.'

'She never does, but I'll find out, don't you worry. Brrr! That's better,' Maria exclaimed, entering the long, low living-room where logs blazed in the stone hearth.

The air was sweet with pine resin and pot-pourri, the carpets of Persian design, the furniture deeply cushioned and chintz-covered, the decor in tune with the black-beamed antiquity. Horse-brasses winked, dried flowers stood in pottery vases, there were landscapes in gilt frames, bronzes on the overmantle and willow-patterned china on the pine dresser.

Yet the cottage had been completely modernised and extended, a secluded dwelling where antisocial guests might hide away. It even had its own jacuzzi and massage-couch, and a private walkway leading to a discreet entrance at the back of the main building. The most media-shy star could reside there with perfect confidence. No one would disturb their privacy.

It was an ideal rendezvous for lovers.

Maria unpacked her bag and stowed the contents in the kitchen: flour, packets of herbs, fruit teas and coffee in the oak-fronted cupboards; milk and fruit juice in the fridge, vegetables, meat and fish, too, though meals were usually delivered from the house. But according to her shopping-list, this one enjoyed cooking.

When she got back to the lounge it was to find Kevlin sprawled in a deep armchair. His flies were undone and he was fondling the thick shaft and glistening bare glans of the erect penis emerging from a nest of brownish curls. A pair of plump testicles in their crinkled sac bulged beneath it.

She knelt on the floor between his legs, level with his exposed tackle, gazing at it intently. 'I get all hot when I watch you do that,' she whispered, her roseate nipples chafed by her bra. She unfastened then removed it, along with her sweater, her body bathed crimson in the light of the dancing flames.

His large calloused hand was slippery with the milky pre-come juice pearling his cock-head. There was an intense expression on his face, a glazed look in his eyes. She knew he was teetering on the edge, the pressure building. A touch more, a lightning rub and the fluid would spurt from that narrow slit, jetting up to cream her face. She could almost taste it, salty and strong, on her tongue.

'Sit on it,' he muttered, and left his dick unsupported, viewing it proudly as it stood up straight as a spear. His hands came out to tug at her leggings.

Fired by his urgency, Maria peeled them down and kicked them aside. She could smell her own essence permeating her panties, heady and pungent. When she had removed them she held them to his nostrils so he could share it. His cock leaped, and she could not resist flicking the end of it with her fingers.

She knelt astride him, feathery-fringed pussy wide open. He weighed her breasts that filled each of his hands, drawing her above him so he might mouth each of the nipples in turn. Her eyelids drooped, the touch of his lips stirring atavistic longings deep inside her. A potential earth-mother, the time would come when an infant sucked at her teats. Just for now, Kevlin fulfilled this role.

Pleasure ripped through her as he slipped a finger into her pouting vulva, tapping the reserve of honey-sweet liquid and sliding it over her clitoris, wetting and frigging it at the same time.

Maria moaned and writhed, arm braced against the chair, the other enclosing his upward-curving prong that searched blindly for an entrance. He gave a shuddering groan and masturbated her harder. A series of spasms began deep inside her, heralding climax, while a flush suffused her entire body, and the need became a compulsion, hurling her towards the mini-death.

As Kevlin rubbed her frantically, so her hand moved skilfully on his prick, the foreskin slipping backwards and forwards over the purple-red head. She wanted him to make her orgasm – wanted him to slow down – to take his finger off just for a moment, to make it last.

It was no use. Her climax swept over her like a mighty tidal wave, carrying her to the peak, dropping her slowly down – down—

Even before the last contraction had swept through her, Kevlin lifted and impaled her on his turgid cock, thrusting into her with delicious violence. She fastened her thighs around him, her body like a piston as she pumped on that thick organ which was almost too big to fit into her tight tunnel.

Kevlin flung back his head, a tortured expression contorting his features. He convulsed and jerked, and Maria felt every spasm as if it was her own. She slumped forward across his chest, knees drawn up and wide apart, her naked backside raised. Slumped and rested and wanted more.

'Good Lord, what's all this? Who's been a very, very naughty girl, then?' A voice asked from the doorway.

She craned her head round, those thrilling, cultured tones sending apprehension bolting through her. Lance Manwaring, in a spread-legged stance, was in the doorway staring directly at her.

He emanated classy sex, with a firm jaw, long straight dark hair, a thin nose and narrow, cruel lips. Whiplash lean and elegant in a hacking jacket, his beige jodhpurs fitted like a second skin, underscoring his large, prominent member. He was impatiently slapping the side of his leg with a silver-headed crop.

Her employer, master and teacher. Maria shuddered and thrilled and needed to come again.

A woman stood beside him, in coat, riding breeches and boots of unrelieved and sombre black, a low-crowned topper covering her flaxen hair, a misty veil thrown back from her face.

'Sorry, Mr Manwaring – Mrs Steadson. Kev and me – we were just – getting everything ready,' Maria stammered, making no move, very aware of the smooth, contoured cheeks of her arse thrust high into the air.

Lance Manwaring, mouth set in a grim line, steel-grey eyes glittering, reached her in a couple of strides. 'No. Don't move until I say you may,' he commanded sternly. 'What happens to naughty girls who fuck on their boss's furniture, *and* in their boss's time?'

'They get punished, sir.' Maria's face was scarlet with shame.

'And how do they get punished?' His clipped accent cut like a knife.

'They get caned and spanked, sir, sometimes

whipped,' she whimpered, nerves juddering at the sight of those strong, finely-shaped fingers gripping the crop.

'They do indeed. Shall she be punished, Mrs Steadson?' Lance cocked an eyebrow at Inga who smiled coolly while perusing the alluring spectacle of Maria's bare backside, the deep cleft between the sweet pursed lips under their light coating of hair.

'Of course,' Inga agreed, slowly working her fingers out of her supple black leather gloves.

'I'll get out the way,' Kevlin offered, staring up at the gorgeous woman who was looking down at him calmly, as unmoved as if this scene were common-place.

'Stay where you are. Keep your cock rammed in her. Inga, make sure it's stiff as a poker.' Lance sounded in control, but Maria noted the enlarged and upraised line of his truly unique phallus spoiling the cut of his breeches.

Still wearing that austere smile, Inga opened her coat and the silk blouse beneath, revealing a pair of little breasts crowned by rose-pink nipples.

Standing by the chair, she was just beyond Kevlin's reach. With an infinitely sensual gesture, she massaged the undersides of the taut mounds with her delicate hands and fondled the tips, scratching over them with almond-shaped, red-lacquered nails.

Kevlin's eyes were glued to her, his tongue coming out to lick his lips. His cock was still embedded in Maria and she felt it growing larger, filling her wet channel, nudging against the neck of her womb.

Her bud was swelling, too, one orgasm never enough for her. She was trembling yet desirous, knowing what punishment to expect from Lance. Even so, she was taken off-guard when his crop connected with her bare backside. She yelped and jerked. Kevlin's prong responded to the movement. The hardness of his cock-base put pressure on her clit, shocks of pleasure mingling with shocks of pain.

She arched her back, staring up into Inga's eyes, ice-cold sapphires shining in that perfectly sculptured face. She yearned to have her mistress slide those scarlet-tipped fingers over her breasts, teasing them into points, circling and pleasuring them, as she had done on many occasions. But it was Kevlin's small male nipples that Inga fondled.

Maria's bottom stung, laved in heat. The crop swished and came down again, laying another scarlet trail across the ivory skin. Kevlin was bucking beneath her in time to each blow, and now discomfort ebbed away, replaced by a spreading warmth that quivered through her, transformed into exquisite pleasure.

She felt a finger inserted between her mons and Kevlin's pubis, a much needed finger stroking her clit. Inga was leaning over, her bare breasts close to Maria's mouth. By extending her tongue to the limit, she was able to brush the end over one of her mistress's tight nipples. The taste of her silky, pampered skin was divine. The humid smell rising from their heated flesh exacerbated the excitement – love-juice and spunk, sweat and Inga's expensive perfume, overlaid with leather and the ripe odour of horse that clung to her clothing.

Maria braced herself, fearful yet longing for another blow, but instead felt Lance dabbling his fingers in the copious nectar oozing each side of her vulva and spreading it up the amber crease between her nether cheeks. He inserted one into her puckered anal-ring till it was buried to the knuckle. He added a second, then a third, preparing the way for something bigger.

His fingers were withdrawn, replaced by the bulbous head of his penis pushing against her forbidden entrance, stretching it, easing it, as slowly, inch by inch, he penetrated her, till the entire length and thickness of his weapon was lodged within her.

She bore down on it, taking it deep into her rectum, accustomed to receiving this attention. He grasped her hips and pulled her even harder on to him. Her loins were filled to the utmost, Kevlin in one opening from below, Lance occupying the other from behind, and Inga rubbing her clit till she reached a shattering climax that left her weak and trembling. Kevlin grunted as he attained fulfilment, and Lance rode her in furious frenzy till he, too, achieved his goal.

'"Cheveral Court: the magnificent historic mansion stands in two hundred acres of tranquil park-land on the borders of the ancient and lovely New Forest. When you arrive there, you leave your problems behind and enter the ultimate health resort, taking the first step on your journey to a fitter, more rewarding life".'

Tamzin read the brochure aloud over coffee in the motorway services restaurant, then remarked, 'Are you quite sure this is me?'

'That's their publicity blurb, designed to encourage "normal" clients and it's all true, but—' Janice paused and smiled at her across the round formica-topped table, 'there's a great deal more than that. I know Lance

Manwaring and his partner, Inga Steadson – I was at finishing school with her – and this ain't like no other health farm you're ever likely to come across, lady.'

'So you've already said. That's why I agreed to come, though you're being evasive. What's the score? Do they practice Satanic rites, or something equally sinister?' Tamzin crossed her legs in their warm black stretchy ski-pants that fitted without a wrinkle and disappeared into the tops of tan leather cowboy boots with elaborate silver buckles.

'Cool it. All will be revealed,' Janice promised, tapping the side of her nose.

'I feel a bit of a fraud, really. It's been a long holiday and I did nothing but eat, sleep and watch the telly. I guess I could do with losing a pound or two, but I'm not particularly stressed out.'

'I know that, but I suspect you haven't taken a proper break for ages, not since you got on the staff of *Chimera*, and even a superwoman like you needs to lighten up.'

'It's been at least two years,' Tamzin admitted, pouring another cup of coffee, and wondering if this was the last caffeine fix she would have for a while. 'And that was a week in Greece on the trail of an egocentric rock guitarist who refused to cooperate with the press in any shape or form. I got an interview out of him and, though I generally stick to the rules about not mixing business with pleasure, enjoyed having him shag me senseless.'

Janice pulled a face, amused and admiring, remembering Dennis's party. Lust stirred in her groin. 'You were happy in your work, I take it?'

'Those were good days,' Tamzin replied reflectively, while on either side travellers came and went, looking for tables, bearing trays of convenience foods – a lot of chips were being consumed. 'I miss being out there under fire. I could usually get a story, by fair means or foul.'

'So I've heard. I was scared shitless when I knew I was to meet the formidable Miss Lawrence. They said you were brilliant, determined and ruthless.'

'I'll admit I trod on a few toes to get where I am today.'

Little vignettes flickered across Tamzin's brain, incidents of which, in retrospect, she was not proud – stories she had sold to the highest bidder, confidences she had betrayed, never mind what effect exposure had on the interviewees. She had received handsome cash payments, and furthered her career from investigative journalist to the plum position she now occupied. Even so, conscience pricked at times.

'We all do that,' Janice cut in quickly. 'Who hasn't a skeleton hidden somewhere in the ethics cupboard?'

Tamzin seemed edgy, despite the extended Christmas break, maybe because of it: some people needed to keep busy so they had no time to think about themselves. She had come to the conclusion that Tamzin was a workaholic.

They were avoiding the moment of leaving the warm womb of the Little Chef and stepping into the grey afternoon, where cold knifed the lungs, the breath hung on the air, and the traffic crawled along roads gritted against treacherous patches of black ice. So far, the snow had held off since yesterday, but the sky was pregnant with it, that curious steely, dirty colour presaging a heavy fall.

Tamzin leaned her elbows on the table and pushed back the springy curls that fell across her brow. Had Janice not known it was natural, she might have assumed she'd spent three hours in a salon with her hair wound round rods to achieve a spiral perm.

'I miss reporting,' Tamzin confided, gazing across at her friend's high camp garb that consisted of layers of violent-coloured wrappings – a poncho, heliotrope tights, earrings like neon lights, a Peruvian bowler hat. 'I got a tremendous buzz out of it. That's lacking now. Someone else goes out and rustles up copy. I'm the one who has to vet it, approve or disapprove, consult with Mike.'

'Ah, so it's your chauvinistic co-ed that's bugging you,' Janice said sagely.

Sharp green eyes, frosty as the afternoon beyond the double glazing, pierced hers. Tamzin's lip curled slightly. 'It's not him – though he can be a pain – it's the whole restrictive set-up. I'd like to land a sensational scoop myself.'

'Maybe you can.' Janice sat back and, rummaging in her enormous designer bag, produced a mirror and prinked into it. She spiked her fingers through her hair, now more purple than plum, and stared critically at her matching lipstick and eyeshadow.

'At Cheveral Court? I don't think so,' Tamzin said dubiously.

'Leave it to your old Auntie Janice,' she answered with a mischief-inspired grin. 'Inga passed on an interesting snippet of gossip when I rang to confirm we were on our way. This was to go no further, but she and I are close mates so that's all right. Guess who she's expecting to stay?'

'I don't know. Brad Pitt? The Princess of Wales?'

'Nearly as good. Guy Ventura!' There was a wicked glint in Janice's eye as she triumphantly announced this.

Tamzin was impressed. Ambition reared its head, along with her predatory reporter's instincts. If she could only meet him, do an indepth piece, that would boost her self-esteem, proving she hadn't lost her touch. Guy Ventura, the dynamic, world-renowned concert pianist, with the face of an angel and the temper of a devil. He was reclusive, unpredictable, rude – and punchy if pushed. The paparazzi hounded and hated him.

She had attended one of his performances at the Barbican Centre, bewitched by the fire and force of his playing. He was a giant, not only physically, but as an acclaimed exponent of his chosen instrument. His face had appeared everywhere, he had granted Melvyn Bragg an exclusive on the South Bank Show – then vanished into limbo. Rumour had been rife: he was in America – in a Buddhist retreat in the Himalayas – he had given up the piano for ever. No one knew.

'I saw him play,' Tamzin mused, tipping her lighter end to end, needing to occupy her restless fingers. 'He's something else.'

She recalled the menacing aura that hung about him as he stalked on to the stage, marking out his territory.

Six foot four of raw sex and blistering talent in a flawless black evening suit. The blood had boiled in her veins as, in the midst of the rapturous ovation, she had stared at that strikingly handsome face, product of mid-European descent, the broad high cheekbones, strongly pronounced nose, full sensual mouth and heavy-lidded, come-to-bed eyes.

And his hair – this was what had really got to her – wild, shaggy, intensely black, flowing over his shoulders. The fans had gone mad, the atmosphere charged with a tension that was intense adoration and naked sexual desire. She had felt it juddering down every vertebra of her spine to the heartland of her womanhood. Neatly gowned middle-aged ladies, musical *aficionados*, scruffy students, demure housewives – even the critics had not been immune.

He was a sorcerer, and this was before he had nonchalantly flipped back his tails, seated himself on the piano stool, poised his large, sinewy hands over the keys, and cast an eye at the conductor. The first notes of Prokofiev's third concerto had rung out, and Ventura had started to play.

Never had Tamzin experienced such a powerful, gutsy rendition of the work. She had an Ashkenazy recording of it, but no other pianist succeeded in matching Guy's brilliance and energy, astonishing bravura and wonderfully piquant lyricism. During the interval, she had rushed to the foyer and queued to purchase his CD.

'Maybe you'll be able to meet him.' Janice's voice brought her back to the present. 'Sounds like you might have the hots for him.'

'That's an understatement,' Tamzin admitted. 'Back in my flat on the memorable night of his Barbican concert, I played the CD I'd just bought and reached for my dildo.'

'Wish I'd been there to watch,' Janice murmured, pressing her bottom against the hard seat, wriggling a little, feeling the drag of silk tights over her damp cleft. Tamzin had given her no chance to repeat the pleasures they had shared in Dennis's hammock, and she was hoping for a renewal of their intimacy when they reached Cheveral Court.

'She's beautiful,' Janice had told Inga down the phone. 'But too controlled, needs bringing out.'

'Does she swing both ways?' Inga had asked, in her mellifluous dusky voice.

'As far as I know she's new to the delights of Sappho.

I've done it with her once and she's a natural, though a little shy.'

'We'll have to do something about that, shan't we? I can't wait to meet her, darling.'

'She's beginning to appreciate discipline,' Janice had added.

'Lance will be pleased,' Inga had replied, laughing softly. 'And not only him, as you well know. Remember the object of this exercise?'

'Our mutual friend has arrived then?'

'Oh, yes. He's arrived.'

Now Janice gathered up her bag. 'We'd better get on,' she said, rising to her feet, her bizarre attire attracting interested glances. 'With any luck we'll reach the house before it starts to snow. Once we're tucked away inside, it can blizzard as much as it likes. We'll be too busy to notice the weather.'

They were travelling in Tamzin's car, with Janice map-reading. Her sense of direction was nil, and there were delays as they shot past the motorway exit, went off course, and had to drive several miles out of their way before getting back on the right track.

A flake of snow settled on the windscreen as if on a journey of reconnaissance. Almost at once the air was full of them, thick, white, whirling feathers that reduced the world of spacious sky and wide fields to a narrow orbit of road.

'We're almost there,' Janice said, index finger on the map. 'Yes, I remember it now. There's the King's Arms – the village pub. Now, take the next turning on the right.'

'Damn this snow!' Tamzin snorted, eyes slitted as she peered ahead. 'Can't see a bloody thing!'

They drove down a narrow lane, the hedges on either side rapidly vanishing in the drifting whiteness, icy ruts under the wheels. Then a dark shape loomed out of that dancing glitter, forming into a pair of imposing gates, lacy iron etched with frost.

Janice, swearing, ventured to place her fashionable boots into the slush, picked her way across and spoke into the intercom. Within seconds the massive portals ploughed through the fresh fall already piling up against their base.

'Here we go!' Janice cried, jumping in and brushing flakes from her poncho. 'Don't know about you, but I could slaughter a gin and tonic.'

An avenue lay ahead, guarded by beech trees, their filigreed branches lost in the enveloping flurry. The head-lights cast a yellowish beam barely a foot in length, and

Tamzin slowed to a crawl. She didn't relish having to abandon the car and trudge the rest of the way, hefting her luggage. She began to regret falling in with Janice's plans and leaving her cosy apartment.

Then, without warning, the solid bulk of a Range Rover appeared out of the gloom. It slewed to a halt. So did Tamzin. A man climbed down and strode towards them.

He was tall and he was strong. 'It's Lance,' Janice said, immensely relieved, winding down the passenger window. At once she was covered in flakes. She wound it up again.

He tapped on the glass, shouting, 'Thought I'd better come and meet you. I'll go ahead and you follow.'

'He's a babe,' Janice informed Tamzin smugly. 'You'll like him.'

Independent and liberated lady though she was, Tamzin was thankful he had come to the rescue. It was easier now, following his wheel tracks, and soon lights shone ahead. No details could be determined through the obliterating storm, but Lance's vehicle swung round the side of a building into a courtyard. Double-doors opened by sensor, and the Range Rover trundled through. Tamzin parked alongside and sat back with a sigh of relief.

Janice made the introductions as Lance helped them unload the boot which was crammed with Vuitton suitcases. Though Tamzin liked to travel light, Janice didn't, and had managed to convince her that one couldn't arrive at Cheveral Court inadequately kitted out.

'Give a hand, Kevlin,' he said to a rugged young man in an Arran jumper and jeans who was giving Tamzin an impudent, appraising stare.

'The local talent,' Janice hissed in her ear. 'And not bad at all.'

They left the integral garage by a fire-proof door connecting with the house. 'It was once the mews,' Lance explained as they walked along a warm, well-lit passage. 'But we've made alterations. There are stables on the other side and several horses for those who like to ride. Do you, Miss Lawrence?'

He threw her a look that made her stomach clench, so dashing was he in his country clothes – green Barbour jacket, Hunter wellingtons, a tweed cap at a jaunty angle on his straight brown hair. He wore it long, and this always inspired her interest. She could not resist men with long hair.

His accent, too, was one that caressed her ears and

slid sinuously over her senses. He sounded like the arche-typal upper-crust Englishman – public school educated, varsity trained. She had no doubt that he was a sports-man through and through. Cricket, rugger, polo – he'd excel at every one.

'I can ride, Mr Manwaring, though I'm rather rusty,' she replied, wondering how it would be to go for an early morning canter with him.

He'd be bound to mount a thoroughbred, maybe even a stallion. A Spanish Arab from an Irish studfarm, prod-uct of selective breeding which included the blood of the indigenous Connemara ponies.

'Capital. We'll go together.' There was no question of asking her: he had decided and there was no more to be said.

Arrogant, she thought, and decided to stand her ground. Aristocrat he might be, but she had no intention of being ordered about. 'I'll see how I feel, and it rather depends on the weather, surely?'

Janice shot her an amused glance. Lance would find he had met his match. He was too accustomed to getting his own way, relying on his flagrantly masculine sexual allure.

He did not betray by the flicker of an eyelash that he

was anything but enchanted by his new guest. He did, however, exchange a look with Kevlin – one which was immediately understood. A few days at Cheveral Court and the austere Miss Lawrence would change her tune.

Chapter Four

Inga leaned forward, pressed her hands against the stone wall and stared through the spy-hole at Tamzin. Concealed in a secret passage leading from a walk-in cupboard in her bedroom, it was a never-ending source of delectation and delight for the voyeur, offering an uninterrupted view of the adjoining apartment.

She and Lance had discovered it when studying the plans of the original Elizabethan manor, to which there had been structural additions over the centuries. They had found it to be honeycombed with hidden corridors, priest-holes, attic rooms tucked away under the eaves and a complex network of cellars.

The occupant of the room beyond had no idea she

was being scrutinised. From her side of the wall the narrow aperture for the use of salacious eyes was artfully concealed by a large landscape in a gilt frame. The vista of fields and woods, à la Watteau, gave no hint of the cunning device by which everything taking place there could be observed. It was in direct line with the massive, ornate four-poster bed. An article of furniture too heavy to be moved, it had stood on the same spot for over three hundred years, as if taking root like the oak from which it had been fashioned.

Inga knew of several other peep-holes in various quarters of the house, and trick mirrors, too. Lance shared this knowledge. It was part and parcel of the bonds welding them together – kinship, an overweening pride, the love of money, an even greater love of power.

Passion came into it, of course, and Inga was all too aware of this. If, despite her calculating cold heart, she loved anyone on earth, then it was her cousin Lance. He had taken her virginity at a tender age, and together they had explored the killingly marvellous, sometimes destructive and terrible wonders of sex.

Her girlhood had been far from normal, orphaned young and brought up with Lance, rampaging through his parents' stately pile near York, and running wild over the moors till tamed by boarding-school: on the surface anyway, as was he. In reality neither had altered one whit, headstrong, amoral people determined to drain sensation to the dregs.

She had been canny enough to avoid love, marrying a rich old man who, on his demise, had left her a fortune. Lance had remained a bachelor, but also inherited wealth on the death of his father. They had pooled their resources and sought a business enterprise which would give them career satisfaction, a substantial income and the opportunity to indulge their predilection for the bizarre.

Cheveral Court had just gone on the market, a run-down property in need of complete renovation. It had come at a time when health consciousness was to the fore, and those who could afford it were desperately seeking temples dedicated to the pursuit of fitness and longevity. Lance and Inga had seized on this as a God-given opportunity.

Within a year the manor had been opened as a resort to rival Champneys. They had employed an outrage-ously expensive and competent advertising agency who had launched a multi-media campaign emphasising the exclusivity of this club. Inga and Lance maintained a house-party atmosphere in the warm and secluded ambience of an elegant country house where privacy was respected, the service impeccable, the views peaceful, and the staff dedicated to the guests' comfort and happiness.

In every way, Inga mused with a slow smile, and her skirt rustled as she raised it slowly, slipped a hand between her legs and caressed her cleft. We're very discreet, but as sexual gratification plays such a vital role in well-being then special attention is paid to any particular desires our clients may express.

This was no hardship as she, Lance and their carefully selected assistants were experts in the art of love, priding themselves on their skills. Inga and her cousin always personally vetted any applicants for the posts, subjecting them to intensive research, judging their aptitude by a series of amorous tests and expecting them to perform superbly.

Inga's tongue crept out, snakelike, to lick her lips as she scrutinised the Embroidered Room where Tamzin was unpacking her suitcases and hanging clothes in the armoire. The thrill of viewing any aspect of Cheveral Court gave Inga supreme pleasure, second only to that of orgasm. It was her creation, rising like the Phoenix from the ashes of neglect, a supremely desirable residence, and she gloried in her achievement.

She fondled her silky blonde bush, her fingertips and the sensitive skin of her pubis in perfect harmony. She liked to rub herself in a leisurely fashion, the sight of Tamzin and visions of what they had planned to do with her firing her imagination. With a stifled moan, she found her core, eased back its tiny hood and massaged it swiftly. The needy little organ responded by bringing her to orgasm in a lightning burst of sensation.

'She is lovely, isn't she? I can see you agree,' murmured a voice in her ear, and she jumped, her inner muscles still contracting, clitoris throbbing. He had crept up on her unawares.

Quickly regaining command of herself, she moved aside so that he might view Tamzin, saying, 'Yes, she's very lovely.'

'I knew I had to have her the first moment I saw her. She roasted me in her damned magazine. Gave no quarter. But when I met her, very briefly, you understand, I knew she could be one of us.' The cadences of his voice were like syrup, but with a slightly rasping edge that rippled along Inga's nerves and settled in her belly, filling it with rekindled warmth. She suddenly wanted a phallus inside her – hard, pounding, thrusting against her inner contours.

The passage was dark, its constriction forcing her close to him, and she felt the broad shoulder against her narrow one, the leather-clad thigh pressed to hers. She could smell him, freshly showered male body, damp hair, a hint of aftershave. Prickles like minor electric shocks ran under her skin, the fine down rising on every limb as she thought about their plot. Anything dark and devious excited her.

Secrets!

Like those she had shared with Lance as a child. Things the adults forbade, a smoky world of hidden actions, guilt and defiance. A religious child, adoring the paintings of saints and martyrs, the crucified Christ, the agony and the ecstasy of denial and sacrifice, she had revelled in her burden of sin, laying lilies at the feet of the Magdalen.

Secrets! She was aware that he suffered from guilt, too. It showed in certain aspects of his work, transformed it from slick, facile competence into the visions of a tormented genius. Beware of those with flawed personalities, she thought. We are dangerous. We know how to survive.

'It's our secret,' he whispered, echoing her thoughts, his eyes glistening in the gloom, still fixed on Tamzin. 'I don't want her to know I'm here. Not yet. Or anyone else, except Janice and Lance.'

'She won't.' Her voice trembled, her body, too. She was loosening again, vaginal fluids wetting her labia that were still flushed and swollen from the orgasm just passed.

'Look at her,' he murmured and seized her arm in iron talons. 'She has no idea the very fabric of her life is about to be ripped apart.'

I'll be branded with the marks of his fingers for days, Inga thought, voluptuous pleasure surging along every nerve and culminating in her bud. It demanded to be pleasured again. He straightened up and she peered through the opening.

Tamzin took a book from the smaller of the cases and placed it on the bedside table, then lifted out a teddy bear, kissed him on his button nose and sat him on her pillow. After this she sat on the lower step of that mighty edifice, crossed one knee over the other and tugged at her boots.

First one, then the other was removed. Her sweater came next, peeled off over her head, followed by the

T-shirt and leggings. Naked except for two small coffee and gold underwired cups supporting her breasts and a matching triangle that barely covered her mound, she stretched her arms above her head in a sinuous and graceful movement.

Inga looked her over with the eye of an expert, then nudged her companion. He bent his tall head and gazed at his prey with a sharp intake of breath. Inga almost felt it on her nipples – warm wet breath awakening them to acute sensitivity, sharp teeth nibbling.

She was dressed for dinner in a full-skirted moire gown with long tight sleeves, a bodice that gripped her ribs and had a low, square neckline, vaguely reminiscent of the costumes worn by some of the ladies in the portraits that adorned the walls of the Queen Anne drawing room. But beneath this fabulous couture creation, her firm boyish buttocks were bare, as was the scented avenue between them. She ached for him to be aware of it, too, imagining the tight feeling as he inserted his cock in the taut mouth of her rectum.

He was excited. How excited? There was only one way to find out. Dare she touch without his permission? She decided to risk it. Her small strong hand, used to controlling high-mettled horses, reached unerringly for his crotch. Like a solid bough, fully erect, his penis surged against the imprisoning leather trousers. He made no move as she felt for the zipper tag and eased it down. His cock shot forth like an animal freed from its cage.

Darkness is so good, she thought, her hidden self surging with freshly aroused want and dusky memories. Murder in the Dark. Hide and Seek. How she and Lance had loved those games played in and around the Yorkshire castle. Not always alone, inviting neighbouring children to tea sometimes, when Nanny gave permission. A stern woman, Nanny, but no match for them.

Birthday parties – Christmas. They'd scared their little friends half to death. Ghosts. The Headless Horseman. The Grey Lady. A potent brew: fear, a hint of cruelty – and sex. Their whimpering victims had been only too ready to agree to anything they wanted to do.

He did not react, remaining standing, watching Tamzin. But his prick had a mind of its own, twitching as Inga ran her fingers along the thick stem and worked the foreskin over the slippery wet head. His juices, hers too. Her fingers still bore traces of her own nectar. His balls were stirring, that little clench and spasm she recognised, the spunk welling up, demanding release. She sank to her knees, her back pressed to the wall, her mouth reaching for his tool.

She took it between her lips, but he dug his fingers into her hair and pushed in hard, the glans jabbing the back of her throat, his urgency heralding an almost immediate climax. She knew she'd not come this time, but no matter. Her orgasms would be enjoyed later. He would give it to her in his own peculiar and exciting way, inflicting the pain-pleasure she craved.

His penis spasmed. Creamy liquid spurted out, filling her mouth, running down her chin, hot and saline on her lips. She swallowed, making no sound. Neither did he. It was their secret.

'Enter,' Tamzin called at the tap on the bedroom door. She was bathed, fragrant with exotic oils, wrapped in a white towelling robe provided as part of the service with the initials CC embroidered on the collar.

'Welcome to Cheveral Court,' said Inga, sweeping in, yards of skirt swishing round her. 'Miss Lawrence, isn't it?'

'That's right. Tamzin Lawrence – Janice Kent's friend.' She was transfixed by the sudden arrival of this ravishing creature who blended so perfectly into the sumptuous surroundings.

The pale blonde hair, the pale gold skin, those eyes darkened to purple, reflecting the colour of her gown. Why was she hidden away in Hampshire instead of gliding round as a mannequin, displaying garments for some top fashion designer? Tag would go ballistic at this wicked waste of talent.

'Lance told me you'd arrived. Such a terrible night. We'll be well and truly grounded. But this makes it all the more fun, don't you think?' Inga came nearer, and even on close inspection her skin was flawless – like delicate porcelain but with a warm glow as if she moved through perpetual candlelight.

'I'm glad to be inside. Just for a moment on the journey, I thought we were lost, but Lance saved the day.'

'He's such a hero!' Inga exclaimed, her laugh spiced with irony. 'I hope you'll enjoy your stay. We're a small group at present. The weather, you know – and people still abroad after the New Year celebrations. You'll meet some of our other guests at dinner, though a few are on strict diets and prefer to have their meals served in their rooms to avoid temptation. We have separate cottages for those who wish to avoid the public. Guy Ventura is in one of them at present.'

'Janice told me. Shan't I meet him? That's a shame. I admire his playing.'

'Don't we all? And as for the man himself – to die for, my dear!' Inga enthused, then shrugged. 'He may relent after a day or two. Who knows with a man of such unpredictable temperament?'

'Dinner is formal, I take it?' Tamzin gestured towards Inga's gown.

'The choice is yours, but here we think women should be encouraged to dress up, their escorts, too,' Inga purred. 'They enjoy it, especially as the days pass and they become fitter, prettier. That's what Cheveral Court is about – helping people to reach their full potential.'

'Janice warned me that your methods can be unconventional,' Tamzin ventured, inadvertently letting her robe fall open at the neck.

She pulled it together and fastened the girdle more tightly. The bright awareness in Inga's eyes put her on guard. Lance had made her feel the same – undressed somehow, even though fully clad. She wished Janice was there, and suddenly felt shy, all that cool confidence she displayed in the business arena deserting her.

The room was pleasantly warm, the central heating system supplemented by an open fire, one of the luxuries of this fiercely expensive accommodation. Damask drapes with deep, fringed pelmets curved round the large bay windows, but outside the blizzard could be heard sheeting against the panes. The wind boomed in the carved stone fireplace, and snow flakes dropped down the wide chimney to hiss and melt on the logs.

Inga draped herself on a settee upholstered in velvet, feet tucked up under her. 'It rather depends on one's point of view,' she declared, the table-lamp gleaming on the linten hair piled high on the shapely head, and touching sparks from the diamond drops swinging in her ears. 'Tonight we will relax, but tomorrow we'll begin an exercise regime to suit you. You don't need to diet, maybe simply taking fruit or vegetable drinks and vitamins to rejuvenate you.'

'Lance suggested I might like to ride with him, Miss Steadson,' Tamzin put in, dropping on her heels by the hearth and enjoying the sight of living flames and their kiss on her face.

'I expect he did, and please call me Inga,' she replied in her throaty voice. She leaned across and ran a hand over Tamzin's curls, then her fingers feathered down her cheek and touched her lips. 'You have unusual hair,' she added, her eyes pure amethyst. 'It's the colour of butterscotch. Is it the same everywhere?'

Tamzin looked up sharply, meeting her stare. 'I don't have a lot of body hair, and what there is happens to be brownish.'

'You don't dye it, like Janice?'

This is one foxy lady, Tamzin decided, shaking her head. Has she seen Janice naked? She could have done during massage and sauna sessions, I guess. Or is there something more? Just how intimate are they?

'I neither bleach nor dye,' she announced and then added pointedly, 'I'm going to dress now.'

'Don't mind me. We can talk while you do so. Tell me about your work. Janice says you run *Chimera*. How thrilling. It's my favourite glossy. What a fascinating life you must lead, mixing with the stars, attending functions, first-nights, film premières.'

'It's not like that. Very little glamour comes my way,' Tamzin said, wondering why Inga was being deliberately provocative.

Disconcerted by the woman's blatant interest, she walked across to select a gown from the wardrobe. It was an antique piece which had occupied that space for generations. The doors were carved with acanthus leaves and vines, and when opened wafted a sweet, musky smell like incense or the memories of long-ago ball dresses and withered posies. Many an innocent young girl must have stood where she did now, anticipating the night, hopeful of meeting her true love on the dance floor.

'I'm mad about old furniture,' whispered Inga, close behind her. 'I wonder if this door leads to Narnia?'

Tamzin spun round, startled. Inga was staring at her with blazing eyes, a pensive smile curving her poppy-red lips. She stepped back, and Tamzin squeezed past her, dress on a hanger hooked over one finger.

'One likes to believe so,' Tamzin said, keeping a grip on her emotions, though thoroughly disturbed by the close proximity of this alluring woman. 'There's the child in all of us, isn't there?'

'Playmates. Yes, indeed. Cousin Lance was mine.'

Tamzin laid the dress across the bedspread which matched the window curtains and those of the four-poster. Without removing her dressing-gown she stepped into black lace panties, pulled them up and adjusted the ribbon ties at each pointed hip bone. For some reason she couldn't fathom, she was reluctant to appear nude before Inga. Everything she said seemed to have a sub-text, even the passing reference to her relationship with Lance.

Tamzin had chosen a plain gown, its sage-green silk suiting her colouring. Still possessed of this curious modesty, she turned her back on Inga and let the robe drop to the floor. Slipping her arms through the shoulder straps of her bra, she felt round behind to fasten it.

Cool fingers touched her skin as Inga let her hand move up the taut length of her spine, lightly touching every vertebra. 'Let me,' she offered, and deftly hooked the straps together.

Tamzin did not move. Despite her reservation she relished the feel of those silken fingers and remained motionless as Inga's hands appeared from beneath her arms, gently settling her breasts in the bra-cups. She ran a finger across the top of the tight satin, and skimmed the hard peaks of Tamzin's nipples.

'You have gorgeous breasts,' she said. 'See how the tips rise, hungry for caresses.'

The softly lit room, the dance of firelight on tapestried walls, the spicy smells redolent of passions both recent and far-off, were casting a seductive spell over Tamzin. The blonde woman behind her could have been any handsome being from any era – male or female. All that mattered was appeasing the need glowing in the pit of her belly. Already the silk triangle between her legs was damp.

She picked up the dress and dropped it over her head, settling it round her waist, covering those wanton breasts. Inga acted the lady's maid, brushing aside the mane of curls and holding the gap firmly together as she pulled up the zip to just above the line where the bra fastened. Bare shoulder-blades, a deep cleavage, the skirt cunningly cut to fit the hips sleekly.

'Have it, darling, as a Christmas present,' Tag had insisted when Tamzin had admired it at his charity show.

'I can't possibly,' she had protested.

'You can. You will. Just give me a good write-up.'

'Lovely gown,' Inga murmured, bringing her back to the present.

'Designed by a friend – Tag Pedra.'

'The designer? I said you were lucky, didn't I?'

Tamzin had already put on her make-up before Inga arrived and there was no reason to delay longer, but she hesitated, wanting to stay in this warm, sensual world with Inga. It was comforting to feel her caring touch, exciting to feel those delicate fingers smoothing the folds from her skirt, lingering on the hidden apex of her thighs, pressing against the silk a little, connecting with her cleft, lingering on the tiny bulge of her protruding clitoris.

'I want to kiss you,' Inga whispered, soft arms around her, sweet woman's breath brushing her face.

Tamzin felt palms cupping her face with the most delicate of gestures, nothing hard, nothing harshly masculine, all fragile, languorous delight. She did not resist, feeling the tip of Inga's tongue moving over her lower lip, first the corner, then the full central pout.

The sensation was ecstatic, the taste and texture so different from the men who had kissed her. Red mouth on hers, moving warmly, deeply, tongue slipping between to coax her lips apart. The shock of her own response, her tongue eager to meet Inga's, curling round it, encouraging it, and her hands reaching for Inga's breasts, feeling her quiver with excitement as she brushed over the small, taut nipples.

She was sinking, caught in the silken coils Inga was weaving around her. Her knees were weak and, still kissing, arms entwined, they moved to the couch. She was accepting, moulding herself to Inga's curves, lava creeping through her, gathering in her core, needing, wanting. A sound woke her from her slumberous daze. The echoing boom of a sheepskin covered hammer on brass.

Inga lifted her head, smiled into her eyes, and said, 'The dinner gong. We'll have to put this off till later, darling.'

The diners were positioned each side of the refectory table in the middle of the Great Hall. A linen cloth stretched like a snowy plane between them, crimsoned by patches of fire and candlelight.

The hall was steeped in history, decorated with tattered flags and crossed pikes, suits of armour and swords. A minstrels' gallery was situated halfway up one wall above a carved screen sheltering the door. Logs the size of a man blazed in the wide hearth of the inglenook fireplace. Its stone canopy was ornamented with a central crest, its apex lost in the dimness of the oak rafters.

Orange tongues of flame licked round the roaring logs, reflected in silver and cut glass, on the flower-filled epergne shaped like a goat-legged satyr in the centre of the table, on the vibrant oriental patterns gracing the Royal Doulton service.

Inga sat at one end, looking down the board to where Lance occupied a thronelike chair. Kevlin was helping to serve as they were short-staffed, jeans and T-shirt discarded in favour of a dark uniform. The butler, Harper, middle-aged and hatchet-faced, opened bottles of wine and received the covered dishes as they were wheeled in on heated trolleys.

Tamzin was hungry. She'd had nothing but a cup of herbal tea since her arrival. The meal was superlative – as Inga explained, smiling at the half a dozen couples enjoying it, 'Your first night here, so we've relaxed the rules a little. Make the most of it, for tomorrow I'll not be so lenient, though I assure you we're definitely not cranky or spartan with our food.'

There was a ripple of polite laughter, and Harper stepped forward with the wine bottle, topping up glasses. Janice nudged Tamzin, saying, *sotto voce,* 'Well, what d'you think of it so far?'

Tamzin was engrossed in the dessert, the finale to a gourmet meal of melon dredged in ginger and brown sugar, melt-in-the-mouth smoked salmon and caviar omelette, tender roast lamb stuffed with truffles, and a selection of seasoned vegetables tossed in a sinful concoction with a buttery base. Now she was enjoying profiteroles smothered in a veil of rich, dark chocolate sauce.

'If this is healthy eating, then I'm all for it,' she smiled, tongue delicately licking a trace of cream from her lips.

'Healthy eating? That's codswallop. Call it self-indulgence,' snapped the man seated on her other side. 'Where I've just come from we were lucky if we found nice fat juicy grubs lurking under logs.'

'Really, Alex, must you?' Inga dimpled at him, forkful of choux pastry poised on its way to her mouth.

He grinned wickedly. Some of her more conventional guests were grimacing and shuddering – the colonel and his wife, grey-haired but spritely – the honeymoon couple aware of little but each other – the mother and daughter, rivals in beauty.

'The jungle Indians swear by them. Full of nutrients. You should try them some time,' he continued, raising his wine-glass to Inga, eyes toasting her over the rim.

Tamzin had been introduced to him earlier. Alex Fenton, wild-life photographer and explorer, recovering from a harrowing trek into the Brazilian jungle.

He was conspicuously attractive, his light brown hair streaked by a tropical sun, his tan that solid chestnut colour only achieved by months of living in a hot climate. Of average height, lean and wiry, there wasn't an ounce of spare flesh anywhere on his body. A humorous face, the eyes of a crystalline blue, hedged by sandy lashes and crinkled at the outer corners as if he was forever staring into the distance in search of enemies.

Now she said, 'Will you tell me about your trip, Mr Fenton? I'd like to interview you for my magazine. Maybe we can have a photo session. I've brought my camera.'

He turned the full force of his gaze to her, and she decided that this was his most compelling feature – the clear blue power of his eyes. 'And may I ask the name of your paper, Miss Lawrence?'

'*Chimera*,' she answered, almost defensively.

This hard, blunt-tongued individual would no doubt scoff at appearing in a fashion magazine. Others had before him – intellectuals professing to scorn the popular press. She liked to think *Chimera* was a cut above the average.

He gave a derisive snort and asked, 'Why is it called that? According to definition a chimera is a fabled fire-spouting monster with a lion's head, a serpent's tail and a goat's body. Are you and your staff monsters, Miss Lawrence?'

She bristled at his rudeness, her cheeks growing hot, but her secret lips even hotter. He was insolent, mocking, yet her body was drawn to his as by a magnet, and she leant towards him as Kevlin appeared at her other shoulder, removing her plate and replacing it with a minute gold-lined porcelain cup filled with thick, black Turkish coffee.

She gathered her wits and mentally leashed the wayward desires coursing through her. Sitting up straight, she answered crisply, 'It also means any wild fancy, Mr Fenton. Ours is a cosmopolitan periodical – we cater for all tastes and air unusual views, photos and stories. I suppose you could say we were monsters, depending on the angle we take.'

'Ah, so I'll have to be careful what I say, shall I? Or you'll feel free to kick shit out of me. Don't worry. I'm used to that. The press invariably misunderstand my motives and write crap about my love-life.'

'One of the prices you have to pay for being a celebrity, dear boy. You love to shock 'em, don't you, Alex?' Lance butted in, cupping a brandy glass between his hands.

'It's dead easy. They lap up anything I care to lay on them,' Alex said with a dismissive shrug.

Tamzin decided that he was far and away the most difficult yet desirable man present, though Lance came a close second. Janice, it seemed, was enchanted by Kevlin. Every time he bent over to retrieve her plate or refill her glass, her hand disappeared under the table in the direction of the impressive bulge behind the fly of his tight black trousers.

Coffee finished, the lady removed her reluctant daughter, and the colonel and his wife made their good nights, saying something about a brisk session in the exercise room early in the morning. The honeymoon couple went up, too, so starry-eyed that Janice remarked to Tamzin, 'Why on earth did they come here? Surely they won't have any energy left once they've finished bonking each other brainless?'

The atmosphere lifted. 'Now it's down to us chickens,' Inga said, pouring herself another brandy and sucking sticky droplets from her fingers like a greedy child. 'We'll go for a swim in a while. You've not yet seen our indoor pool, have you, Tamzin?'

Swimming while a snowstorm raged sounded wonderful to Tamzin, as a part of this strangely unreal ambience where the past met and merged with modernity. She could feel stress melting away under the soothing influence of first-class cuisine, fine wine, stimulating company and that aura of sensuality which Inga and Lance engendered.

She relaxed in her chair, aware of every movement Alex made. These were many for he was a volatile person, given to expansive gestures as he argued with Lance over the vexed question of whether what remained of the Amazonian rain forest should be left undisturbed or if road-makers should cut a swathe into remote regions to bring education to the natives.

'Leave the poor buggers alone, I say,' he declared, banging his fist down on the table and making the glasses rattle. 'They've more education in their little fingers than the rest of us put together. They know about the things that matter – the environment, the jungle gods and spirits. They're wise about tribal laws, and have a great respect for the elders.'

'What about medicine? You surely won't deny they need this?' Lance demurred, refusing to back down.

'Bollocks! I'd rather put myself in the hands of a shaman than any quack from medical school. They know all there is to know about herbs.'

'Darling, such zeal! But I really do need a swim,' Inga interrupted, turning the conversation which threatened to become boring.

Alex shrugged, rose slowly to his feet and went to her. She gave him a smile of lazy intimacy and rested the tips of her fingers on his arm as they strolled across the parquet flooring.

'Speaking of swimming,' he said, 'did I tell you about the tiny fish that lurks in the South American rivers?'

'No, you didn't, but I've a feeling you're going to.'

'It has a nasty habit of penetrating any orifice, particularly fond of diving into the anus or up inside the penis. Very difficult to remove, entails a painful operation,' he announced, adding with a quirky grin, 'That's why it's best to keep a finger up your bum if you feel like a dip in the Amazon.'

'Darling Alex, much as I adore listening to you, doesn't anything nice ever happen there?'

'Not a lot,' he said. 'I sometimes wonder why I bother.'

Tamzin watched as they drifted towards the door with Lance and Janice. She was replete and lazy, in no hurry to follow, but finished her drink and pushed back her chair. Then suddenly she stopped, a sense of danger, urgent and primordial, prickling down her spine. She looked round sharply. The hall was deserted, yet she had the strong feeling that someone, somewhere was watching her.

Giving herself a mental shake she tried to forget the warning bells insinuating themselves into the recesses of her mind, and set off in pursuit of the others. They had not used the main door, but a smaller one to the side.

As she passed through it her nostrils immediately responded to the strong miasma of overripe vegetation and leaves on the point of rotting. It was far from unpleasant, reminding her of midsummer days holidaying on Exmoor, when she had hidden away in a forest of ferns and waist-high heather, curlews lamenting overhead.

'Which way to the pool?' she asked Kevlin who appeared from nowhere. He had changed, now bare-chested with the briefest of swimming trunks cradling his bulky tackle.

He grinned, and she warmed to the look in his impudent eyes. 'I'm going there meself. Your friend Janice wants me to fuck her. I'll fuck you, too, if you like. Come with me, miss.'

Rendered speechless by this unabashed invitation, she followed him into a conservatory designed in the Gothic style, with convoluted ironwork, ecclesiastical arches and gargoyles carved round the capitals of stone columns.

Plants grew thick on every side, twisting vines coiling serpentwise to the glass roof; banana and rubber trees with large shiny leaves; palms and cacti and exotic, fecund creations with huge white trumpets and scarlet stamen poking forth like penises. They reminded Tamzin of the devil's Stink Horn fungus, emitting a powerful odour, fascinating yet repellent.

'Inga calls this her Garden of Eden,' Kevlin supplied, smiling widely over a dazzle of strong white teeth. 'I don't know about that, but it's better than being outside. Terrible bad road conditions, so the weatherman said on telly. Looks like you just made it in time. It's kind of like a dream in here. A wet one, if you get my drift.'

Voices ahead, and laughter, the sound of splashing. They emerged from the hot-house into a large construction surrounding a blue pool of irregular shape. Set as it was amid palm trees and luxuriantly leafy shrubs, it looked like a lagoon. A waterfall cascaded over rocks and churned the azure deeps into foam. Totally enclosed and secluded, this mock Polynesian paradise was crowned by a high, stained-glass dome.

Inga was sitting on the tiled edge, shoes and stockings discarded, feet dangling in the water. Her skirt was wet and hitched high over her thighs, the fair floss of her pussy displayed. She was laughing at some remark Alex had just made, holding a champagne flute between her scarlet-tipped fingers.

Lance, naked, lay on a half submerged rock, his superbly muscled body lapped by wavelets. But he rolled over as Tamzin approached, bracing himself on one elbow, forming his hands into the shape of opera-glasses through which he studied her with evident fascination. It was embarrassing, possibly rather sinister.

'Come to me, Kevlin,' Janice commanded, her voice slurred, waist-deep in the pool, her evening gown cling-ing wetly to every curve. She waved a bottle at him. 'Have a drink, darling. Get your dress off, Tamzin. We're all friends here.'

Somehow, she could never quite remember how it happened, Tamzin found herself lying in the water with Alex. He was nude and so was she. Though at first she had resisted, her glass had always seemed to be brim-ming, no matter how often she emptied it, and now events seemed jumbled, as confusing as a sheaf of num-berless pages.

She was submerged in steamy fragrance with aromatic middle notes and a sensual woody marine base, through which ethereal trails of meditative ambient music swirled and condensed. Floating on her back, neck supported on the rim of the blue mosaic-lined basin, she looked down her length, shocked by the sight of her nipples, flat belly, and the wedge of wet woolly hair divided by the deeper darkness of her sex. Alex was looking, too. His body was whiplash lean, marked here and there with crooked scars.

Old wounds, perhaps? The idea of him as a battle-toughened mercenary sent her clitoris into needy convulsions and made those rosebud tips crowning her breasts harden with something more than the passage of air over wet skin.

Now he was staring up at the coloured cupola, eyes contemplative as he quoted, '"In Xanadu did Kubla Khan a stately pleasure dome decree: Where Alph, the sacred river, ran through caverns measureless to man down to a timeless sea." D'you suppose Inga decreed this Disney-land bayou, Miss Lawrence?'

'I've no idea.' She stumbled over the words, her tongue feeling too big for her mouth. With a supreme effort she added, 'Why don't you call me Tamzin? Seems odd to be so formal, when we're mother-naked.'

'So we are!' His ice-blue eyes registered mock astonishment. 'Why, my dear Tamzin, how did that happen? Oh, my goodness me, now you've seen my prick.'

She had indeed seen his prick, marvelling at it. Long and lean like its owner, it was very hard, with a splendid curve that pointed towards the illustrious dome overhead. The red glans had risen from the foreskin which now formed a ridge around it. The shaft was pinky-beige, ornamented with pulsing veins, the base disappearing in the brown thatch sprouting on his underbelly. As he spoke, he tensed his muscles and his cock danced for her.

Over on the other side of the pool Janice, soggy skirt peeled up, was on her hands and knees as Kevlin mounted her. His tight buttocks rose and fell and she squealed her appreciation. Inga, stripped to her garter belt, lay on her back below her, tonguing the enlarged clitoris protruding from Janice's labia. And Lance knelt between Inga's spread thighs, his massive dick plunging in and out of her vagina, while his fingers rubbed Janice's nipples.

'They look like sculpture on an Indian temple wall,' Alex murmured, turning towards Tamzin under the water.

She felt it slosh, felt his hand coasting over her breasts, lingering on the hungry points and teasing them till they became even harder. The liquid of her arousal joined that of the water poking libidinous fingers into her entrance.

His legs were entangled with hers. She could feel the jutting prong of his erection. He pressed it against her thigh, captured between his. There was a heaviness in her groin, that thick, hot sensation which could only be eased by orgasm. He smiled into her eyes, lashes spiky, surprisingly thick and curly.

'Well, Tamzin,' he whispered, his hand moving from one excited breast to the other. 'It's time we got better acquainted.'

He let his fingers wander down the concavity of her belly, skim past her navel, and cruise over the feathery maze of wet hair darkening her pubis. Tamzin shuddered, her hand closing round his penis, working it under the water, reaching beneath for the spongy pouches that carried his seed.

He turned her, back pressed to his chest and, soles touching the pool's floor, she felt the nudge of his cock between her buttocks, gliding in past her anus, pushing through the tender leaves of her labia. The head touched her clitoris and she rocked against it, the water buoying her up. Alex held her firmly, finding her love-hole with his cock tip and pushing it inside her cavity. The muscles tightened around the length of him and she gasped as he plunged in deeper.

His hands were at the juncture of her legs, one holding the swollen wings apart while the middle finger of the other stroked her clitoris. Water and her own torrent of juices combined to aid his slippery, exquisite massage of that throbbing organ. Her nipples ached, her loins were on fire, and Alex was wise to her needs.

'I want it,' she gasped, possessed by carnal madness, head flung back against his shoulder, her voice rising to a wail as he lipped her ear.

'I know you do.' His voice was like rich cream. 'I'll give it to you. Come on, darling – do it for me.'

His words were the final aphrodisiac. They tipped her over on to the wild ride towards climax. She was spinning in a vortex, screaming her need. Her eyes, rolled back and wide open, fastened on the glittering cupola, its dazzling facets holding all the colours of the rainbow. Her body and mind echoed it. The brilliant hues splintered into fragments as she reached a shattering orgasm and lost herself in that moment of supreme pleasure.

His hunger-stiffened phallus thrust into her again and again, and she shared the tremors as he came, her inner walls throbbing round his mighty shaft.

Drifting, dreaming in the water like a baby in the

womb, she rested against Alex, quiescent now. Lapped in perfect peace, she wanted to stay there for ever.

Vaguely she could hear the others gambolling over on the far side, changing partners, playing games, splashing and ducking, then pairing off and mating. She was drowsy, satiated, held in the pool's warm liquid embrace, Alex's chin against her shoulder, his hands still fondling her mound.

'Sex, sex, sex,' he murmured, laughter rumbling in his chest. 'Life at Cheveral Court is one big horn.'

She was about to reply, when something delayed on the periphery of her awareness came sharply into focus. She sobered, grabbed at her wits through the web of sex and champagne, and stared around.

The water gave back an innocent smile, the setting resembling a fantastic dream grove in fabled Ancient Greece. Yet Tamsin felt that shivering under the skin that warns of danger. As in the hall, she knew in her gut that something unseen was watching her.

Chapter Five

The shadows were pitch-black among the trees, but moonlight marbled the forest floor with shining silver. There was no sound except the rustle of night-hunters on the prowl.

Naked feet pressing lightly over a pine-needled carpet. Naked flesh caressed by the breeze. I'm dreaming, thought Tamzin, surfacing momentarily. I must be. It's snowing outside.

No trace of bitter winter in this dreamy wood. Spring, maybe, a balmy, ensorcelled spring night. She was drawn towards some unknown destination – aware of whispering voices, of hands touching her intimately, impudent fingers and slavering tongues penetrating the tight moue of her anus, opening the petals of her labia. Her nipples were twin points of fire. Her clitoris a third needy peak.

She moaned in her sleep and fidgeted restlessly under the damask canopy of the vast four-poster, the quilt tangling round her legs. Her loins throbbed, making her wet and desirous. Unconscious, caught up in her sensual dream, one of her hands went down between her legs, cupping her mound and finding her centre, rubbing the diamond-hard tip.

Then, out of impenetrable darkness, he came to her.

She swam to the surface, awake now. He was real, a physical presence, holding her fast, moulding her body against his. A stranger in her bed, and terror gave her added strength. She kicked, threshed, struggled furiously but was helpless against muscles that scarcely felt her blows.

'Be still,' he said, his voice low, harsh and grating. 'Don't fight it – relax.'

That unfamiliar tone held a hypnotic quality. The strength drained from her limbs and she was suddenly passive in his arms, yielding to her excitement as she had yielded to the man's mastery, vitally aware of the powerful body pressed to her own. The texture of leather lay under her fingers, its compelling odour filling her nostrils, overlaid by the chill of frost-sharded woods.

Her hands, wedged between her breasts and his bare chest in a feeble attempt to keep him off, encountered a pelt of hair over iron muscles. His erect, naked phallus forced itself implacably between her thighs, the heat of it filling her with a savage hunger that obliterated fear. His lips on her cheeks were arctic. Ther was something else, too, brushing her face. An alien substance, not human skin.

She raised her hands, fingertips registering the smooth feel of leather shrouding his features to the upper lip, and tracing round the eye-slits. He was masked and hooded. A long shudder passed through her. This man, this aberration from nowhere – why was he masked? And what was he? An incubus come from hell to brand her as his own?

His purpose was clear, and she grew weak under the consummate artistry of his touch on her nipples, first circling the areolae, then rolling the hardened crests till she was roused to a sobbing frenzy. One hand moved to her clitoris, magical fingers now hard, now light, always wet. Within seconds a violent orgasm surged through her entire body, rushing up from her toes, searing her cortex.

Her dream lover gave her no time to recover, driving a gasp from her lips as he thrust his tumescent organ into her pulsating sex with a force that suggested he wanted to drive his way to her heart. It seemed to go on forever, stretching the ridged walls with its thickness, the blunt glans penetrating deeply to butt against the end of her vagina.

Such enormous size was shocking, almost painful, intensely satisfying. Never before had she been so completely filled. He plunged and bucked, large hands cupping her buttocks, lifting her pelvis to meet each thrust, slamming into her again and again, driven by a furious, compulsive need.

She cried out as his teeth fastened on her throat when his climax took him. He convulsed and shuddered, his frantic movements subsiding.

Pinned beneath him she whispered hoarsely, 'Who are you?'

Without answering he took his weight on his arms, his semi-erect cock slipping from her body, leaving her empty and bereft. She heard the mattress creak as he left the bed. Sitting up, she fumbled for the lamp, cursing because she couldn't locate it, determined to look at him.

She contacted the switch and banished darkness. Swinging her legs over the side of the mattress, she staggered to her feet. The fire was a heap of smouldering ash on the hearth, and snow tap-tapped persistently against the windows, but the room was empty. Her ghostly lover had vanished.

For a dazed instant she wondered if he had been a mirage, then caught sight of herself in the dressing-table mirror. A bruise was beginning to purple on her throat. She felt the slither of juices running down her inner thighs. This had been a close encounter with a flesh and blood man, not an apparition.

Her first instinct was to press the intercom and wake Inga. Her finger hovered over the handset, indignation raging through her. A man had broken into her room and raped her. They must call the police. Then her thudding heart slowed, resuming a normal pace. She calmed down, replacing the receiver in its cradle.

Had it been rape? In all honesty she couldn't say it was. She had experienced a dark, sinfully carnal pleasure in the ravishment of her flesh. Lust, pure and simple. Primal satisfaction in being dominated. Even now her skin crept at the memory of it. She had not been forced but controlled – even mastered. And she shivered, heat flooding her secret self, nipples standing out proud on the flushed surface of her breasts.

You're getting kinky, she scolded herself. It's Janice's fault, and the sexually tense atmosphere of this house, hot, heavy and thick. Anything might happen, and probably will, with Inga and Lance wily puppeteers pulling everyone's strings.

But it started with Mike before Christmas, you have to confess, she continued in self-analysis. When he bound your eyes you almost had an involuntary orgasm. What is it with you? I never thought you'd go for the odd quirks which some use to whip up their appetites.

That man just now – his hands, his lips, his stupendous cock – I couldn't see him and it was deliriously exciting. He was in charge. He could have done almost anything he liked to me, performed any debased act and I should have been helpless to do anything other than go along with it. I may have been his victim, but he also gave me tremendous freedom. Because of my helplessness. I could revel in depravity, exonerated from blame. As with Mike, I was entirely in his hands.

Was this scenario orchestrated by Inga and Lance? Tamzin drew her silk kimono about her body and ruminated. The more she thought about it the stronger her conviction became that Cheveral Court's owners were at the bottom of this weird escapade.

Was her mysterious lover one of their friends, or maybe a servant? Had they ordered him to take her in the dark? Was the room bugged? After their uninhibited behaviour at the poolside, she was convinced this was entirely possible.

In the circumstances, she decided to say nothing. Besides, the possibility of his return on another night made her shiver with anticipation. Her hand went to her throat and she fingered the tender bruise. What a brute! she thought, and smiled at the trite description. Even so, longing tightened in her womb like a coiled spring.

She glanced at her wristwatch. It was half past five, too early to rouse the household or even Janice, who'd probably not thank her if she was tucked up in bed with Kevlin's dick buried inside her.

The Embroidered Room was equipped with a kettle and cups, tea and assorted beverages, milk and cream. Tamzin selected drinking-chocolate, and retired to bed, the television set's remote control to hand. She could not concentrate, however – the news dominated by the weather, England caught unawares, as usual. There were reports of gritting lorries buried in snow-drifts and the standard warnings about the inadvisability of travelling unless absolutely necessary.

Tamzin's eyelids grew heavy as she stared at the mesmeric screen. So, they were stranded here till conditions improved. The magazine would have to carry on without her. Somehow, this did not throw her into her customary panic.

She could not stop thinking about her mysterious assailant. It was maddening not to know his identity. Could it have been Lance, or Alex – even Kevlin? Not Alex, she was sure. The demon lover's cock was too big. As for the others, she had not yet experienced their size.

Only one way to find out, she decided. Fuck them as soon as possible. On this intriguing thought, she snuggled down and surrendered to sleep, the gnomish little weather person still rabbiting on cheerfully.

Pop music reverberated through the gymnasium. Sunlight reflecting on snow struck the plate-glass windows and gleamed on state-of-the-art equipment.

A tall woman with cropped ash-blonde hair, wearing petrol-blue leisurewear swung her arms above her head and swooped down to touch her toes in time to the beat.

A dozen others of assorted sizes and gender, united in their adoption of a uniform similar to hers, were copying her movements with mixed success.

'Oh, Christ!' muttered Janice, eye-catching in bright green gym gear. 'The torture begins! Start grooving, Tamzin. Feel the burn! Don't think you can get out of it just because Inga said you don't need to lose weight. We're in this together, comrade.'

'That's what I came for,' Tamzin replied with a resigned smile. 'Positive health and positive thinking.'

'Thank you for sharing that with us, Miss Lawrence.' Janice was already jogging on the spot in her white Hi-tecs, breasts bouncing as if they would pop out of her oval-necked top.

The instructress left her class heaving and panting, and strode over to the newcomers. She held out her hand, announcing brusquely, 'I'm Astrid. You'll work out with me at this time every morning.'

Her fingers were thin and strong, her body amazingly supple and muscular, custom-built through pumping iron. She had the sort of physique Tamzin envied – a vibrant, irresistible animal.

As their hands met she felt an electric thrill shoot through her, and wanted to caress the smooth tanned skin, touch those hard nipples poking against the tight blue fabric, palm the flat breasts. Almost wanted to be Astrid, to slide under her skin and experience the joy of inhabiting such a perfect machine.

'I'm Tamzin,' she said, meeting eyes of blue-grey flint.

She could sense Janice's interest as she introduced herself. She, too, lusted after Astrid. Images of the three of them making it together somewhere private floated across Tamzin's inner vision. Making love with Astrid would be like screwing a young man fresh from the football pitch – a triumphant warrior – sex incarnate. She could almost taste the sheen of sweat on Astrid's face and naked arms, wanting to drink where it had pooled at her bare collar-bone.

The thought lit up her mind like a laser: if she were a man, what beautiful children we could make. And this was strange because, till then, Tamzin had never felt in the least broody.

Putty in Astrid's hands, Tamzin and Janice were put through their paces. She looked down her handsome Roman nose at shirkers. Wouldn't allow it in her class. No, sir! It was useless to moan if one's muscles shrieked for mercy.

'Up, down – step – step – swing those arms – reach for

the ceiling – when you think you can't stretch any further, do it a little bit more.'

And they followed her, this lithe, agile taskmaster. Tired though they were, none dared gainsay Astrid.

'I'll never walk again!' groaned Janice when, the session ended, she collapsed on one of the benches.

'You will, and better than ever,' Astrid assured her, stalking over, a towel draped round her neck. 'You're out of condition, my friend, yet Inga tells me you've been here before. Didn't you keep up the exercises she taught you?'

'I did for a week or two, but then let them drop. It's not so easy to be disciplined on your own,' Janice admitted shamefacedly.

'And now you're suffering for it.' The grey eyes flecked with cobalt smiled in Tamzin's direction. 'How about you?'

'I don't take enough exercise either,' she said with a shrug.

'Come with me,' Astrid ordered, already marching towards the door.

'Where are we going?' Tamzin dragged herself to her feet and plodded after her.

'You need a sauna and a massage,' Astrid proclaimed over a decidedly biteable shoulder.

'Sounds like heaven to me,' Janice said, limping in their wake, dark arcs spreading from her armpits, turning the glowing green to bottle. 'Anything to get out of this torture chamber. Just wait till I see Inga. She didn't warn me they'd been joined by an Amazon slave-driver.'

She did not have long to wait. Inga was lying on the wooden slats in the sauna, hair pinned closely to her scalp, succeeding in looking elegant even in that swampy heat. She turned her head to observe them as they entered, naked, like herself.

'I'm bushed!' Janice declared, slumping down beside her, the sweat pearling her skin.

Inga smiled through the haze of steam and placed her hand on Janice's thigh. 'Never mind, darling. Borg is a brilliant masseur. He'll make you feel wonderful in no time.'

'I'm as good as him,' Astrid declared sulkily, seated with her legs far apart, thighs knotted with muscle, the triangle of pubic hair between them matted and wet.

Tamzin looked at it, fascinated. It covered the base of her belly with a thick straw-coloured thatch. The lower angle was wide, a brown line dividing the two plump halves of her pussy. Astrid smiled, aware of her scrutiny, slipping her hands down to wind a finger in that dense thicket, and Tamzin quickly averted her eyes, the flush of embarrassment adding to her body heat.

The atmosphere was somnolent, breathless with the increasing warmth of water hissing over redhot bricks. Tamzin lay back, resting her head against the pine-panelled wall. Her eyelids drooped, rivulets of sweat running from her hairline, down her face, dripping from her chin to hang in heavy drops on her nipples. They fell, continued their journey across her stomach and vanished between her legs, lost in the mystery of her sex.

No one spoke. The effort required was not worth it. They sat in companionable silence, an elite group. The other members of the class had dispersed to different areas. Because Janice was Inga's friend she and Tamzin enjoyed special treatment.

The sauna was claustrophobic. Tamzin was not too sure that she enjoyed such confinement. Scents hung heavily on the air – female emanations of hair, perspiration and the humid, oceanic essences of their secret places. It roused visions of intimate caresses, of hands that fondled and lips that fed, divine, accurate and understanding because they were women who knew women's needs.

Inga was watching her beneath lowered eyelids, a

pensive smile playing around her lips. Tamzin wondered if she was remembering an earlier scene, perhaps, when a mysterious visitant had entered the Embroidered Room. Had she been party to this?

She decided to sound her out, breaking the silence by saying, 'There was a man in my bedroom in the early hours.'

'Really, darling, do we want to know that? Stop showing off,' Janice murmured, waving a languid hand.

'Seriously, he broke in and—' Here Tamzin stopped, unsure how to continue.

'Did he touch you?' Inga asked in her throaty voice.

'Yes. Look at the marks on my neck.' She pushed back her hair and displayed the bruises.

'Wow! A vampire! Did he look like Tom Cruise?' cried Janice, pulling ghastly faces and pantomiming with her hands. 'If he did he can come and drink me dry any night.'

Inga ignored this interruption, asking, 'What else did he do? Tell everything that happened, Tamzin.'

They were all alert now, even Astrid, who moved closer to Tamzin, her large hand closing on her arm, fingers stroking the slippery wet skin. In that torrid heat Tamzin could not help but respond, liking her touch, wanting more, nipples rising like pets reaching up to be fondled.

'He made love to me,' she whispered, and Astrid's hand came to rest on her shoulder.

'What a quaint, old-fashioned term,' Inga mocked. 'You mean he fucked you? And did you enjoy it?'

'I did. I couldn't see him because it was dark and he was masked, but he was a big man and his penis felt huge. He was strong and I was powerless. I had no choice in the matter,' Tamzin continued, longing to feel that giant serpent inside her again, shivering as Astrid's fingers trailed across her breast and touched the tip of her nipple, flicking it with her nail.

Janice leaned forward eagerly, wet hair straggling around her face. 'Is this your latest entertainment, Inga? Can I expect a visit too?'

Inga stood up, her slender, lean-hipped body rosy-hued. 'Who can tell? He didn't hurt you, did he, Tamzin?'

'No. He was forceful – powerful—'

'Masterful?' Inga was in front of her now, partially depilated pubis on a level with her eyes.

Her fragrance brushed Tamzin's senses, her own strong musk coupled with that of the flower-fields of Grasse.

'Yes.' She could hardly speak for the thickening in her throat. Desire was like a boiling cauldron in the heart of her sex. To be bound, helpless, with this woman pleasuring her! Heaven held no greater promise.

'And you liked being mastered?'

'Yes.' Tamzin's voice was barely a whisper.

'You recognise it as a glorious release for a woman like you who is used to being in control.'

'I've never thought about it before.'

'I'll ask Lance to talk to you. He will explain.'

Tamzin didn't want talk, she wanted action, and the three women moved in on her so that she was lost in a welter of silky wet limbs and caressing fingers. Astrid and Janice attended to her nipples, teasing and arousing them to aching points as large and hard as fruit pips. The pleasure was intense. Her legs opened wide, sex curling like a leaf at each caress, her love-juice running from her perfect vulva, pink and tender as a damask rose.

Inga knelt on the hot floor and worshipped at the altar of her womanhood. Then she bent forward and licked it, holding the fragile lips apart gently with two fingers and inserting her tongue into the pink fissure, finding the swollen clitoris, caressing it and settling down to a steady sucking. With a cry, Tamzin toppled over the edge of passion, a swirling, almost painful sensation that made her writhe and shake.

She came to herself to find arms still holding her, but the women were now pleasuring each other with mouths and fingers, the narrow space redolent of female lust and female satisfaction.

There followed a moment's relaxation, then the icy plunge into the cold bath and permission to enjoy the hot one. The rectangular pool was tiled in white and turquoise. At the far end, a wall fountain sent a jet gushing into the water beneath it.

'This is an original Regency feature,' Inga said, lowering herself into it. 'The man who had it built had spent much time in Turkey. That's why it's called the *hammam*. Similar baths were used in the harems.'

There had been a modern addition, and the swirling waters of a Jacuzzi caressed Tamzin, lapping her skin, penetrating every hollow, stimulating and soothing. As she lay there she remembered her dream, the invisible lecherous tongues seeking intimate knowledge of her folds and crevices, the little knowing fingers. They had roused her, prepared her, made her a more than willing sacrifice for him.

Who was he?

She shifted restlessly, the whirling water a bubbly cushion of sensation beneath her. A jet rushed up to play over the tight rosebud of her anus. Another shot along her furled labia, touching its apex, her hidden clitoris awaking in immediate response to the pressure on its enfolding cowl.

Who was he?

She wanted him, shivering in the warm water, thighs tensing, nipples pricking as if penetrated by needles. Inga wouldn't tell, though she was sure she knew. And was Janice as innocent as she made out?

She glanced at her companions where they sat, half submerged, on the marble steps that stretched the entire width of one side, and she blushed as she remembered their recent intimacy. Inga had an arm looped over Janice's shoulders, a hand reaching down to cup her breast while the other fondled the tinted pubic bush. Astrid was flexing her long limbs, resting back on her elbows, ribs lifted, nipples peaking like tiny islands from a blue sea, lynx eyes watching Tamzin.

The desire to masturbate was becoming uncontrollable, the whirlpool rolling around her secret parts unrelentingly. She rocked her hips, straining to catch the ripples. Her groin felt heavy and under the warm, fanning waves her sex-lips were growing engorged, plump, red and slick. Her clitoris was thrumming, hard and greedy, desperate to be rubbed.

Her hand hovered over it. Her eyes closed and her brain experimented with images, disconnected and form-less but exciting. Then they coalised into a series of dicks – Martin's, Tim's, Mike's – Dennis's and others from way back whose owners she had forgotten. Big dicks, small dicks, pink, brown and red ones. Thick stems, purple glans. Some cut, some *au naturel*. She never could make up her mind which she liked best; a penis with a foreskin or one without.

Phantoms assailed her, gigantic cocks thrusting her legs apart, pushing into her vagina. One after another in ceaseless motion they plundered her treasure-trove, end-lessly flooding her with libations, large – larger – largest of all: that of her unknown lover.

No longer caring if she was seen, she abandoned herself to her desire, her hand descending to her cleft under the water. Her middle finger began that gentle motion which would soon bring her to orgasm. Then she felt a hand close down on hers and Inga was there to move her finger aside and insert her own. Without a word, she used a circular motion on Tamzin's clitoris and brought her to an almost instantaneous orgasm.

Before Maria reached the cottage she was aware of the sound of a piano. Uneducated musically though she was, a devotee of pop and rock, her ears responded to the heavy chords that seemed to contain a conglomeration of anger, violence, love and unendurable suffering.

She paused at the back door for a moment, head cocked at a listening angle as she worked the snow from her boots against the iron scraper. Then she inserted the key in the lock and opened the door cautiously, embraced by warm air and the smell of freshly percolated coffee, a heartening combination on such a cold day.

The music continued without pause. 'He's really going for it,' she muttered, recognising without knowing why that this was a live performance.

One of her jobs was to tidy the cottage, make the beds, clean the bathroom, leave the kitchen spruce. In so doing she could hardly avoid coming across the occupants, no matter how shy. She always arrived there hopping with anticipation when someone new had moved in. There was no knowing who it might be.

Maria was starstruck, an avid movie and TV fan, even more besotted by rock bands. In her eyes these were almost superhuman. She lapped up everything the media put out about them, and thrilled to sensational stories concerning their wealth, love-affairs and untamed behaviour.

The present guest was a different kettle of fish, however. The world of classical music was a blank to Maria. Yet she had seen his picture in the newspapers, and caught a glimpse of him on BBC2 before a bored Kevlin had seized the remote and started channel hopping.

However, his swarthy brand of louche sensuality had not been lost on the unsophisticated Maria. A wave of lust had dampened her panties as she sat on the settee with Kevlin in front of the television set. And this time it hadn't been her raw young buck of a lover who had made her pleasure-bud pulsate. It was the sight of Guy Ventura.

Her heart racing, she now removed her boots and slipped her feet into a pair of moccasins she had taken from her tote-bag. She padded silently towards the source of those glorious sounds – the black Steinway grand in a window recess at the far end of the living-room. Maria had recently seen a reissue of Walt Disney's

Fantasia, and was reminded of the great rolling abstracts inspired by a Bach fugue with which the cartoon opened.

Firelight flickered across the white walls and snow-light crept between the latticed panes. The air was sweet with the scent of smouldering pine-cones, like couch-fires on an autumn afternoon. The sound was louder now, and Maria stared at the pianist.

He was seated with his back to her. She could see the mane of raven hair tumbling across the shoulders of a burgundy velvet embroidered waistcoat, and the powerful movements of his arms under the white shirtsleeves. His hands rose and fell as they attacked the keyboard, controlled yet vigorous.

'Who are you? What d'you want?' His heavily accented voice rose above the song of the piano.

Maria jumped, not realising he was aware of her. He continued to play without glancing round. She took a few steps closer, wanting to touch him.

'I've come to tidy the cottage,' she said, standing just behind him. 'Sorry if I've disturbed you, sir.'

The music died. He balled his hands into fists, then spread them on his knees. He turned his head and Maria was speared by the power and beauty of his face. Paralysis struck. It was as if she had been hit by a curari-tipped dart. She loved Kevlin, would no doubt wind up as Mrs Scully, yet still she retained those secret dreams and longings to be swept up and borne away by a knight on a white charger. Guy Ventura was Sir Lancelot reborn.

A haughty smile lifted his marvellously shaped lips. 'That's OK. I've finished practising now,' he said, the cadences of his voice causing mayhem in Maria's core, vibrating that mystical chord connecting the G-spot and the brain.

He pushed back the stool and stood up. Maria gaped. He was the tallest man she had ever seen. Her head did not reach the pit of his throat. Wide shoulders, a narrow waist and those strong hands, he was a striking figure, staring down at her with smouldering, peat-dark eyes.

As usual when he had been playing, he was energised, needing to express the inspirational, creative force which had possessed him, awesome in its power. He felt edgy, unsettled, though this was minor compared to the mood that tore through him after a recital. Then the need to translate that power sexually was almost uncontrollable. Fortunately there were always women ready, willing and eager to leap into his arms, wrap their legs round him and impale themselves on his cock.

Now, relaxing at Cheveral Court prior to a gruelling

stint in American concert halls, he knew he could summon Inga who would either glue her gorgeous body to his or find him a suitable mate. But staring at the girl who had appeared so unexpectedly at his side, he recognised the sturdy peasant stock from which she had come and the bough of his phallus sprang erect. Rosy cheeks, hazel eyes and blonde hair, wide hips and big, luscious breasts, she typified the women who had been his nursemaids back home in Eastern Europe.

Left in their care on the demesne while his conductor father and opera-singer mother had been on tour all over the world, everything he knew about sex had been learned initially from them. They had taken his virginity, those laughing, motherly wenches, each in turn introducing him to some fresh earthy aspect of coitus. By the time he was fourteen, Guy had been acting the rooster over a barnyard of hens.

'What is your name?' he asked, one tanned finger stroking the side of her face.

'Maria,' she breathed on a sob, capturing his hand in her own. She licked his fingers greedily, drawing them between her lips as if they were miniature penises, sucking on them as she wanted to suck on his manhood.

She felt him tremble, and tipped back her head,

staring up into that intense, beautiful face. He towered above her, the neck of his shirt thrown open over a darkly furred chest, the velvet waistcoat giving him an even more romantic aspect, as if he was a poet or the swashbuckling hero of a costume movie.

Maria placed her hands at his waist, girded by a leather belt with a buckle shaped as a dragon. She was standing close to him, acutely aware of the long, slanting upward shape of his cock beneath the black denims. They were so tight that she could make out the ridge below the head where the foreskin had rolled back.

At the same moment, she felt her breasts cradled in his hands as he squeezed the plump flesh. She moaned and he pushed the sweater high over them, admiring the large round globes suspended in their white bra-cups. He was silent, his eyes burning and a tense line to his chiselled lips.

The wild gypsy hair, his beauty and foreign accent, the awe she felt because he was educated, talented, as far above her as the moon and stars, all combined to fill her with a need to worship.

And Maria knew only one way to express her adoration.

She sank to her knees on the Persian carpet, pressing

her face against his crotch, biting along the hard smooth outline of his phallus, her nails gently scratching over the material encasing his balls. He shuddered, his fingers gripping her shoulders and winding into her hair as her damp, hot breath excited the skin beneath his jeans.

Maria was wearing jeans, too, and as she knelt they strained over her crotch, the seam gouging a line between her sexual fruits which swelled on either side. It pressed against the fringed lips and dug into her clitoris, the friction enough to take her to the edge of orgasm.

Guy's erection was a bold swollen bar of flesh beneath the black fabric. Infinitely desirable. Saliva flooded her mouth as she thought of taking that arrogant organ between her teeth and running her tongue over it, tasting the cock-juice smearing its head.

The fly of his jeans was strained to the utmost by the bulge beneath. The buttons were cold and metallic against her lips. She raised her eyes to Guy's. His were hooded, watchful, his face expressionless. No movement, except for the bite of his fingers against her scalp, the nails digging deep.

Still holding his gaze, she undid the waist-button and the rest followed suit, the fly gaping, showing bare skin and crisp dark hair. Lower still and his penis shot out like a sword. He was big. Maria's fingers played with it, delighting in this new toy. The extraordinary variation in men's dicks never ceased to amaze her.

This was so tempting that she could not resist opening her mouth and taking it into her throat with a hungry thrust of her head. She closed her lips tightly about the shaft, working it hard, every movement a caress. At the same time she fondled his balls. They were big and pendulous, bursting with semen. He groaned and pleasure shot straight to her clit, his admittance of pleasure making him seem more human. For one precious moment in time, humble Maria Banting meant more to him than fame or fortune, and even his career was of no significance compared with the overwhelming need to ejaculate.

She ran her tongue round his glans as if she was tasting the most scrumptious ice-cream cone. His breathing became shallow and rapid. His pelvis rocked slightly, pressing towards her face. He began to thrust in and out, faster and faster till he spurted a great, creamy-white tribute into her mouth.

Maria, almost choking on it, swallowed down the thick juice. It had a bitter after-taste that made her hungry for more, her sex desperate for the feel of that mighty cock inside her, rubbing the walls, driving its dome against her cervix. He lowered his head and kissed her, tasting himself on her lips, then said, 'Take your clothes off.'

Maria could not wait to obey and when she was naked he lifted her effortlessly and sat her astride his waist, her legs spread wide. His penis was erect again, standing at a ninety-degree angle, and he lowered her on to it. Maria felt herself expand as it slid into her vagina like a massive prong, first the helmet, then the thick shaft. At last the whole of it had disappeared, his hairy pubis pushing against hers.

Tears sprang into her eyes as she raised, then lowered herself on his cock. It was so huge, she could hardly take it all without discomfort, yet pleasure outweighed this. The deep satisfaction of being possessed by a handsome, famous man, a star who could have had almost anyone at the lift of his little finger. Yet he had chosen her. It was her body he penetrated, her juices that bathed his tool and would bring him to ecstasy.

Let Kevlin screw the arse off Janice Kent or play the stud to Inga Steadson. Maria had the edge on them in possessing this wonderful creature. The balance had been adjusted. She was happy.

Chapter Six

Darkness, humidity, the persistent hum of the heating system in the bowels of the house. Wine cellars and storerooms, and the dungeons still in existence on a lower level, in use, too, for certain clients of macabre predisposition who required a little extra by way of entertainment.

Inga entered through the gloom, sure-footed as a cat. She edged towards the faint glow of crimson in the distance, and came out in the boiler-room. There she found herself facing the tall, powerful, thickset figure silhouetted against the blood-red flames roaring in the mighty monster whose breath heated Cheveral Court.

'Master,' she whispered reverently, alert at his sudden movement, but he did not touch her.

She knew the rules. The game was afoot.

'What do you want, slave?' he demanded in a sneering, contemptuous tone, slipping into his role.

'To serve you, Master. Only to serve you,' Inga vowed, hands pressed to her needy breasts stimulated by the prick of steel studs, the drag of leather biting into her secret lips from the tight harness cinching her waist and dividing her nether cheeks.

'Where is the other slave?' He sounded displeased, and a thrill chased over her skin as she heard the sibilant sound of a thong being drawn between his mailed fists.

'We couldn't both be absent. It might have roused her suspicions. Janice has stayed with her. Later, we will bring her to you.'

'Not till I command it. Leave matters as they are for the moment,' he ordered, pacing closer till her senses quivered at the smell of him, an odour reminiscent of past joys and ripe with the promise of more to come – the musky, primitive smell of leather and sweat and sex.

'Anything you desire. You are in control,' she murmured submissively, a frission of anticipation raising the hair at the nape of her neck.

'You'd like to disobey me, wouldn't you? I know you, Inga. You are rebellious.'

'I'm not. I swear it.'

'But you are,' he purred. 'You've already had her. I told you to wait, didn't I? I saw you with her in the sauna. Have you forgotten that I have eyes everywhere?'

Inga hung her head. 'I'm sorry. It was too tempting – her glorious tits, those succulent nipples, that pink, fleshy cunt slippery with juice. She spoke of you, and how you had taken her in the dark. The urge was so strong. I had to do it. I couldn't help myself.'

'You're a wicked, lustful woman,' he sighed, shaking his head, more in sorrow than in wrath.

'I know. I want to obey you, truly I do,' she whined, cringing before him, excitement like a thick red tide flowing inside her.

'Show me how much,' he commanded, reaching for her. She heard a faint chink, felt the snap of cold metal cuffs round her wrists and the restriction of chain-links.

'Anything you say, Master,' she breathed, far removed from the cool woman neatly dressed in a Chanel suit who had welcomed late arrivals half an hour before, congratulating them on battling through the snow.

Such deception thrilled her. She adored posing as the sophisticated operator of a health resort while depravity lurked beneath her businesslike exterior. The need to

166

partake of the rich, heady draught of perverted desires had throbbed in her belly. A trickle of nectar had bedewed her labia even as she conversed with the new-comers in the most light-hearted, charming manner possible.

During several years of feverish living among the glitterati before she found Cheveral Court, she had plumbed the depths and scaled the heights of decadence. Then she had met Orlando Thorne and recognised that she need seek no further.

He had become her mentor, introducing her and Lance to the exclusive secret society dedicated to the pursuit of pleasure over which he presided. Inga had risen to a position of power, but Janice was still a novice. One of their duties was to lure initiates. Orlando had taken offence at one of Tamzin's editorials in *Chimera* but been roused by the challenge of her beauty, pride and independence. A word from him, and Inga and Janice had done the rest.

Now Inga was to receive her reward.

Soon they were in the dungeons, an area of dank stone, prison bars, chains and unnameable objects resembling implements of torture. Delapidated when Inga took over, this was now a make believe centre of incarceration, but realistic enough to excite those who sought corporal punishment as an adjunct to fulfilment.

Inga stared up into Orlando's face illumined by the wavering orange flares set in iron cressets on the grey walls. It was a memorable face, austere and large-boned. A famous face – Orlando Thorne, director – *enfant terrible* of the film-world.

Some said he was a difficult, arrogant charlatan, others that he was an inspired saint. Many considered him mad. But even his deadliest enemies grudgingly admitted to his genius. Actors fought to work with him. Critics loved or hated his brain-children. He pushed the boundaries to the limit and there was no sitting on the fence when it came to his screen creations.

His dark hair, winged with silver at the temples, was swept back into a pony-tail. His tigerish eyes, yellow flecked with green, contrasted with his olive skin. He was a mature man, broad-chested with every muscle honed. Inga had to ensure that one of the gyms equipped with weights was available for his exclusive use during his stay and carefully balanced meals served on the dot.

Dictatorial, manipulative, he was the one man who, apart from her cousin, had complete control over Inga

Steadson. Indomitable in every other aspect of her life she was more than willing to be his slave.

A stone slab formed a table in the space between the cells. Inga lay face down on it, the cold surface searing her bare breasts and pressing the harness more closely into her love-lips. She wriggled her hips slightly to position it against her thrumming clitoris, already swollen, red and begging for attention. Orlando bent over her. By turning her head she could see his black leather trousers, so tight that they looked as if they had been sprayed on, accentuating the massive bump at the crotch over which the brass buttons strained.

She longed to cradle it in her palm but her hands were manacled to solid iron rings. He stared down at her, eyes gleaming like quicksilver, then shifted closer, that bulky package on a level with her lips. Inga's mouth parted, reaching for it, managing to caress it with her tongue-tip. He permitted this salutation, the area she licked growing larger, more solid. Her nipples chafed the stone beneath her and her needy bud ached.

He drew off his gloves and one of his large, carefully manicured hands went to the fly buttons, unfastening them with tantalising slowness. They opened, one by one, and she feasted her eyes on the shadowy 'V' before he lifted out his enormous penis and began stroking its hardness. A lengthy sigh escaped Inga's lips.

It was thick and long, and as he rubbed it little droplets oozed from its single eye. She yearned to lick the clear fluid, to run her tongue round the bulging naked glans, twin-lobed and shiny, slip a hand into his fly and cup the hairy balls that hung there, heavy and mobile in their scrotal net. She could do none of these things, a prisoner to his will. This acted as a spur to the wildfire of her lust.

'Confess,' he whispered, a catch in his throat. 'Tell me your basest desires.'

'I want to feel your cock inside me, pumping in hard. I want you to ride me, fuck me, come all over me,' she breathed, lips wet and slack, eyes slitted in an agony of longing.

'Dirty little slut,' he scolded, moving his hands over her naked bottom, the fingers still moist with the slippery, cock-head lubrication. 'I suppose you want me to fondle your arse? Stick something up it?'

'Yes, oh yes,' she whimpered.

'Why should I pleasure a filthy slut like you?' he ground out, his cock swaying stiffly just beyond her reach.

'Punish me first, Master. Please!'

He moved out of her sight, then returned with a thick black dildo in his hand. Leather strips dangled from its base. Thus it could be used as the handle of a whip or an instrument of penetration. Curved, mighty, it was an accurate representation of a penis, the shaft knotted with veins, the helmet bare, domed and glossy. Inga's legs parted slightly and she raised her hips, the deep amber furrow between her buttocks ready for its attention.

Orlando unbuckled the harness, freeing her to his purpose. He stroked across her body with the thongs – her shoulders, spine, back of waist, rear, and eagerly jutting pelvis. His hands spread her wider and she felt the smoothness of leather trailing between her twin openings. He eased it backwards and forwards, the hide strips soaked with her fluids. She felt him slide a hand under her pubis, and the unerring touch of a finger pressing on her clitoris. And then her body jerked and spasmed at the searing pain as he whipped her across the bottom.

She gasped, while he pinched the head of her clit and she felt his tongue licking over the welts left by the lash. He struck her again, rolling her clit under his finger. She lay, legs sprawled open, longing for more. Then, while he rubbed her, he inserted the dildo into her anus, first the cap, then the whole thick length of it. He wriggled, spiralled it, withdrew it only to plunge it in again. He left it rammed in there, his hand flying to his cock.

Inga writhed and screamed, her pleasure mounting to an erupting volcano and, as she came in a paroxysm of bliss, she felt the scalding heat of his seed pouring over the scarlet stripes marking the tender flesh of her buttocks.

Nothing would satisfy the intrepid Alex but an expedition into the great white wilderness. Restless, with a fierce surge of energy coursing through him, he was already tired of being idle. It went against the grain.

'Is there a sledge anywhere about?' he asked Lance.

'Tackle Kevlin. He'll know. A couple of the inmates have taken skis out,' Lance replied, twirling his racket, stunning in pristine shorts and T-shirt, owner of a year-round tan. He was raring to make up a four on the covered badminton court. 'Why don't you come and knock hell out of a shuttlecock instead?'

'No, thanks. There's only one cock I want to shuttle and that's my own. I need to fill my lungs with fresh air.' And Alex strode off to find Kevlin.

He returned shortly to winkle Tamzin and Janice out

of the television room where they had hidden away, curling up on a feather-cushioned Chesterfield to watch an old black and white movie. Still aching from Astrid's aerobics session and enervated by the sauna, they were wrapped in towelling gowns, enjoying Cheveral Court's casual atmosphere. They had not even been required to dress for lunch, partaken in the conservatory with some of the other guests.

'I won't take no for an answer,' Alex said, squatting on his hunker's beside Tamzin. 'Come on, lazybones. Stir your stumps.'

He looked fit and glowed with health, his tanned face split in a wide grin over even white teeth, his eyes so intensely blue that his glance was like a lightning flash. Tamzin's nipples crimped in response, and she hoped she could persuade him to allow *Chimera* to print an account of his adventures. Photos of him, all bronzed, rugged and gorgeous, would have her female readers wet with desire, and probably some of the male ones, too.

'I'll go up and change,' she said, willing to cede if this might induce him to talk.

'Wear something sensible,' he advised, dressed as he was in a pair of green sweatpants and a kagoul over a designer cashmere sweater.

'Don't worry. I can cope.'

'May I come and help?' he grinned, and the lift of his brows, the slant of his sensual lips betrayed that he was re-living their encounter in the swimming-pool.

'Not if we want to get out before dark,' she murmured, and placed her fingertips lightly over his mouth. He licked them appreciatively.

The blizzard had let up earlier and now it was a crisp afternoon with an invigorating sparkle. The air was like chilled wine. Ice crunched beneath their thick-soled boots, and the runners of the sledge made a soft swishing sound as Alex hauled it along. They crossed the white lake of lawn, frost lying like crystallised sugar on top of every bush and wall, glittering in the pale sunlight.

Several groups, red-cheeked and exuberant, trudged determinedly between the trees and out of the gates. A few figures on skis stood out starkly against the purity of the slopes beyond.

'There you are,' Alex exclaimed, his breath rising about him in a cloud of vapour. 'I told you it was a good idea.'

Janice remained unconvinced. 'I'd have rather stayed and watched *Jezebel*,' she complained. 'I adore Bette Davis as the spoilt Southern belle shocking polite society by wearing a scarlet ballgown instead of a white one.'

'How could you tell? It wasn't in colour.'

'Oh, Alex! Typical man! Use your imagination.'

The snow shone like wedding-cake icing on the hillside and Tamzin remembered how it had been when she was a child, tobogganing near her family home. Suddenly, her father materialised in her mind's eye, that laughing, good-looking man calming her fears, holding her tightly as they sped down a steep incline. She hadn't been afraid while his arms pressed her close to his chest. That was before the break-up. It had never happened once her parents were divorced. The split had been far from amicable, riddled with bitter animosity.

Kevlin kept the sledges and skis in order, greasing the runners for just such an eventuality. The one Alex had selected was painted in cheerful, fire-engine red, and Tamzin took her place with her lower back against the warmth of his loins. Janice was in front between her legs, poncho tucked round her, hat jammed down.

'Keep your feet up. I'll steer,' he shouted, his arms imprisoning Tamzin as he grabbed the guide rope in both gloved hands.

'Whoops! I don't think I like this. Can I get off?' Janice yelled.

'No. Hold tight. Here we go.'

They were away, careering over the glassy surface. Tamzin felt the rush of icy wind stinging her cheeks, heard the whoosh of the runners gathering speed as the wintry landscape flashed past. She clung on like grim death, aware of a crazy exhilaration. Alex's steel-muscled thighs gripped her, his upper arms clenched around her, the heat of his crotch penetrated her clothing. She suddenly wished Janice had stayed home, wanting him to fuck her, then and there on a bed of snow.

As they flew down the slope she saw a cottage part-hidden among the trees. Wisps of blue smoke coiled skywards from its chimney pots. It would be an ideal love-nest. Alex could screw her before the hearth, curtains drawn against the outside world, enclosing them in firelit intimacy.

She was conscious that the longing for this completion and companionship had been buried somewhere deep in her psyche, dragged to the surface by the snow, the speed and the male body pressed against her spine. And what would my shrink make of that? she wondered as they tumbled off at the bottom of the hill.

She staggered to her feet, slipping and sliding, with Alex's arms supporting her as she laughed up into his face.

'What a buzz! Let's do it again,' shouted Janice, converted.

They laboured up the slope, leg muscles burning, to begin all over again. But this time the toboggan veered off course and ploughed into a deep drift. They sprawled there, winded but unhurt.

'Well, troops, what say we have a rest?' Alex suggested, brushing the snow from his jacket, then peeling off his gloves and dredging a pack of cigarettes from an inner pocket.

'I've had it. Let's go back,' Janice grumbled, sitting on a log and lighting up. 'I'm bloody freezing. This wasn't one of your better ideas, Fenton old sport. I think I'll find Borg and get him to give me one of his marvellously relaxing massages.'

'Oh, yes?' Alex cast her a glance from his tip-tilted eyes. 'Inga's told me about the renowned Swede, six foot five of solid meat with a cock to match.'

'I love it when you talk dirty,' Janice mocked, blowing smoke-rings in his direction.

One of Alex's hands shot out, gripping her round the ankle and hauling her down beside him. 'And what exactly is it you expect from Borg that you couldn't get from me?' he asked, eyes twinkling, but hard line to his lips.

'You think you could do better?' Janice was never one to pass up an opportunity.

'I've never had any complaints. Ask Tamzin.' His hands slid to the zip of her boot, easing it down slightly, fingers disappearing inside.

Tamzin ignored him, arms clasped about her humped knees as she stared in the direction of the cottage. They had piled up close to its gate, a winding path leading to a front door. She had been about to suggest that Alex investigate it with her. Now she preferred to go alone.

She got up with difficulty, bracing herself against the bole of a tree. Her eyes bright as emeralds, she looked down at Alex and Janice, half-seated, part lying in the drift. 'I wonder if anyone is staying there,' she said, jerking her head towards the cottage.

'Probably one of Inga's celebs,' Janice answered carelessly, warmed by the feel of Alex's caressing fingers worming their way under her sock and stroking her bare skin.

'I'm going to take a look.'

'Better not,' Janice said, suddenly serious. 'Inga doesn't like her guests disturbed. It's bad for her reputation. Leave it, Tamzin.'

'Come on. Let's get back.' Alex rose and righted the sledge. 'It'll be dark soon.'

'Catch you later,' Tamzin said and walked off. Having started this, there was no way she was about to back down.

Alex was right about one thing. It was getting dark. And deadly cold. It wouldn't do to have a fall. One could die of exposure out there. The sun, invisible in an overcast sky, was sinking with a peculiar radiance, casting a glow that flushed each cloud with pale boreal hues. Then this faded. The heavens turned to iron and large flakes swirled through the dusk. Tamzin thought of the walk back. It would be exhausting, fighting against the rising wind, blinded by snow, stumbling into treacherous drifts.

I hope someone's at home, she thought on arriving at the cottage. Her footsteps were muffled, and she hesitated before inching round to one of the diamond-paned windows. It was shuttered. She returned to the front door. It was snowing in earnest now and the cold bit deep. She was wet and freezing, badly in need of shelter.

She reached for the brass, lion-headed knocker but before she could lift it the door was wrenched open. A form stood outlined against the golden glow within.

Tamzin stopped dead, her heart thundering in her chest. She had the swift impression of height and power, of a lean face, ebony hair and dark eyes. Recognition swept her back to the Barbican Centre.

'What the hell do you want?' he demanded, and his voice rolled over her like a church organ, making her inner core vibrate. It was the deepest, richest voice she had ever heard. The fact that he was furious did not matter a jot.

'I'm cold,' she answered through chattering teeth.

'Are you a reporter?' He stared at her from under the bar of his black brows.

'No,' she said, telling herself this was the truth, mostly. 'I'm lost.'

He looked as if he might slam the door in her face, then he stepped back grudgingly. 'You'd better come in. Are you from Cheveral Court?'

'Yes.' She followed him inside.

'I'll phone and ask them to send someone over to fetch you.'

Music filled the room. Warmth permeated the atmosphere. Logs from trees felled in the grounds crackled in the wide grate. The resinous smell mingled with that of joss-sticks, strong coffee and the rich, gamey scent of garlic, onions and cooking meat. She was aware of her snow-stained boots, but he did not suggest she remove them. Neither did he go to the phone, pouring her coffee instead and handing her a mugful.

She warmed her hands round it, then opened her calf-length black redingote, took off her Cossack hat and thawed out on the hearthrug, hardly able to believe the ease with which she had gained entrance.

He ignored her, dropping back into his armchair. It faced a large TV screen where a video was playing. She recognised the music as that of *La Bohème*, but the set and costumes were unusual – the 1950s instead of the 1800s. It brought *West Side Story* instantly to mind.

He was engrossed in the performance. It was as if she didn't exist.

'I thought you were going to phone the house,' she said edgily, for she liked to exist, most emphatically, and for people to know that she did.

'I'll do it when this Act is finished. Please be silent.'

He's rude, she thought indignantly, then reflected that he had every right to be, considering that she had imposed herself on him uninvited. He had upped the sound level and the glorious, heartbreaking music of Act III swept her away. She sank down on a footstool, mesmerised by this work which, hackneyed though it sometimes was, shone through brightly in this dazzling new production. No fat, elderly divas or tenors past their sell-by date, but a vibrant, lively company of superbly trained, slim and good-looking young singers who could act.

'Who directed this?' she asked, carried away by enthusiasm and forgetting his request for silence.

'Baz Luhrmann, for the Sydney Opera House,' he growled.

She had heard of the *avant garde* movie-maker and had seen his film *Strictly Ballroom*. But now she became caught up in the reworking of the tragic events on stage. Love in the winter among poverty-stricken students. Young love, with the consumptive heroine desperately ill. Tears rose in Tamzin's eyes, spilling over to run down her cheeks as the curtain descended on the star-crossed lovers swearing to put off parting till the sun came out again in spring.

He pressed OFF, blanking out the screen. Looking across at her, his expression softened. 'It moves you?' he said, and she felt herself falling into the dark mesh of his melodious, accented voice. It was like a potent drug.

'Oh, yes. I'd like to see the whole thing. I love opera. Puccini most of all.' She managed a watery smile.

'What's your name?' He was serious, immobile, watching her.

'Tamzin Lawrence.'

'I'm Guy Ventura.'

'I guessed. I'd heard you were staying here. Inga told me, but don't worry. I won't shop you to the paparazzi.'

'You work at Cheveral Court?'

'I'm here to get myself in shape.'

'It doesn't look as if you need it, Miss Lawrence.'

Her coat was open and she felt suddenly shy before his intent gaze, aware that her sweater was tight and the cold had made her nipples bunch like wild strawberries beneath the silk and wool-jersey cloth.

Her cheeks flushed with more than the heat of the fire as her green eyes met his dark ones. He was an even more beautiful specimen of masculinity than she remembered, on the lines of a Renaissance nobleman. Aquiline nose, square jaw, a clear swarthy skin, blue-black hair that sprang back from a wide brow. He was broad-shouldered but lean, well-balanced and graceful as a fencing champion.

His clothes seemed to be deliberately nondescript, as if he had no time for flaunting designer labels, and was disinterested in fashion, yet Tamzin recognised them as top of the range. An elegant shirt and tight jeans.

Tamzin could feel herself melting into lubriciousness, the roseate tips of her breasts rubbing against the jersey. Her thighs had parted without her knowledge, the soft-fringed margin of her love-lips engorged and moist, her clit rising from its vestigial foreskin. She felt as if Guy had already penetrated her, as if his voice had opened her whole being to him.

If this presignifies love, she thought, then it could be said that I'm in danger of entering that delirious state verging on madness.

Stop it! she nagged inwardly. Don't be a fool! He's only a man, and probably a bastard into the bargain. Haughty, pig-headed, unreasonable. You've avoided being in love so far, and I suggest you go on avoiding it. I've never seen it do a woman any favours. Quite the contrary. It turns them into doormats, then when the gilt has worn off the gingerbread, they become tyrannical shrews. No thank you!

She stood up and he, too, rose. 'I'd better be going,' she said. 'I know it's not far to the house but I'd be grateful if you would make that call. Maybe Lance will come in the Range Rover.'

He was regarding her with a grave expression, those impenetrable eyes never leaving her face. 'Do you have to go yet?' he asked slowly. 'Why not share a meal with me, and then we can watch the rest of the video, if you like?'

Tamzin's pulse was running away with itself. Here was a heaven-sent chance to get that interview, but this was not foremost in her mind. Rather, she was concentrating on his face, saffron in the firelight, on his body so close to hers, feeling the heat of his phallus and seeing the swell of it in his jeans.

She gulped and forced a smile, when the situation was so fraught that smiling was the last thing on her mind. 'Thank you. That would be great. But I don't want to put you to any trouble.'

He shrugged, spreading his hands wide. 'I shouldn't have asked you if it had been trouble. I like to cook. Besides, it's been in the oven for some time already.'

She draped her coat over the back of a chair to dry and pushed her hands through her ruffled curls, then bent to unfasten the double straps of her leather boots, saying, 'I'm hardly dressed for dinner.'

His lips curled in a brief smile. 'We'll be informal, shall we?'

The truth was that Guy was a little tired of his own company. The first day had been blissful – no agent, no manager, no press, only the self-imposed regime of piano practice. There had even been sex in the voluptuous form of the obliging Maria. He remembered her mouth and his penis lifted. She gave great head.

He thought about this as he moved around the kitchen, assembling the rest of the ingredients for the meal. She would be in every day to tidy up, see to his wants, including paying lip service to his prick, but this lovely woman who had come in out of the snow intrigued him.

'"Man cannot live by cock alone,"' he murmured to himself, amused as he changed the quotation. It looked as if she had brains and sensitivity, besides the most exquisite face and figure he had seen in a long while.

'Can I do anything to help?' she said, startling him from his reverie.

'I think not.' His long hands wielded the knife expertly as he prepared salad. The oven emitted a mouth-watering odour and a pan bubbled on the stove.

She peered into it curiously, wondering at the domesticity of this scene while aware of the current pulling her towards him. It was as much as she could do to stop herself from grinding her body against his.

She felt like a schoolgirl in the throes of her first crush. Aching, confused, trembling with the desire gathering in her womb in a knot of lust. Blushing, almost shy in his presence, she told herself firmly not to be stupid. She'd had more men than she cared to remember and had recently sampled women, too. So why was she shivering as if still an unpenetrated, inexperienced virgin?

In her overheated state every item on the chopping-board suggested sex. The thick upward curving shaft of a cucumber, a fat courgette, tomatoes lying side by side like plump testicles, the bananas in the fruit bowl nestling against downy-skinned peaches with the dewy bloom of female labia. Exotic, dusty purple grapes lay on a bed of flat vine leaves. She imagined their crisp pop as her teeth punctured them, the juice flowing into her mouth in the same way as Guy's spunk would flow on to her tongue.

She was rabid with need. Her fingers tingled to touch him. Her breasts throbbed, nipples supersensitive. Her vagina spasmed with the longing to have him in her body. Her clitoris was a burning nub, ready for his lips and teeth to suck and nip it. But she did nothing, made no move, controlled her distress as Guy calmly played at chef.

'Where did you learn to cook?' she asked: anything to keep her mind off the firm waist she wanted to clasp, the hard male nipples she wanted to tweak through the thin cotton shirt, the branch of flesh she wanted to fondle through the denim jeans.

'At home, near Budapest. I spent a lot of time in the kitchens when I was a boy.'

'With your mother?' I'm truly interested, she thought, this isn't the reporter probing.

He shook his head, his hair falling forward as he arranged the salad in an earthenware bowl. 'She was a singer – away a good deal. My father, too. He was, still is, a conductor. You may have heard of him. Petru Groza.'

'Of course I've heard of him.' Good God, she thought, no wonder he's so talented. Groza was in the top league, along with Sir George Solti, James Levine and Simon Rattle. 'You don't have the same name.'

'Ventura is a pseudonym. I didn't want to use his influence to help my career, preferred to make it on my own.'

He's proud. I like that quality, she mused, moving closer. I've met too many prepared to take advantage of their connections to further ambition. Mike Bishop, for example.

'Is your mother still singing?'

'She's dead.'

End of conversation, Tamzin realised, and could have kicked herself. That sombre look lingering beneath the surface of his face had returned with a vengeance.

She helped to lay the table. Handmade lace place-mats on the shiny oak surface; Sèvres dishes; Georgian silver; Baccarat crystal. Nothing was too good for Inga's renowned guest. No doubt he was paying in telephone numbers for the privilege.

The suite she was sharing with Janice cost the earth. Cheveral Court did not come cheap but this was an inclusive tariff. One could play bridge with experts, create a fashionable image or conquer stress with the help of lifestyle consultants. The only stress Tamzin needed to conquer at that moment was the tension tormenting her core, and she had the remedy to hand, if she was bold enough to use it.

Supposing he rejected her? For all she knew he might be gay. As they sat down to eat, she ferreted around in her mind for gossip concerning his private life. There was precious little to go on.

He poured red wine from a dusty green bottle. 'Tokaj,' he said. 'It goes well with Rakott *Vesepecsenye*.'

'Come again?'

'Hungarian hotpot.'

'Ah, so that's what it is.'

'You like it?'

'Indeed.'

She found him surprisingly easy to talk to once he relaxed, accepting the fact that she wasn't a member of the gutter press intent on persecuting him.

Firelight and wine, the main course followed by *tarte tatin,* glistening with caramel and swimming in cream. 'I must confess that I didn't make this,' he said with a smile. 'Maria brought it over from the house. I'm well supplied here. Try the olives.'

Purple-black and sage green, they were piquant on her tongue, and he followed this up with a further pot of strong coffee laced with cognac. He lounged on the couch, his eyes hooded as he stared into the heart of the flames and Tamzin settled beside him, her legs folded beneath her. She watched his hands clasped lightly round the wineglass, long strong fingers, a dusting of dark fur over the backs.

'What do you do?' he asked suddenly, turning to look at her.

'I'm an author,' she answered at once, thinking that it was almost the truth. Hadn't she wanted to write once, long ago before ambition swallowed her up?

'Oh? What do you write?'

Damn, she thought. Now I've dug a hole for myself. 'Novels – romantic fiction for women. You know the sort of thing.'

'D'you get them published?' He pushed an errant lock of black hair from his forehead, every movement going through her like a knife, piercing her heart with his beauty.

'I – er – I'm only a beginner,' she stammered.

'"Don't give up the day-job." Is that it?'

'Something like that. I'm fortunate in having my own private income.' God, but I never knew you were such a liar, Tamzin Lawrence, she scolded herself sternly. Talk about expedience.

Yet none of this was strictly untrue; she was or had been a writer – of gossip columns. Her parents had left her comparatively well-off – not madly rich but comfortable.

To hell with it, she decided. I'll do and say anything to stay here with him. He mustn't get the slightest suspicion I'm involved with *Chimera*.

He put down the glass and rested back on his elbows, long legs stretched out. Silence yawned between them like a third presence in the room. The tension was mounting.

'D'you want to watch the video?' he said at last.

'Not now. I'm surprised you like Puccini. I'd have thought it too bittersweet for you.'

'My mother was Italian, and a singer, don't forget.'

Small talk that meant nothing, a prelude to the inevitable. He closed in with panther-like speed, catching her off-guard. He seized her by the shoulders, pulling her on to him, running a hand over her breasts and gathering her into the dark thrall of his embrace.

She was above him, looking down into his eyes shadowed by curling black lashes, feeling herself drowning in their inky depths. His hand was at the back of her neck, urging her mouth to his, her hair falling over them like a tangled curtain. Closer his lips, warm, wine-scented breath, her willing mouth opening like a flower to the sun, tongue meeting his in welcome and celebration.

A shock shuddered through her. It was as if she was dissolving inside, her mind floating with bright colours, the blue of the sky, a green river flowing. To her horror she felt that merging of her spirit with someone else's from which she had always fled.

Now, still holding her, he sat up, turning her on her back so he was above her. His lips trailed from her mouth to her throat, and he began to undo the tiny pearl buttons that fastened the front of her sweater. He spread it open and looked down at her breasts, his eyes gleaming, lower lip sensual and full. She waited but he delayed so long in his perusal of her that her nipples were aching when at last he took the fullness of her breasts in his hands. At once the smooth petal of each areola contracted.

He grazed the tight buds with his teeth, and Tamzin's clitoris responded to the quiver of the tender tissue, sending out its own miraculous signals. His hand sought hers, guiding it to the zip of his skin-tight jeans. She could feel his cock beneath the denim, her fingers roaming over the tell-tale outline of hardening flesh.

Deftly, she undid his belt, snapped open the waist button and slid down the zip. Her hand explored between the open flies, finding him naked beneath. His cock was in proportion to the rest of him, big enough to fill her completely, maybe even too big for her to take fully.

His eyes were unfocused, almost as if he was looking through her as she started to stroke his phallus, easing the foreskin over the flushed glans. She bent her head, wetted it with her lips, allowed her tongue to be a butterfly fluttering under the tip. She was rewarded by a groan that betrayed his excitement. Sap trickled from the slit and she licked at the salty libation, wanting more and more, the dark, wet depths of her needing the completion of his cock.

He was almost there, the long vein running up the underside of his shaft swelling, his body falling into that jerky rhythm, but he suddenly clamped his hand down on hers.

'Stop,' he gasped, and slid to his knees between her legs. 'I want to see you come first.'

She ripped off her leggings and tore away the damp silk panties. Guy's hands caressed her thighs, and his fingers tangled in the light brown bush. With extreme delicacy, he parted the leaves of her labia and gazed at the shiny pink gem of her clitoris, the membrane so swollen as to be almost transparent. She had never been more warm and pliant, smelling the perfume of her essences, feeling the fluid spreading over her folds.

Guy dabbled his finger in it and stroked her quivering bud. But, before the sensation on the head became too intense, he massaged each side of it, then round and round the stem, following it back to where it joined her pubic bone. He wanted complete control and who was she to deny him?

She moaned, adding to the sensation by fingering her nipples, allowing the waves to build up and up. Having roused her clitoris to perfection, Guy stopped admiring it and lowered his head, his tongue finding her secrets. Hands freed, he reached up and replaced her fingers with his own, a great rush of feeling communicating from the pads to her teats. Now the tide was getting stronger, the first foaming waves beginning to break, lifting her high on their crests.

She was riding the magical serpent-fire of Kundalini, heat spreading from the tips of her toes straight up her spine to her head chakra. She cried out in her extremity – blinded by the glory of it.

As she came, Guy thrust his cock into the clenching core of her sex. His teeth champed at the tender skin of her neck and face. He seized a fistful of her hair in the throes of his mounting passion, her cries the most beautiful of music as he joined her in a fathomless orgy of pleasure.

Chapter Seven

Janice stepped through the swing doors into the section of the house devoted to beauty-treatment rooms. Alex had refused, making a beeline for the bar, but she did not allow herself to be sidetracked, not even by this dashing adventurer and the promise of a few drinks followed by a lecherous hour in her bedroom.

A slender Japanese girl glided towards her, wearing a silk kimono embroidered with gilt-threaded chrysanthemums and scarlet birds, an obi girding her doll-like waist. Bowing politely, she ushered her into a warm cubicle, its walls glazed with azulejo tiles. There were mirrored shelves containing unguents of perfumed oils, the air sweetly scented. Apart from these the room contained a shower stall and a padded massage couch.

'Is Borg available?' Janice asked, admiring the sloe-eyes and traditionally dressed black hair of this smiling creature who looked as if she might have stepped straight down from a painted screen.

A diminutive geisha, she was stunningly exotic, attractive to both men and women. Janice was sorely tempted to slide a hand into the opening of the robe and fondle those immature breasts. She knew there would be no resistance – the girl was instructed to meet all the guests' needs. She moved so smoothly and wore such a happy expression that Janice wondered if she had a set of Ben-Wa balls inserted high in her vagina.

'He is, madam,' the girl replied, smiling knowingly with her cupid's bow lips.

Janice could feel those supple fingers helping her remove the damp, snowy outer garments. She pulled the sweater over Janice's head, unbuttoned the blouse beneath and assisted her to roll down her tights.

Because of the cold, Janice wore a red satin and lace teddy next to her skin – skimpy, seductive, fastening under her feather-frilled labia. This was an adjunct to pleasure, keeping her in an almost permanent state of arousal. It was impossible for her fingers not to brush her love-lips every time she opened the crotch in order to urinate. And when she stretched her arms or twisted her body, that strip of crimson silk forced itself into her furrow, chafing the sensitive clitoris.

Now her pussy tingled as the geisha's fingers worked their way round the side, touched the pubic hair, undid the press-studs and stripped her of the garment. Her self-effacing attitude was that of an odalisque and Janice, who was herself learning to be submissive, enjoyed the sensation of power but decided against taking it further.

She was curious about the Swede, and was deliberately stoking her mounting desire. He should be the one to slake it. When she was naked, she stepped into the shower and the girl retired, shutting the frosted glass door behind her.

Janice, senses thrumming by her contact with this pretty oriental, allowed the jets to wash away the sweat of her exertions on the slopes. She hurried, eager for the next stage, intrigued by Borg, whose reputation so preceded him. Inga had been cagey when questioned, simply smiling mysteriously and telling her that he was remarkably well-hung, but she must wait and see, then form her own opinion.

Though hinting otherwise to Alex, Janice had not yet enjoyed the attentions of this masseur, glimpsing him only from a distance. Now, after wrapping herself in a heated bathtowel, she emerged from the stall to find him already there.

He smiled widely, showing an expanse of perfect teeth. He was overwhelmingly masculine in a white T-shirt that clung to his muscular torso, and sky-blue denims against which his thigh muscles strained. He indicated that she should climb on to the couch, and she threw aside the towel without the slightest hestitation, eager to exhibit herself. She took up a position, face-down, the rosy globes of her buttocks, the dark crease between and the lines of her slender spine presented for his inspection.

He set to work and she lay supine under his minis-trations, limp as a rag-doll, head to one side, arms outstretched. Her naked pubis rocked gently against the firm surface beneath her as, almost unconsciously, she sought pressure on her love-bud. She purred like a cat, his touch transporting her to blissful realms.

His hands were large, but gentle as a woman's. He was large in every way – a big, tanned, white-blond giant, whose knowledge of the human body, its sinews, tendons and tensions was masterful to an awesome degree. Janice was on fire, consumed with wanting, confident her heat was contagious, sure that so virile a man would be unable to resist her.

He hammered lightly up and down her spine with the edge of his hand, then kneaded the muscles, releasing the knots, pressing on the backs of her thighs, her calves, circling her ankles and working on her toes. He pulled them, and she wanted to giggle but held herself still, a torment when he was attacking those ticklish places – the ball of her big toe, the tender arch of her foot.

Next he fastened pads to his palms. These were covered in rubber nodules that vibrated over her skin, rippling and stimulating as he slowly moved them up and down, down and around, skimming over the mounds and dipping into the hollows. They passed across the surface of her inner thigh and Janice's legs eased apart, the honey seeping from the gate of her vagina, trickling between the pouting lips and dampening the sheet beneath.

Then, 'Please to roll over,' he said.

Anything for you, babe, she thought, but found she could hardly move, so relaxed it was as if her bones had dissolved. Her nakedness excited her. She yearned to open herself to him, turning gracefully with a provocative flash of her glistening wet crevice.

As he brushed close to the couch the solid bar of flesh behind his fly was on a level with her eyes. She longed for him to unbutton, to display this extension of himself, and imagined him getting it out and laying it on her belly for her to admire.

He gave a secretive, amused little smile and she knew he was fully aware of her desire. Her heart throbbed and her clit swelled in anticipation. It was part of his job to relieve tension, and she was sure he would carry this out, a professional through and through.

He took a phial from the shelf and poured a puddle of oil into his palm. It smelled of sandalwood. Her thighs trembled. Her legs splayed and she raised her pubis, almost in supplication. His hands ignored this, moving across her body skilfully in long, rhythmic sweeps. They climbed to her nipples and revolved round them. Janice mewed quietly, laved in heat that travelled from her breasts to her core. It was as if her whole body was a sexual organ, every inch sensitised.

He shifted to her shoulders and arms, inner arms, lower arms, wrists, then returned to her agonised nipples, rolling them, grazing them, nearly bringing her to orgasm. He was still silent, but she could not keep quiet, gravid with lust.

'Borg,' she whispered hoarsely, 'do you think I'm beautiful?'

He nodded, that smile still playing round his full lips. 'Very beautiful, madam,' he said.

'Then why don't you fuck me?' she asked, her breath jerky.

He made no reply, but her hopes soared as one of his hands left her and moved to his fly. He flicked it open and his penis uncoiled. It was huge, even in repose. No erection? Didn't he fancy her? She reached for it, but before she could take it in her hand, he moved away, shaking his head with that enigmatic smile.

His hands slid to her lower belly and feathered through the burgundy pubes. His two thumbs pressed between, spreading open her labia like the petals of a flower. Her clitoris grew stiff at his touch, the silvery moisture of her juices joined that of massage oil. He worked his fingers each side of her cleft, and finally concentrated on the crest, as expert with this fleshy, heated organ as he was with the rest of the body.

Her excitement soared. This was to be for her pleasure alone, then? He permitted her to view him to add to her arousal, but he would not enter not, not yet at any rate. So be it. Janice lay back and surrendered herself to enjoyment.

One of the most satisfying climaxes she had ever had crashed over her and tore her apart. She convulsed and yelled. Borg continued to stroke her throbbing clitoris for a moment more, then straightened his shoulders. He stood back, hands hanging at his sides, large but limp penis still exposed.

'That was wonderful,' she murmured languidly, puzzled as she watched him moving to the glass shelves, replacing the bottle of oil. 'But what about you? Don't you need satisfaction?'

His blue eyes lit up, and his fresh-complexioned face wore a quizzical expression as he returned to her. 'You'd like to give it to me, madam?' he said in his rather guttural accent.

'You bet your life I would.'

'You'd not question it, no matter how unusual?' he asked, standing with his legs apart, knuckled fists resting on his hips, his jeans still gaping wide over the pinkish brown phallus resting in its blond nest.

'No,' she answered, then wondered if this was rash. She had learned much from Inga and Lance, but even so there were kinky areas still foreign to her. Supposing he was to attack her? She'd be helpless as a kitten in his hands. 'What is it you want? Shall I suck your cock? Is it a whipping you need? Or anal intercourse?'

He was so long replying that she grew impatient. With an exasperated snort, she flounced from the massage couch and snatched her clothes from the hanger, intending to dress and write him off as an impostor.

In her haste she dropped the scarlet teddie. Swift as a striking falcon Borg snatched it up and buried his face in the shiny material. At once his prick sprang out of his fly, straight and smooth and inflamed.

'This is what I want,' he gasped, burying his nose in the crotch, sniffing it all over like an animal, fingering the lace, smoothing the satin.

Janice could feel a heaviness in her groin. It spread out through her pussy as she responded to the sight of her underwear in his hands. Her nipples stiffened as she watched him taking his pleasure.

'You're welcome to it,' she replied, her voice low and shaky. 'But why? I don't understand. Are you a transvestite?'

'No, but the texture of silk, the fragrance of cunt

clinging to soiled knickers turns me on,' he panted, taking his penis in one massive hand and dragging the foreskin back from the helmet.

It shone with pre-come tears dribbling from the slit. He used this is a lubricant, rubbing his weapon thoroughly, up the length of the stalk to the pulsing acorn-shaped head and back again.

Janice stared, her own hand diving down to tangle with the dyed hairs of her bush, tweaking and stroking them, then clutching at her mound. She was soaking from the first orgasm, but wanted more, needing to be filled, exchanging warmth and essences, her female crevice aching to hold and keep, suck and clench round a solid prick.

Borg positioned himself in front of her, wrapping the teddie around his rampant cock, caressing it with the silk, the wet tip appearing over the lace edge with every stroke. He smiled vaguely, eyes half closed, moaning and jerking as the friction summoned up his orgasm. Janice frigged herself hungrily, gasping with ecstasy as a stream of semen shot from his tip with such force that it sprayed her face.

Then he wiped his flaccid organ on the teddie, inhaled the sea-washed mixture of his own spunk and her vaginal secretions, before stuffing the sodden, silky bundle into his jean's pocket.

Tamzin swam up to the surface from the ocean of dreams. Slightly disoriented, she realised she was cradled against Guy's chest and stomach as they lay, spoon-fashion, on the couch in front of the fire.

His penis rested between her thighs, the glans nudging her stickily wet entrance. They were still part clothed, their mating so violent they had not stopped to undress, his cock plundering her sex, almost hurting her with its force and size, her breasts bared to his hands.

The cottage was quiet, except for the sounds of logs crackling on the hearth and the wind buffeting in the chimney. The snow settled outside, transforming the land into an Arctic waste. The track to Cheveral Court would be completely covered. Sleepy, but with little flames of passion starting to lick at her intimate places again, Tamzin had no desire to break the spell, though a thought kept intruding. Janice might be worried about her.

'I'd better phone and let them know where I am,' she whispered, turning and winding her arms round his neck, fingers buried in the hair growing thickly at the nape.

She breathed deeply of the rich, pungent smells wafting between them, seminal libation and sharp male sweat, her own elixir and softer woman-scent, and wanted to capture him in her depths, a prisoner of passion for all time. She hoped he would think the world well lost for love and demand that she remain with him.

'They will send someone to fetch you,' he answered, his lips on her brow. Then he pulled back, giving her a strange, penetrating look. Rebuffed, she released him and he rose to his feet, tucking his shirt into his jeans and fastening up.

She bristled, aware of acute dismay and thoroughly nettled by his reaction. He was so cool and arrogant, completely controlled, as if she meant no more to him than one of the foolish women who hung round his dressing-room door. He had rid himself of the seed pressurising his balls and needed her no longer.

What did you expect? she chided herself. That he'd ask you to stay all night? Share his bed, maybe his future?

She was not sure if she would have agreed, too wary of becoming dependent on another person for her well-being. It was better this way, the golden gift of magic retained. It would never become tarnished by usage and familiarity, like her relationship with Tim, and others before him. They would both be left wanting more – and this was how it should be.

She found her leggings, but could not locate the silk G-string. No doubt it had been kicked under the couch during their frantic coupling. Now she almost regretted not taking it slowly, savouring every moment, but Guy had been so urgent in his need, brooking no denial, and her lust had matched his own.

Good old healthy lust. That's all it had been, she assured herself.

Fully clothed again, sweater buttoned over her breasts, she combed her fingers through her hair and struggled to regain her composure. This was easier to do if she did not look at him, though it was nigh impossible to resist.

He was lounging carelessly with an elbow on the over-mantel, one foot resting on the fender, the other taking his weight. He held a wine-glass in one lean, brown hand, staring down at it as if he was reading his destiny in the clear, blood-red liquid.

Tamzin's clitoris pulsed and her womb contracted at the sight of him.

Damn! she thought irritably. I don't want to feel this ridiculous, melting feeling – as if it's in my heart.

'Can I make a call?' she asked briskly, dragging her

dignity together and remembering who she was – the editor of *Chimera*, sought-after, renowned – able to make or break careers or reputations.

He did not reply for a moment, looking down at her, then shrugged his wide shoulders under the crumpled shirt. 'Of course, Tamzin.'

The way he pronounced her name caused further havoc with her hormones, but she marshalled her wits and took the cordless telephone from the low buhl table. A voice answered at once from reception.

'Cheveral Court.'

'Tamzin Lawrence here. I'm at Fir Cottage. I need to be picked up.'

'Certainly, Miss Lawrence. It may be a little while because of the blizzard.'

'Thank you. I'll wait.'

The silence stretched out between them as she laid down the phone. It was almost impossible to believe that only an hour before Guy had been kissing her breasts, moving his penis in her mouth, passionately possessing the glove-tight tunnel of her sex. Her body hungered to feel it again, but she gave no sign, picking up her black coat and fur hat.

He shifted position so that she was under the full

appraisal of his velvet-dark eyes. 'Would you like a cigarette?' he asked, the timbre of his voice plucking at her nerves so they quivered like harp strings.

'Thank you.'

She took one and his lighter clicked, twin flames, jets of amber, reflected in his pupils. He seemed absolutely calm, his face proud and strong, and her body leaned into him despite her resolutions.

He did not move, but it was as if his penis was penetrating her core. The smell of his night-black hair seduced her nostrils, the sight of his full lips urged her to lick them, suck him into her mouth, swallow and absorb him, make him a part of herself. She could not stop looking at those powerful hands that could coax the most beautiful sounds from the piano or woo her clitoris, bringing her to feverish climax.

Her breath shortened, and she felt giddy – a girl again in the presence of an adored teacher – an underage fan screaming her obsessional passion for a rock-star. She shed years in a millisecond, possessed, infatuated – every vestige of sense deserting her.

A sound clawed her back from the vortex, just in time to stop her pressing the self-destruct button, a car horn proclaiming rationality.

'My lift. I must go,' she said, instead of mouthing those three dreadful, powerful, wonderful words that would have condemned her to despair.

Guy held her coat as she slipped her arms into it, then he settled it about her shoulders, his hands resting there a second longer than was necessary. She could feel his fingers burning into her like a branding-iron.

'I'll phone you tomorrow,' he murmured, close to her ear, the movement of his warm breath causing further mayhem. 'Come to dinner again.'

'I'd like that.' Control was part and parcel of her everyday life, and it stood her in good stead now when she was wondering how she could possibly cope with separation, even for a few hours.

He accompanied her to the door. The cold air fitted over their faces like masks. The Range Rover was a rugged silhouette against the stark whiteness. Lance's lean features appeared to drift, ghostly yellow, at the driver's window.

'Don't come out,' she murmured, her mouth turned up to Guy's, almost in search of a farewell kiss. He did not offer it.

'Good night, Tamzin,' he said, a hand resting on the lintel.

'Good night, Guy.'

What's wrong with me? she wondered as she crunched through the snow towards the car. I've never in my entire life felt so reluctant to leave a man.

'All right?' Lance asked, leaning over to open the door for her. 'Horrible night. We thought you'd got yourself lost.'

'No need to worry. I had dinner with Guy Ventura.'

She settled herself in the seat, wrapping her coat round her, snuggling down. Cars always seemed suggestive of cosy intimacy, like a nest or animal den. One could be incarcerated there with a companion and forget one's identity and the world outside. No wonder they were sometimes christened 'passion wagons', boon to courting couples, adulterers and illicit lovers.

Even though Tamzin's thoughts were still with Guy, her physical self was vibrating in harmony with the man beside her, aware of his dormant phallus resting beneath his corduroy trousers, and the spunk-filled testicles pressed between his legs. Even as he moved to operate the gears, so this equipment would be stirring, too.

He was attractive, his profile like that of an eagle in this weird snow-light. The peak of his tweed cap was pulled low over his eyes and he stared out intently from under it, studying the road with the keenness of a rally driver. The conditions were bad and this added to the thrill of adventure spreading fiery tentacles under her skin.

His gloved hands did not leave the wheel, but he stabbed her a quick glance, mobile lips curved. 'I'm surprised the elusive pianist let you in.'

'He didn't want to, not to begin with,' she admitted.

'Does he know you run a magazine?' Lance had an annoying habit of getting to the crux of the matter.

'I didn't tell him,' she said chillingly. 'What business is it of yours, anyway?'

'Let's hope he never finds out or it will be "bye-bye, baby". I suppose he shafted you?'

'God, is nothing private round here?' She answered his question with another, allowing anger to override the uneasiness engendered by his brutally truthful statement.

He chuckled. 'The stars in your eyes are so bright we hardly need the headlamps. Beware, Tamzin. I've the uneasy feeling you're about to commit the unspeakable folly of falling in love.'

'That'll be the day!' she returned sardonically, trying to forget that had he not arrived in so timely a manner she might have declared her passion for Guy.

'Really?' he sounded unconvinced. 'You wouldn't be the first. He's a handsome savage. Oversexed, of course, like most tormented geniuses.'

'Don't worry, Lance. I'm not some silly little slapper. I've no intention of falling for him. I never get too serious about men. It's not worth the aggro.'

'That's my girl.' He gave her a sideways beam of approval. 'You see, I have high hopes for you. There's a lot we can teach you at Cheveral Court. For some it is simply a health farm. For others—?'

'What?' Her attention was captured by his tone.

'A place where they can let their hair down, in every sense. I think you've much to learn, Tamzin,' he observed in a soft, concerned voice. 'Have you, for example, ever played a submissive role?'

Tamzin's face flamed and her thighs clenched as she remembered Mike. 'It's not exactly my bag,' she answered. 'I'm in control at *Chimera*, and don't submit to anyone.'

'I know. I'm not talking about work. Have you never enjoyed being dominated?'

'Well, no, not exactly,' she prevaricated, guilty feelings tormenting her. It was as if Lance was her confessor.

'That's not what Inga says.'

'Inga doesn't know anything about it.' Tamzin's face was growing hotter, and that embarrassed heat was communicating itself pleasurably to her secret self.

'There's nothing to be ashamed of. It's perfectly normal. Bondage can be fun, as you've already discovered, according to Janice. Have you ever considered taking it a stage further – into corporal punishment, perhaps?' Lance spoke as calmly as if he were discussing stocks and shares.

'No,' she lied, remembering that she had wondered how it would feel to have Mike tie her up and whip her.

'You should try it some time,' he continued as they swung between the snow-capped gates and approached Cheveral Court.

'Do you do it?' she asked levelly, and the thought of him pulling down her panties, bending her over his knee and administering a hard spanking with his bare hand was one that made her nipples crimp.

He steered the car round the back and into the garage, then swivelled towards her in his seat, leaning close. Her senses quivered to the faint, pine smell of aftershave.

'I've been known to take the dominating role,' he said,

the shadow of a smile in his eyes. 'SM releases tension, takes away guilt, accentuates pleasure. Would you care to give it a whirl?'

'I don't know,' she said slowly, but there was no denying the furore his words created in her epicentre. 'I've never liked being hurt, but have sometimes fancied venting my rage on someone else!'

'You just felt like lashing out?' he said with a grin, and his hand came to rest on her knee. 'Maybe it's time to expand your experiences. There are so many interesting facets to sexual enjoyment, and the greatest of these is the unexpected.'

'How d'you mean?'

'Have you ever watched Parliament in session on television and wondered if it's your imagination or is there really a suspender button showing faintly under the tailored trousers of a leading politician?'

'No, I haven't,' she answered, but the picture he conjured up was intriguing.

'Or watched one or two of them wriggling uncomfortably on the bench as if their bums still stung from the previous night's beating by a dominatrix?'

'Lance! What a thought! I love it,' she laughed, and the pressure on her knee increased, then the hand moved to open her coat and travel up the black-legginged thigh, pausing when it reached the damp apex.

'We must talk more. Maybe you'd like to watch it happening to someone else?' And his middle finger pressed between her legs, opening the lips through the material, digging in gently.

'Later,' she murmured, wanting this, but also needing to be alone to think about Guy.

He withdrew, climbed down, then came round to her side of the vehicle and helped her out. 'I'll tell Inga. She'll be pleased. She thinks you have great potential.'

The room was large, lofty and filled with treasures, but the bed dominated everything.

Fully six feet across and seven long, it was reached by three shallow steps on either side. Darkly magnificent, with bulbous posts and a headboard intricately inlaid with rosewood marquetry. Its towering domed tester resembled the canopied tent of an eastern potentate, and a large mirror hung at the foot, angled to give an uninterrupted view of whatever was taking place on the bed.

Here Inga loved to recline between black satin sheets, indulging her desires and concocting the deepest mischiefs. Now she shared this opulent couch with Lance.

'She's almost ready,' he said, burrowing against her, biting into her breasts, delaying the moment of possession, a perfectionist in foreplay.

'I think you're right,' she murmured, reaching down to run a long, red-lacquered fingernail over his scrotum, making him shiver.

Music drifted through the dimness, piano music rising and falling, the arpeggios seducing the senses and stimulating the imagination.

'"*Le jardin sous la pluie*,"' Lance remarked, his fingers circling Inga's nipples, making them bunch and flush to a deeper pink. 'Debussy's tone poems are so sexy. I hear a fountain splashing at twilight in a dark forest inhabited by nymphs. They are being leched after by grotesque satyrs with outsized dicks.'

'It's a CD of Guy Ventura playing,' she answered, watching their reflection as she raised his fingers to her lips and sucked two into her mouth, licking them with the careless pleasure of a cat.

'Just so. Guy Ventura. Did you realize that Tamzin has the hots for him?'

'Don't we all?' she answered in a slow, languid voice. 'Would you refuse if he wanted to shaft you? I certainly wouldn't – haven't, in fact. We had quite a thing going at one time, but he's too temperamental. Spits his dummy out all over the place if he can't get his own way.'

'She had dinner with him tonight, and that's not all, if my experience of a cock-struck woman is anything to go by. I think, my sweet, we may lose the delicious Miss Lawrence if we don't do something about it pdq,' he answered, sliding down and taking one of Inga's shapely naked feet into his hands.

'Can't do that. You know we have our orders,' Inga reminded, stretching luxuriously, arching her spine and thrusting her breasts out, the roseate nipples like two eyes staring back at her from the mirror.

'What do you suggest?' he murmured, the point of his tongue licking at her instep and between her toes.

'Oh – ooh,' she responded, eyes narrowed with enjoyment. 'Do? Put a stop to it, of course. Leave it to me. Then we will begin to train her.'

'Now?' he asked, releasing her toe momentarily.

'Well, maybe not quite yet.'

He made love to her foot, laving each toe in his warm saliva, lapping and tonguing. He cleverly varied the pressure and suction, sometimes fierce and hard, sometimes light as a whisper. It was as if her toes were in line with her clitoris. She wriggled her hips impatiently, dying for the touch of his mouth on her breasts and pudenda. He deliberately held back, even though his penis was fully erect and his cods swollen in their velvety purse.

Inga, almost screaming with frustration, cupped her breasts in her own hands, teasing the nipples into points with the ball of her thumb. Slowly, Lance moved up from her foot, nipping at her calves, her knees and the sensitive flesh of her thigh.

She squirmed, thrusting her pubis against his mouth, but he did not stop, going upwards to her breasts. He paused, carefully spread a single layer of the satin sheet over her aching points, then bent his head and sucked at one hard peak through the fabric, pinching the other firmly with his fingers.

The friction of wet silk over roused nipples was excruciatingly pleasant. Lance sucked hard, drawing as much of her into his mouth as he could, then impatiently pushing the material away and attacking the bare nubs beneath, nipping at them, plaguing and tormenting them.

Inga thrashed against the sheets, her skin very pale in contrast. But he sat back teasingly, leaving her hanging on edge. She wanted to fly at him, nails ready to claw that smirk from his face.

'Bastard!' she hissed. 'Why have you stopped?'

'Remember Orlando's orders?' he said, wagging an admonishing finger. 'If he thinks Tamzin's getting too involved with another man he'll have a major sense of humour failure.'

'Damn her!' Inga slumped against the black pillows, her eyes stormy, red lips drawn back from her pointed white teeth in a snarl.

'Patience, my love. I'm going to give her a call. You'll be satisfied, never fear, and so shall I.'

Inga calmed down and her eyes became heavy-lidded and smoky. 'Sport, d'you mean?'

'Of course. Haven't we always had fun together?' He leaned over and kissed her lips, running his tongue over the pouting lower one. 'And while we're about it, I'll give Orlando a bell, too, just to make sure he has a ring-side seat. OK?'

'Anything you say, cousin. Haven't you always been my guide?' She lifted her hand and, slipping it between the opening of his thigh-length dressing-gown, tweaked his hard male nubs.

Lance smiled and picked up the intercom. There was no reply. 'Humm,' he said, frowning and displeased. 'She's not in her room, or already asleep.' He flicked back the sleeve from a wrist darkly coated with smooth hair and glanced at his Zeitner watch. 'I didn't realise it was after midnight.'

'Never mind,' Inga cooed, happy to have him to herself, her delightfully flawed cousin who was so close as to be almost a part of her. They rarely had the opportunity to play alone these days. 'We'll start the indoctrination tomorrow. Meanwhile, I have a call to make myself.'

And, shiny tongue tip appearing between her smiling, cushiony lips, she took the phone from him and dialled a sequence of digits.

Chapter Eight

Tamzin moved cautiously on the couch. Flat on her back, arms held straight at her sides, her naked body was completely coated by a sludgy, strong-smelling – though not unpleasant – mixture of pulped seaweed and ocean mud.

The therapist, an exquisite person with the golden curls and worldly blue eyes of a Botticelli angel, had just finished wrapping her in silver foil as if she were a precious possession.

'It's to keep in the heat, Miss Lawrence,' he cooed, so tall and willowy in his crisp white tunic and slim-fitting trousers that she regretted he was, like Tag, of the faith. 'Are you quite comfortable?'

'Yes, Andy, but it feels a little strange,' she said, aware of invisible muddy fingers inching over her body, worming between her legs, entering every private fold and crevice. Even her face had been covered, except for mouth, nostrils and eyes, her hair protected by a bandana.

'Oh, it will, to begin with, but it's fabulous. Takes away all the wrinkles and leaves your skin as smooth as a baby's. I swear by it, and have it done at least once a week,' Andy declared enthusiastically.

'It seems to work for you,' she vouchsafed with a hidden sigh. He really was quite stunning. Such a wicked waste.

'It's a duty to look after the gifts one has been given. Beauty must be treasured, encouraged and pampered. That's my philosophy.' He posed in front of her, hand on one hip, and then added, 'How old d'you think I am?'

She made a guess, erring on the low side, not wishing to offend him. 'Twenty-four?'

He prinked in the mirror and rearranged his quiff. 'I'm nearly thirty, but I don't look it, do I? That's because I've always taken care of myself.'

'And how long do I have to stay here, looking like the Bride of Frankenstein?' she asked, finding it hard to smile under the mixture caking her face.

'Half an hour, dear, and then I'll rinse you. I promise you'll be all of a glow. I see you're booked in for aromatherapy, and that's my speciality, too. We'll have you looking great by the time you go.'

'These are the best weeks to stay at Cheveral Court,' commented Janice from the couch alongside Tamzin's. She was also swaddled like a mummy. 'So few guests that we get the full VIP treatment.'

'I'll leave you girls for a while,' Andy said, drying his hands fastidiously before applying barrier cream. 'When I come back I'll bring some herbal tea.'

'He reminds me of Tag,' Tamzin said with a chuckle when he disappeared in a flash of white.

'Gays are tuned in to both sides of their sexual nature,' Janice said with a yawn, the soothing action of the slippery warmth making her sleepy. 'It's a pity heterosexual men aren't so in touch.'

'Indeed,' Tamzin answered meaningfully. Guy had not phoned as he had promised.

She had awakened with that lovely, bubbly feeling of something wonderful about to happen, kidding herself it had nothing to do with the anticipated call. She had a grapefruit for breakfast, then attended Astrid's classes, followed by a sauna, a shower and a light lunch. Every time she heard a phone ringing in the distance she was aware of that tightening in her sphincter, that tingling down her spine. But the call was never for her.

Why? she brooded, as the foil acted like a blanket on her thickly plastered flesh. Where did I go wrong? I really thought he was sincere when he said he wanted to see me again.

She would have liked to talk with Janice about it, but her pride would not let her. It was best if no one knew Guy Ventura had given her the brush-off.

When Andy had finished with her, showering away the last remaining traces of seaweed, Inga poked her head round the door. 'How d'you feel?' she asked blithely.

'Limp but wonderful,' Tamzin replied and put up a hand to unbind her hair.

Inga restrained her, fingers on her shoulder. 'Not yet. A Jacuzzi is next on the agenda. Come along.'

'I'll take it off anyway. It gives me a headache. Has there been a telephone call for me?' Tamzin nerved herself to add.

'No. Are you expecting one? I hope it's not business, darling. You're to be left undisturbed.' Inga's voice was a trifle tart, and Tamzin did not like to pursue the subject. Her spirits dropped a few more notches.

Hearty, friendly sounds were issuing from other treatment rooms, and the tock, tock of balls hitting rackets was pleasant to the ears as they passed the indoor squash court. A lecture on the Alexander Technique was taking place in one of the drawing rooms. A little gaggle of aspiring athletes in jogging gear were drinking tea in the lounge and comparing notes on their loss of poundage.

Inga, smiling and exchanging pleasantries on the way, guided Tamzin and Janice to her own apartment with its en suite bathroom attained through her boudoir and bedroom.

Tamzin was rendered almost speechless by the beauty of the surroundings, the sumptuous drapes and deep-pile carpets, the antique furniture. Everywhere she looked there was a superb example of the rare, exotic and beautiful. There was something about this *fin de siècle* luxury and the density of the atmosphere that stole across her senses like a narcotic.

'Is this where you sleep?' she murmured, pausing to touch the purple bed-curtains with reverent fingertips.

Inga laughed, deep in her throat, and ran a hand lightly down Tamzin's spine. 'Naturally. It came from France and is what is known as a seigneurial bed. Its provenance states that it once belonged to a great lord.

No doubt his heirs were conceived within its depths, something I'm not seeking just yet. Would you care to share it with me? It's fun, isn't it, Janice?'

They exchanged a glance charged with memories and desire. 'You can say that again. Unlike normal beds, it'll comfortably hold several people at once,' Janice answered, her hands going to her breasts, as if that ostentatious couch inspired her to expose them.

'Ideal for an orgy,' Inga agreed, eyes sparkling.

Tamzin was not quite sure about all this. Though willing to try most things, she found to her horror that she was fixated on Guy. I can't go on like this, she thought, bordering on desperation. Other offers, no matter how tempting, mean sweet fuck-all. If he doesn't ring me by early evening, then I'll break every rule in my book and contact him.

She formulated a dozen excuses for his cavalier behaviour – he was absorbed in piano practice – he was stressed out about the next tour – his manager was hassling him.

It was no good. She kept returning to the indisputable fact that there was no valid reason why he should keep her on a string like this. It was selfish, uncaring, ego-centric, and showed a total lack of regard for the feelings of others. If she had an iota of sense, she would erase him from her mental notebook.

Inga switched on the sound system, swaying her hips to a soft, seductive bossa nova. There was an underlying throbbing beat, the melody reminiscent of waves on tropical shores, the wind in the trees – female voices singing, high and sweet and far off.

Tamzin followed the others into the bathroom, extravagant and overblown, with tiles and mirrors and Egyptian decor in turquoise, burnt umber and white. The sunken bath was circular, the water gushing when Inga spun the gold-plated dolphin-shaped faucets. The music throbbed in the background from hidden speakers somewhere near the arched ceiling.

Janice was first in, throwing aside her robe, voluptuous body golden from hours spent in the tanning rooms, her bush freshly coloured, a flaming beacon between her thighs. A brash, outrageous statement of her overwhelming interest in sex, it drew the eye like a magnet.

Inga handed Tamzin a glass of champagne, and gave another to Janice. She toasted them over the rim of her own, eyes brimming with laughter, saying, 'Good luck, girls, and may all your dreams come true.'

'I don't know what Andy would say,' Tamzin giggled.

The wine was strong and she was surprised to find she had drained the glass. Inga topped it up again. 'I expect he'd give me a lecture on alcohol causing broken veins on the face. We only had fruit tea with him.'

'Andy, my dear, is no saint, as you'll no doubt discover,' Inga answered. 'Drink up. If we don't finish the bottle it will go flat.'

She bent with sinuous grace and rested her glass on the tiled floor, and then her hands went to the sash spanning Tamzin's waist, loosening it, peeling away the towelling robe. Tamzin stepped down into the bath, the water deep now, swirling pleasantly, stimulating every inch of her skin. The fret about Guy was receding to the back of her mind.

Inga watched her, slowly unbuttoning her elegant and sensible beige silk blouse and laying it aside. Beneath it she wore an underwired bra of coffee-coloured satin, her nipples peeping over the tops of the lacy baskets. Next came the skirt, long, demure, even prim, but when she removed it her bottom was bare, as was her mons, innocent of panties.

Tamzin closed her eyes, feeling the marble seat beneath her, the water undulating between her legs, agitating her sex. It was enjoyable in the extreme. Everything that had happened to her since entering Cheveral Court had been sensually satisfying. This was indeed a palace of enchantment, a Pleasure Dome as Alex had hinted, though the caves of ice only existed outside.

When she lifted her lids it was to see Inga standing at the edge of the tub. Her slender legs were apart, the rounded globes of her buttocks, thighs and calf muscles exaggerated by the high heels of her black court shoes. Suspenders stretched down tightly from a tobacco and gold garter belt, clipped to the tops of stockings so transparent as to resemble a dark brown mist.

If Tamzin had found it hard not to stare at Janice's burgundy plumes, then it was doubly difficult not to look at Inga's depilated slit invitingly framed by tight elastic and satin. A window on to the magically fragrant world of her womanhood. The inner lips pouted between the outer, forming an enticing, fleshy line crowned by her protruding, lascivious love-button.

She moved, came closer, and the heavily scented nectar seeping from her pussy excited Tamzin's nostrils. She found herself becoming unbearably aroused, wanting to touch that glistening crack, to open and explore it, to run her tongue over the juices and take them into the cavity of her mouth.

Inga stared down her thin, aristocratic nose, an imperious look in her eyes. She towered above her, dominating, even sinister, and Tamzin thrilled, her own honeydew welling at her portal, joining the bubbling water. She could see Janice from the tail of her eye, squatting, wide-legged, over one of the jets, opening the lips of her labia and stroking back and forth, a dreamy smile on her face.

Inga stalked to the vanity unit and selected a lipstick, then renewed her spread-legged stance. She lifted her breasts free of the cups and rouged the nipples lovingly, admiring the picture they presented in the mirrored walls. Opening her legs a mite wider, she held back her tiny foreskin and touched the crimson cosmetic to her clit-head – just there, nowhere else. Now it shone like a ruby, irresistible and alluring.

Tamzin could wait no longer. She rose out of the water to kneel at Inga's feet, her skin cooling, trickling, tingling as she raised her hand. Inga, head flung back, was rubbing her nipples, fingernails red as blood. Her ribs rose and fell with the quickness of her breathing as Tamzin gently stroked that deep cleft, feeling it quiver slightly.

Her heart was thumping wildly, need stabbing her

vagina as she let her fingers explore Inga's avenue, holding back her labia between two of them. It was like touching velvet.

She opened wider, and Inga parted her legs and thrust her pubis high. Crystal liquid covered the rose-pink wings, shining between them. Still holding them apart with her left hand, Tamzin used the middle finger of her right to smooth that silky fluid over the sensitive area and permit herself the joy of wetting the carmine bright nub.

It was as if she caressed herself. Masturbation had taught her to achieve the highest pinnacle of pleasure, and she knew exactly how another woman would react to the same caresses. She varied them, now hard, now a feathery whisper – nothing harsh or brutal, just sublime, joyous strokes producing utterly fulfilling sensations.

If the clitoris became too dry, she simply dipped down into the nectar pooling in Inga's vulva. If the feeling was too intense, she picked up on her lover's distress, slackening off, giving her a respite by rubbing each side, fondling the petals, holding off from touching the pistil. She gave it time to recover, want, ache for more, delaying orgasm, making it last.

Now the whole delicious vista was exposed to her and

she could drink her fill of those swollen lips and the engorged organ surmounting them. Somewhere behind her she heard Janice gasping as she came. A moment later she felt the touch of a hand slipping between the taut mounds of her bottom. Fingers probed the tight ring of her anus, then cupped her pubis from behind. With laser-beam precision Janice's forefinger found the bud which had risen from its cowl like a miniature phallus.

'Don't do it yet,' Tamzin murmured jerkily, and Janice understood, keeping her hand still, her eyes lifted to Inga.

Fingers flicking swiftly over her nipples, Inga was rolling her head from side to side in an extremity of pleasure. Tamzin judged the moment to a nicety. Too much and Inga would have lost the impetus to climax. Too little and it would be over in a flash. Attuned to her need she began to increase the speed. Inga started to buck and moan.

'Now – do it now!' she panted.

'Not quite yet,' Tamzin replied, and could not resist pressing down on Janice's hand, her own love-bud throbbing.

'Yes. Please. I want it,' Inga cried, and thrust her crotch against Tamzin's fingers, grinding her hips, seeking release.

'Be still,' Tamzin said quietly. 'I'll give it to you.'

Faster her finger moved, slick-wet over the fulcrum of Inga's desire, watching her thrash her pelvis as she came in a rushing, screaming frenzy. Her head dropped to her chest and she sighed deeply, still shuddering as the retreating shock-waves of ecstasy gradually subsided.

Tamzin did not abandon her at once, continuing a very gentle stroking on the oversensitive clit-head, then gradually leaving it to recover, in exactly the same way as when she had finished pleasuring herself. One needed time to reflect and enjoy the peace climax brought, that good, empowering feeling to which every woman was entitled.

He watched through the two-way mirror, his face tense in the darkness of the recess behind the wall of Inga's bathroom. Clever Inga, he reflected. So skilled at manipulating situations, his devoted, talented disciple.

Tamzin was possibly the most desirable woman he had ever seen and his experience was legion. So, she'd fancied herself in love with that pretty-boy pianist, Ventura, had she? It hadn't been difficult to put a stop to that. Orlando Thorne had, months ago, marked her out as his own, and what Orlando wanted he usually got.

A sardonic smile lifted the corners of his sensual lips, deepening the grooves each side. His topaz eyes devoured every line of her naked body. She was indeed lovely. Long-limbed, graceful as a gazelle, with that mane of dusky hair in which a man might bury his fears and longings.

Those black-lashed eyes, green as the seas of Galway Bay where he had been born – the finely arched brows – and that mouth: a kissing mouth if ever God made one. As he imagined her lips enclosing his cock, he felt it begin to stir, the glans chafing against the silk lining of his leather trousers.

The women were like the Three Graces, a sight calculated to tempt a saint, the whole show orchestrated by Inga. He had possessed Tamzin by dead of night, creeping into her room like an incubus, so dark, formless and silent that he might have been a part of her dreams. But now he wanted more. She must submit to his desires when fully conscious, her body's responses controlled by his will, and then – once she was his slave – he would reveal his identity.

The thought of her surprise, outrage even, followed by acquiescence made lust boil inside him like molten lava. He would come in her mouth, bathe her face with his libation, then part the delicate membrane of her labia just as he had seen her do to Inga. He would lick it, subject her bud to his tongue until she screamed for release, begging him to possess her.

His balls ached and his penis danced. He opened his fly and cupped the semen-filled balls, then stroked the hard shaft to even greater size. He took it out for easier rubbing, working a drop of viscous fluid over the pulsating head. Trembling, never taking his eyes from Tamzin as she lay on the side of the bath with Janice's face buried between her thighs, he could feel the forces gathering.

His legs shook, and that rushing sensation began at the base of his spine. Out of control, unable to stop, he rubbed hard, working the rampant weapon, squeezing and pumping it. As he lost himself in bliss, his tribute spurted from him in a snowy stream. Frail, emptied and spasming, his lips formed the single word – Tamzin.

She paced the room in a ferment of anger and indecision. What use the time she had spent perfecting her appearance?

The seaweed body wrap, the jacuzzi, followed by a pedicure, a manicure, a facial, and then makeup cunningly applied by a beautician, all wasted now. She might as well take off the strapless, silk apology-for-a-dress she wore and go to bed.

A mistake, probably, at least Tag had said it was, scornful of the inflated price she had paid for it from the Helmut Lang collection. Deceptively simple in cut, it barely covered her silk-stockinged thighs. As she had put it on over a pair of crotchless panties, she had still cherished the hope that Guy might call. But it was time to go down for dinner and the phone by her bed remained maddeningly mute.

'Sod him!' she muttered aloud, addressing the teddy bear who sat, ears pricked, near her pillow. 'Who the hell does he think he is? Good God, in my line of work I've phoned top designers, movie stars, politicians – the *crème de la crème* of society, yet I'm scared to call him. What shall I do, Humphrey?'

It seemed his bright glassy eyes twinkled encouragingly and, on a sudden wave of resolution, she snatched up the receiver. It was annoying to have calls go through Cheveral Court's switchboard, but Inga insisted on filtering them to protect her clients from outside interference.

'Miss Lawrence here. Put me through to Fir Cottage,

please,' she snapped at the anonymous person who answered her.

'Is he expecting you to ring?' came the careful reply.

'Yes. I had dinner with him last evening. We're old friends.'

'Very well. I'll see if he'll take your call.'

There followed a nerve-jangling silence. Tamzin could feel little beads of sweat breaking out on her upper lip and was appalled at her cowardice. Her heart jumped into her throat as a heavily accented, masculine voice said.

'Hello?'

'Guy – it's Tamzin,' she blurted, unsure what to say now the moment had come. 'You didn't phone me. I've been waiting to hear from you all day.' She tried to control that nagging, accusatory tone.

He did not answer at once, keeping her on the rack, nerves taut as fiddle-strings. Then in a voice of pure ice, he said, 'You lied to me. You're a member of the press.' He spoke as if she was something unpleasant he had scraped off the bottom of his shoe.

'Not precisely. I edit a top magazine – *Chimera*.'

'I know all about you, Miss Lawrence. I never want to see you again. I'm warning you – don't come anywhere near Fir Cottage. Good night.'

The phone went dead. She could not believe it, standing there staring at the receiver. Tears of rage stung the backs of her eyes. She had never been so insulted in her life. That damned, high-handed, conceited pig! And she had permitted him to enter the sacred temple of her body. Worse than this: he had invaded her mind. It was horrible. She hated him.

'Fat lot of use you turned out to be!' she shouted at Humphrey, then snatched him up and cuddled his furry body against the pain in her heart.

She refused to cry. Why make her eyes red and ruin her mascara for the sake of a toad like Guy? Instead she replaced the bear tenderly as guardian of her pillow and walked from the room, head held at a defiant angle.

Dinner was served in the palatial dining room, tables arranged between marble pillars and walls covered with heavy flock paper under a ceiling painted lavishly with the divinities of Olympus. Rainbow prisms flashed from the chandeliers, and soft-footed flunkies moved around, bearing trays of carefully prepared food.

Inga was sharing her table with personal friends, Tamzin numbered among them. More guests had managed to pre-empt the storm, and it had not snowed that day.

'A thaw is forecast,' Lance observed over the salmon and monkfish terrine, a delicious concoction despite its low-calorie sauce.

'That's good,' Inga replied, resplendent in black velvet, her shoulders rising from the sombre bodice, iridescent and pearly. 'We're having friends to stay at the weekend, Tamzin. They will be gone by then,' and she gestured towards her other clients with a flash of diamond rings. 'There's a fresh batch booked in for Monday. So we shall have the house to ourselves. I've planned several entertainments.'

She gave a mysterious smile, and Lance reached over to put a finger under her chin and lift her face to his. 'I'm looking forward to it,' he said, and her hand came up to cover his with an affection absent in her dealings with others.

'D'you want us to leave?' Tamzin said frostily, not sure if she could handle a further rejection.

'Good heavens, no!' Inga exclaimed. 'I'm organising it to include you, darling. Janice as well. You'll stay, won't you, Alex?'

'How can I refuse?' he said with his crooked grin. 'Though I don't know if I can really afford it.'

'There'll be nothing to pay. This is on the house,' Inga

insisted. 'Saturday we're throwing a ball, following an equestrian event that will go on throughout the morning and afternoon.'

'In this weather?' Tamzin had wanted to go riding but the snow had prevented her. A brisk gallop might help to clear her head.

'Indoors,' Lance explained. 'There's a covered exercise ring next to the stables.'

'Can I take part?' she asked, leaning towards him eagerly. Mind freed of Guy, she could now appreciate his fine bone structure and tentatively open herself to his charms. 'I can handle a horse.'

Inga laughed, and gave her an odd, sly glance. 'Can you indeed? We'll see, won't we, Lance?'

After a dessert of marinated peaches with low-fat yoghurt and toasted almonds, they were served coffee and cognac in the conservatory. The women lounged on the 1930s Lloyd Loom furniture, while Lance and Alex moved knee-high chess pieces around on the black and white checkered paving.

'Lance tells me you visited Guy Ventura yesterday. How did you get on with him?' Inga remarked from the padded cushions of a pink and gold settee, replacing her cup on a matching round table.

'Fine,' Tamzin rejoined levelly, confident she now had her emotions firmly leashed.

'He's a seriously gorgeous guy, but difficult, and an absolute bastard where women are concerned. I speak from experience, had a fling with him not all that long ago. He has the biggest cock I've ever seen. It almost choked me when I gave him a blow-job. Couldn't manage to take it all. What did you think of it?' Those azure blue eyes regarded her with a bright, inquisitive stare.

'Why ask me? How should I know?' Tamzin was nettled by this information, disliking the idea of Inga practising fellatio on him. She could feel her cheeks growing hot as her mind shot back to the night before when she had experienced every vital inch of that splendid tool.

'You mean to say he didn't fuck you? Who are you trying to kid?' There was the whisper of silk chafing silk as Inga crossed one knee over the other, the tip of her satin shoe showing beneath the hem. The warm length of her black swathed thigh pressed into Tamzin's.

'I don't particularly want to talk about it,' Tamzin snapped, setting down her cup with such force that it rattled on the glass table top.

'Oh, poor darling, has he been unkind to you? Never mind.' Inga nestled closer, slipping a silky-smooth bare arm round Tamzin's waist. 'I think you need cheering up. Don't you agree, Janice? What say we play a little game?'

'What sort of game?' A tocsin clanged somewhere in Tamzin's brain.

Laughter vibrated through Inga's body. 'Call it a form of blind man's buff. Will you take up the dare?'

She was testing her, Tamzin was sure, and her stubborn pride would not admit defeat. This evening was turning out to be far from how she had imagined it when she awoke that morning. No matter. She would close the door resolutely on Guy Ventura and accept anything Inga suggested.

'All right. Let's play,' she said, her voice a tad too loud, sounding brittle in her ears.

Inga stood up, took off the black chiffon scarf wound round her waist and held it between her hands. 'You're it,' she murmured, and before Tamzin could protest, had bound her eyes.

Darkness engulfed her, reminiscent of her office and Mike. Excitement glowed in the pit of her belly, a dark, dangerous and wanton feeling. As on that never-to-be-forgotten occasion before Christmas, four of her senses were tinglingly alive.

She could hear whispering voices, taste traces of coffee at the back of her teeth, smell Inga's perfume, her body odour, too – those spicy essences that lubricated her sex. She knew when Janice approached. She smelled different, of floral spray and deodorant. Now hands touched her and she responded to this tactile sensation.

Men were near her, Lance and Alex, a stronger, more powerful emanation, mingled with aftershave. Someone gripped her under the elbow.

'This way, Tamzin,' Lance said, a skein of something new weaving through his voice. Mockery? Recklessness?

She stumbled, put out her hands as a blind person will. Soft fingers closed on hers either side. Inga and Janice. She was being led through the house. Sounds, echoes – their feet muffled by carpet, the air warm. This changed. A door opened. Her feet encountered stone. It was cooler. They were descending.

Down and down, stone treads twisting and turning. This must be the cellar. A blast of heat, the sound of a furnace roaring. The boiler-room. Then Tamzin went rigid, hearing the clank and scrape of iron on granite.

Was it a gate? Were they about to imprison her? Janice wouldn't let them, would she?

She was pulled to a halt. Felt something at her back, possibly a wooden frame. Her arms were uplifted and outspread. Cold cuffs were snapped round each wrist. Chains clinked. The adrenalin was pumping through every vein, warnings, fear and excitement making her juices flow, wetting the sides of the open-crotched panties.

Footfalls now, coming nearer, a man's – the tap of steel tips on flagstones. For a breathless moment she thought it might be Guy, then she caught the smell of oiled leather. The fine down rose on her skin.

'This one needs to be disciplined, Master,' Inga said with unusual humility.

'Where am I?' Tamzin cried, tugging at her bonds. The game had gone on long enough. 'Disciplined? What the hell d'you mean?'

'You're quite safe,' Inga assured her, and Tamzin's nipples crimped as soft fingers traced them lightly through her bodice.

She hissed in frustration. Who was the man hovering over her? She knew it *was* a man, his male aura seeming to tangle with hers, infiltrating and pervading it.

Could it be Guy? This sort of pre-planned episode did not fit in with his reserved personality. In the pitch blackness, suspended on the cutting edge of fear and anticipation, she remembered the pleasure that had splinted through her at the touch of his large hands, and the sweeping orgasm that had almost frightened her with its intensity. She owed him no explanation, but felt guilty because she had not told him about *Chimera*.

Her thoughts were catapulted into present time as she felt the heat radiating from the body of this stranger who was standing in front of her. Something stroked her mound through the fabric of her dress. Her mind did a flip back to her first night at the manor and the visit from her anonymous lover. She could feel the remembered smoothness as a gloved finger trailed across her bare shoulder, down her arm and around the handcuffs. Was this the same person, and if so, who was he?

Swiftly she catalogued the men who were there: Guy was dismissed. Lance, Alex or Kevlin? The masseur, Borg? Janice had said he was into women's underwear. Andy? Hardly. She could not picture the earthy Kevlin doing other than give a girl a straightforward humping.

None felt right for the part. Besides, Lance and Alex had brought her down there, and they had been wearing faultlessly-tailored evening suits. She was certain this man was clad in hide, exactly like her nocturnal paramour.

He pressed closer. Her ankles were seized. She was spread-eagled and clamped, feet braced against the stone floor. Helpless, vulnerable, whoever it was could do whatever he wished to her and she would be unable to stop him.

Tamzin drank of the heady wine of freedom. No responsibility. No shame. A victim of sensations, prey to the dizzying heights of torment and ecstasy. Tiny pinpricks of fear ran along her nerves as she teetered on the brink of the unknown.

She was entirely in his hands, exposed for his pleasure. The Master, Inga had called him.

It was as silent as the tomb. Even the furnace had died down. No rustle of clothing, no breathing, just herself and the stranger locked in the Stygian blackness.

'Who are you?' she whispered, made up of cold and heat, desire flicking at her core.

'Your Master,' he replied, his voice low, vibrant, the same voice she had heard in the night.

'Why am I here?' she cried, straining against the bonds.

'To learn. This is my School of Correction.' The rich ice of his voice sent tremors through her. In comparison, Mike had been a mere novice.

'I don't understand,' she faltered, gasping as he ran his great hands over her feet, calves and knees, the leather rough on her thighs.

'You will,' he promised and rucked up her short skirt. Bending, he pressed his face against the hard swell of her pubis, nosing between the opening at the crotch of her panties.

She moaned, writhing in the manacles, burning at this humiliation yet stunned to feel a secret part of her welcoming it. Her hips moved upwards against his mouth, almost begging him to continue his examination of her sex.

'It was you, wasn't it, who entered my bed in the dark?' she murmured. 'Why are you doing this?'

'It pleases me,' he answered, rising now, his face inches from her own. She could smell her own juices on his lips.

'Why don't you show yourself?' she began, but before she could say more, he silenced her with a kiss, tongue plunging into the wet cavern of her mouth, ravaging the tender lining.

She hung there helpless, unable to turn her head or escape that violent assault on her senses. Her passion rose like a tempest, her tongue meeting his with a frenzy of her own, lips sucking, teeth biting, needing the taste of blood to mingle with the salty saliva. She wanted him, welcoming the dark gift he offered, her cries muffled by his mouth as he bared her breasts, pinching her stone-hard nipples.

He withdrew with an abruptness that made her judder, and when his hands finally returned to her tormented flesh, the gloves had gone and she felt his cool fingers against her fevered skin. His mouth was on her throat, nipping painfully, then drawing a segment between his lips. He travelled lower, tonguing her nipples till she was ready to scream with agonised longing.

'You must learn to wait, Miss Lawrence,' he said coldly. 'You're too used to having your own way. Spoilt. In command. Now you are my houri, my plaything. Tell me, you want to learn?'

'I do,' she whispered.

He grabbed hold of her panties and jerked the material tight into the wetness of her cleft. 'Say it louder.' His voice was toneless. It made her shiver.

'I want to learn,' she said.

'Again,' he said quietly.

'No!' she shouted, refusing to be browbeaten.

'You're disobedient. It won't do.' He sighed deeply, and his hand dived down to her pubis, pinching her erect clitoris through the lace-edged split.

'Oh – ah – yes!' She quivered with delight, jerking her hips. Too late she realised the folly of expressing pleasure.

He had pulled her skirt high, tucking it round her waist. Then he left her, and she heard him move round behind. Sweat inched down her face, over her chest and between her breasts as she tried to gauge his actions. An alien something, cold and metallic, was inserted under the silk ties at her hip-bone. It sliced through them. The tiny triangle of fabric fell away. Cool air stirred her pussy.

She waited. Nothing happened. Then the breath rushed back into the round O of her mouth with shock as something landed on her buttocks with a sharp slap. The cuffs dug into her flesh as her back arched. The second blow fell before she had time to yell.

'Well, Miss Lawrence? Are you going to confess you dreamed of this?' he purred, arms coming round to press her against him, fingers tweaking her taut nipples.

'Yes – yes,' she sobbed, trembling with fear and excitement.

'Tell me that it makes your juices flow and your clit quiver. Say that you want more. Shall we try the cane instead of the paddle?'

'No. I don't want it!' But she knew it was untrue. Even as she heard the cane whistle and felt it etch burning welts on her body, so the heat was echoed between her legs. She was rabid with desire.

'And you want me to fuck every orifice? To use you as I want?'

'Yes – oh, yes!'

'Then you shall have me, but in my time, not yours,' he said evenly, his breath cooling her skin, his hands caressing her smarting backside. 'Is this how you imagined it would be?' he continued. 'Did you think it would sting like this?'

'I never thought about it,' she said very low, her voice breaking.

'Liar.'

The air rushed as the switch rose and fell, a red mist rising behind the blindfold, her helpless body consumed by fire, jumbled feelings cascading through her. Pain, humiliation, and the evergrowing urgency of extreme arousal.

There was silence and stillness again. She hardly dared breathe, not knowing what to expect. Another blow? A caress?

He came round in front of her, one hand pulling her hips sharply towards him, the other plunging into her sex, forcing the lips open, mauling the slippery interior.

She could feel the long thick bough of his swollen penis pressing against her, and triumph speared her at this evidence of his lust. 'I want to see you,' she cried. 'Take off the scarf.'

'Your wants are not important,' he grated.

'Are you afraid to show yourself to me?' she challenged.

His fingers twisted and turned inside her and she flinched, tried to pull away. Couldn't. 'Slaves have no rights,' he said. 'But I have decided that you should see your Master.'

He left her throbbing sex. His hands tangled with her hair, and she yelled as the blindfold was ripped away.

At first she could see nothing, then became aware of a faint glow – candlelight blocked out by his massive bulk.

He was dressed entirely in black leather. Jeans that clung like a second skin to the bulging thighs and taut buttocks; a shirt that outlined muscular shoulders; high boots that encased his calves. A hood covered his head and the blankness of a mask was turned towards her.

There was no way of telling who he was, but one thing was for sure: it was no one she knew. Had it been, then something would have betrayed his identity – a gesture, a movement – a turn of phrase.

'Satisfied?' he said in that expressionless tone, and she cringed as he moved, but it was only to take up a bottle and pour liquid into the palm of one hand.

He sprang for her, and his oiled fingers snaked down between her legs, massaging her labia with fragrant lotion and her own love-juice. She whimpered as he opened her wider and lifted her pubis high, sliding his fingers past the resisting sphincter and the unexplored haven of her rectum.

Suddenly he unsnapped the manacles, but before she grasped what was happening, he raised her in his arms and laid her across a stone slab, her thighs and legs hanging over the edge. Coldness shocked through her thin dress. Fear shocked through her brain, coupled with a strange admiration of the sinister figure who now inserted a knee between hers and nudged her legs apart.

They were alone in the cellar. Those who had brought her to him had melted away like snow in sunlight. She was as much a gift for this anonymous, faceless being as when the ancient Minoans had left a virgin in the black Cretan labyrinth to appease the appetites of the monstrous Minotaur.

And he was hungry, this untamed, dark thing. She could smell his arousal and hear his raw, ragged breathing. His hands were still coated with oil and she gave small, mewing sounds as he ran them over her breasts, her dress pushed down to her waist. She wanted to be completely naked for him, but he would not wait. He released his iron-hard penis.

Gripping her ankles, he yanked up her legs and rested them on his shoulders. With pelvis canted at an angle, her most private places were completely exposed as his hands cupped her buttocks. She winced, but he massaged her with more of the oil, working it between her thighs, bending to lip her love-bud.

His slanting, vulpine eyes shone through the mask, and his fingers began to move in harmony, brushing her throbbing clitoris, probing into her secret self, smearing her with oil and honeydew.

The great bulk of his rampant cock slipped between

her swollen lips and his first violent thrust lifted her with the sheer power of him. He filled her completely, her muscles gripping him tightly. He withdrew, then entered again, and she strained upwards, trying to find pressure for her clitoris. Then he slid out of her, reaching down to circle it.

White-hot waves rolled over her and she felt the rush and relief as he brought her to the peak and toppled her into heaven. He filled her with his cock, ploughing and churning as her body tightened around him, and she heard herself making animal noises as he thrust into the pulsating depths of her.

Chapter Nine

Maria let herself into the cottage, anticipation warming her belly. Guy had been there yesterday but in such a foul mood that she had not delayed, almost rushing through her chores and escaping to the arms of the easy-going Kevin.

This morning she had walked through the crisp snow from the Big House, her country girl's eye noting the almost imperceptible signs of a change in the weather. The thaw was coming. She could smell it. And spring would be not far behind, violets peeping from the embrace of dark green leaves, bluebells sprawling, lush and vibrant, across the glades, trees bursting into bud, and gawky hares loping over the hillsides in pursuit of mates.

Maria's body-clock was in tune with nature, and she longed for the heat and haze of summer, when she could bare herself to the sun and lie in the hayfields with Kevlin or whoever she selected to plunge his cock into her eager body. Meanwhile there was Guy Ventura, and the weekend party to look forward to.

Maria knew all about Inga's parties; she had been there, done that, wanted to do it again. Game for anything, if it involved sex.

'Good morning, Mr Ventura,' she said cheerfully as she shut the backdoor.

There was no reply. Maria shrugged, ground some coffee beans and switched on the percolator. The smell was bound to make him break cover. Meanwhile, she pulled the curtains back from the windows in the sitting-room and got out the vacuum cleaner. When she inserted the nozzle under the couch to root out fluff she was annoyed to find it sluggish.

'Bugger!' she exclaimed, 'What's wrong with you then, you bloody old thing?'

She hoicked it from under the frill. Something black protruded from the end. Maria flicked the switch and the machine whined and died. Suction released, the obstruction dropped into her hand. It was a minute pair of knickers, little more than a G-string.

'D'you have to make that noise so early?' Guy shouted from the doorway, tousle-headed, hairy legs sticking out from under a silk dressing-gown, his feet bare. 'What the hell time is it?'

'Ten o'clock. The morning's nearly gone,' she said brightly, then dangled the panties from one finger, asking, 'These yours?' Her dimples flashed in a mischievous smile.

'No, they are not!' He scowled darkly at them.

'I can see that, sir,' she went on, dropping her gaze to his lower regions. 'I was only teasing. You'd never get all your tackle in, would you?'

Guy retreated into dignity. 'Miss Lawrence must have left them. I'm surprised you didn't find them yesterday.'

'Didn't hoover under the settee. What you going to do with 'em? Give 'em to her next time she calls?'

'She won't be calling again.' His eyes were moody as he moved towards the piano, as if seeking comfort from routine. 'Mrs Steadson rang to warn me that she works for a magazine. I didn't know. I hate reporters.'

Now what's going on here? she wondered, putting the vacuum cleaner away and seeing to the coffee. She had not yet met Tamzin Lawrence, but Kevlin had been singing her praises. The fact that she had screwed Guy made Maria even more curious. And why had Inga grassed her up?

She carried a tray to where Guy sat before the fire, legs propped up on the settee, the morning papers spread over his lap. It occurred to Maria that he might want a bit of special attention to soothe him. She longed to get her lips round his beautiful cock.

'Thank you,' he said without looking up.

She poured piping hot coffee into a cup. 'I'll just pop upstairs and make the bed, if that's all right by you,' she said, lingering close, fingers itching to toy with his thick curls.

'Very well.' Now he glanced at her and she tingled, glad she'd had the forethought to don her new jeans. They fitted tight as a drum round her bottom, and outlined the swelling lips of her pussy.

'Is there anything else you want, sir?' she asked pointedly, feeling her nipples rising under the 40 D-cups of her bra.

He regarded her steadily, and she could have sworn

she saw something stirring under the newspaper. Hot images of the treasures it concealed made her clit throb.

'Yes, there is,' he said slowly, that dark-brown voice sliding like melting chocolate over her senses. 'You may return Miss Lawrence's underwear to her. Will you do that for me?'

'I'll do anything for you, sir,' she gasped. 'Just name it.'

The paper was thrown aside. The robe fell open and his prick stood out proud through the gap. Maria wanted to fall upon it greedily, but restrained herself.

'Take off your T-shirt,' he growled, and his hand went to his dick, easing back the foreskin and polishing the swollen knob of his erection.

Maria needed no second invitation. The jersey was removed in a trice, her breasts spilling over the top of her bra. Pink-gold skin like ripe peaches, young, healthy and delectable, a sight to reward a man's eyes and make him want to feast at the nipples.

He beckoned her closer and she went eagerly, bending so that her teats swung over him, touching his face. He grabbed at them with that fierce need which was so exciting, his hands pressing the fleshy orbs together, trying to get both tips into his mouth at once. It was an impossible feat. Maria was too well-blessed. Her back arched and she gave vent to soft little whimpers as he went from one to the other, tonguing them hard.

'God, you're a tit-man, aren't you?' she gasped. 'Some men like legs, others are mad about bums, but you can't get enough of these.'

He grunted in response, too involved with his own sensations, dimly recalling the vast bosoms of his nurse-maids back home. Bolster-like, they had seemed to the infant Guy – huge, soft, inflated cushions, smelling of milk and sweat, comfort and love.

He moved over so she lay beneath him, and she wriggled down, taking his cock in her mouth as he rolled her round breasts under his hands. She licked the length and breadth of his powerful weapon. He needed a shower, and she wanted to give him one, imagining soaping him between the legs. Her hands would slither over those pendulous balls and wash the thick shaft, making the cap red and horny.

She unfastened her jeans and, lifting her hips, pushed them over her thighs. Her white briefs were damp between the legs, and she eased them below the neat fuzzy triangle. Her legs were shaking and her sex ready, but he took no notice, concentrating hungrily on the nipples that pointed towards him.

He sat astride her, cupping her breasts, pressing them together. Shifting up, he inserted his penis there, rocking backwards and forwards. It was wet with her saliva and his jism and he slid it up and down, her cleavage imitating a vagina.

Maria enjoyed the feel of his slippery prick rammed between her breasts. Glancing down she could see the head every time he pushed up, its single eye oozing liquid, drop by clear drop. She wanted him to come like that, but her clitoris was throbbing. As his movements became more uncontrolled, driving him towards orgasm, she inserted a hand between her legs, found her pleasure-button, and masturbated.

Her climax came just as he reached his. Hot seminal fluid spurted forth like a geyser, drenching her chest, face and hair. Maria opened her mouth and sucked in the white libation, relishing the spicy taste.

Cheveral Court buzzed. Guests were departing, cars revving up amidst choruses of goodbyes and promises of return visits. When the last sleek Jaguar, sporty Fiat Coupé and suave Alfa Romeo had purred off down the drive, Inga and Lance closed the massive front door and began to prepare for the members of Orlando Thorne's sect.

Tamzin slept late and it was noon by the time Inga tapped on the bedroom door. She struggled up, wincing because her bottom was bruised.

She was hazy about the return to her room, but remembered the Master blindfolding her again, and the giddy feeling as she was slung over his broad shoulder like a sack of potatoes, followed by the jolting, bumping sensation of being carried upstairs. Presumably, he had laid her on her bed, stripped off the remnants of her dress, covered her in the quilt and left.

'That bastard!' she cried, tossing back her tangled hair. 'He hurt me!'

'And didn't you enjoy it?' Inga answered, a predatory smile playing round her lips.

'I'm not sure.' Memories crowded back, thick and fast. She stared at Inga, adding accusatively, 'You knew what was going to happen, didn't you?'

Inga sat down on the floral duvet and picked up Humphrey, running her fingers idly over his honey-hued fur. 'Naturally.'

'And who is he?' Tamzin said, still angry. 'Why did

you let him come into my room, and why the drama in the cellar?'

Inga held Humphrey against her shoulder. He growled jerkily as she absent-mindedly patted his humped back. 'He'll let you see him when he's ready. Suffice to say he's an influential man and you've taken his fancy.'

'Ha! Get real!' Tamzin scoffed. 'He's got a funny way of showing it. I'll bet there are marks on my bum.'

Inga put the bear aside and sat with her hands folded in the lap of her expensive trouser-suit. She regarded Tamzin seriously. 'Was there no pleasure? Didn't you come?'

Tamzin blushed, and in a sudden fit of shyness pulled the sheet over her naked breasts. These people – Inga, Lance, Janice – even Alex – seemed to know far too much about her innermost fantasies.

'Oh, yes, there was pleasure, all right. Fierce, frightening pleasure.'

'You'd like to repeat the experience?' Inga watched her, eyes as blue and slanting as a Siamese cat's. 'Don't be ashamed to admit it. He's my Master as well, and Janice's. In fact, you'll shortly meet others who share the release of submission, or enjoy being the dominating one.'

'But why?' Tamzin whispered, trying to hang on to the concepts that had shaped her life.

'Psychologists would give complicated explanations. We don't bother with that. We simply indulge ourselves, trying out fun things. You, darling, gave an impressive performance.'

'You were watching?' Now Tamzin's buttocks were no longer painful but suffused by a warm glow, and she inhaled the mix of oil and sexual secretions rising from her labia.

'He likes us to watch,' Inga answered simply. 'We enjoy it, too. All four of us pleasured each other while he was initiating you.'

'When shall I meet him again?' A nub of desire smouldered in Tamzin's core like a dark coal.

She yearned to feel the paddle smacking her bottom, the cane slicing across the tender flesh, while she was helpless under his hands, her wants of no significance compared to the force of his will.

'He'll be with us this weekend, and I want you to put conventional ideas on hold.'

Maria came in, wearing a French maid's outfit. Every time she bent over it was to give an alluring glimpse of pink thighs between black suspenders, her tuft encased in transparent chiffon briefs.

She bobbed and said, 'Miss Lawrence? Mr Ventura's

asked me to return your property,' and she laid the scrap of silk on the quilt.

Tamzin was embarrassed that her underwear should be so bandied about.

'This is Maria, ready to help my friends get their jollies,' Inga said carelessly. 'She looks after Fir Cottage. And how is that sexy beast today, Maria?'

'Well, he wasn't in a very good mood when I got there, but better by the time I left,' Maria answered, rolling her eyes saucily.

Tamzin bridled. 'Thank you for returning my panties, Maria,' she said coldly. 'And was it you who told him of my association with *Chimera*?'

'No, miss. I didn't know nothing about it,' Maria answered honestly, her hazel eyes puzzled as they cut to Inga's face.

'It was I who told him.' Inga's voice was as cool as a mountain stream. She placed her fingers over Tamzin's lips before she could launch into an angry outburst, and continued, 'Lance told me you were in danger of making a fool of yourself over Guy, and I didn't want you to get hurt. Besides which, the Master has other plans for you. I hope you're not too cross with me.'

'It was a lousy thing to do,' Tamzin spluttered.

'It would have been far worse if Guy found out later, as he was bound to. He'll be here tomorrow night. I've managed to persuade him to play for us. Calm down, darling. You'll see that I'm right.'

All through the day Tamzin nursed her sense of betrayal, yet beneath it lay that dark thread of inner knowledge she had gained from the Master. By the time evening came she was balanced again, dressing with the greatest care, an electric thrill darting to her epicentre as she wondered if the Master would show himself.

Her dress of the previous night had been ruined, and she took another from the wardrobe.

She had bought it on impulse from *Sh!* and had, as yet, found no opportunity to wear it. She stared at her-self in the cheval glass, amazed at the transformation. It was like wearing a masquerade costume. No one at *Chimera* would have believed their cool, calm and col-lected boss would have dreamed of appearing in public in such an ensemble.

The scarlet leather tunic fastened down the front with buckled straps that left a gap between her breasts. These were pushed high, the bodice supported by shoe-string ties. Under it she wore a thong of soft red kid. Her long legs appeared even longer, bare and smooth, ending in stilt-heeled sandals.

This head-turning little number demanded striking makeup, and she applied more than usual – gold eyelids, mascara, blusher and a crimson lipstick accentuating her pouting mouth. She swept her hair up to one side in a cascade of curls, and added a pair of sparkly earrings.

OK, she thought defiantly. Guy very pointedly sent back my knickers. I'll make damn sure there are plenty of other people trying to get into them!

The crowd in the drawing room were possibly the weirdest assortment Tamzin had yet encountered. Not everyone had arrived yet, trickling in during the course of the evening. Apart from a buffet and late-opening bar, the entertainment was loose until around midnight when Lance gathered everyone together.

'Cabaret time,' he announced, resplendent in a midnight blue velvet tuxedo.

A cheer bounced off the painted ceiling. The odd collection of men in dinner jackets, sweaters, chinos or jogging pants, and the women wearing anything from ball gowns to blue jeans, occupied chairs arranged round the raised boxing-ring in the centre of the polished parquet.

Spots glared down. A pulsing dance track boomed from the speakers and two Junoesque blondes sprang on to the stage and gyrated round the central pole, making love to it. They had huge breasts, tiny waists, and taut muscles. Gold lame emphasised those mammary appendages and sharply defined, depilated pussies. They prowled round one another, crouched, fists bunched, hurling invective. Howling they sprang, instantly engaged in a wrestling bout.

Punching, clawing, first one then the other on top, they went through the motions of the sport, but this game was based on sex not conquest, the blatant exposure of normally hidden areas all a part of the entertainment.

Jeez, will you look at that?' Alex murmured in Tamzin's ear, his hand insinuating itself under the hem of her tunic.

The girls were writhing, blue-veined breasts jiggling, thrusting their naked genitalia at the audience, dry-humping thin air. They stamped and posed in thigh-high lurex boots, their movements increasingly suggestive. One grabbed at her pussy and stuck her fingers into her sex, withdrawing it glistening with juice. This she used to smear the face of the man sitting directly in front of her. He pulled out his cock and frigged it. The crowd whooped.

The two women fell to the floor again, legs locked round each other, every aspect of their pundenda on display as they gave an exhibition of lesbian love. Tongues entwined, hands working at nipples and clits, they appeared to be in a transport of passion.

Excitement shot through Tamzin. She moulded her spine against Alex's white shirt-front as he bit her neck and slipped his fingers into the amber crack that divided her from clitoris to coccyx. The wrestlers were now close to orgasm, egged on by the prurient spectators. Tamzin reached back to unzip Alex's fly, her fingers finding his stiff, throbbing cock.

'D'you like to watch?' he whispered, stimulating her anal opening.

'It's thrilling,' she breathed, parting her legs a shade wider.

'I know. I watched you with the Master while I came into Inga's hand,' he murmured, his chin resting on her shoulder, while she squeezed and teased the hot cock-tip. 'She was sucking Janice at the time and Lance was taking her from behind.'

'And I was having my butt paddled. Great!'

He suddenly jerked and climaxed, coming in lengthy spurts. She held his penis for a moment, then wiped her fingers on his shirt.

'Having fun?' a honeyed voice said and Inga materialised out of the gloom. Her dress shone, close-fitting as a mermaid's scales, sequins rippling with every movement.

The performers were reaching their conclusion, and the room rocked, filled with the sharp, piquant smell of female arousal, perfumes, and musky male odours. Inga's firm fingers circled Tamzin's wrist and she drew her into a recess. Beyond it was a spiral staircase at the top of which lay a small room lit by icy rays of moonlight poking in at the oriel window.

'Another entrance to my apartment,' Inga explained. 'I didn't like to see Alex using you with disregard for your pleasure.'

'I'm sure he would have brought me off,' Tamzin said, staring about her. 'He was aroused by talking about what happened to me last night.'

'It was stimulating, I'll admit. No wonder he couldn't help coming. I ached to possess you, too.'

Inga strolled towards her, darkly mysterious in her spangled gown that cascaded over her breasts and hips. It was backless, slashed to the little hollow just above her bottom crease. The halter-neck made the most of her small firm breasts, and the skirt was slit centre front to show the tops of her black stockings.

She switched on an Art Nouveau lamp with a Tiffany shade and went to a red laquered cabinet. The doors opened and she returned with a tooled leather casket which she placed on the table. Tamzin edged closer, unable to contain her curiosity.

'Do you like making love to women more than men?' she asked.

'I can't honestly tell you. I think women have beautiful bodies, their genitals neatly tucked away, yet opening hungrily when touched, like sea-anemones.' Inga stared down musingly at the contents of her box. 'Breasts are wonderful, and the feel of nipples under the tongue a sweet delight. The clitoris, too, and the smoky taste of it – yet I adore men's semen and their strange, fascinating, ugly equipment. But here are other toys to amuse you, darling. Look.'

'My God!' Tamzin exclaimed.

Dildoes and vibrators lay there, cushioned against the antique silk lining. They were of all the shapes, sizes and materials a fertile imagination might conjure – and not every one resembled a phallus.

'One doesn't need men, you know,' Inga smiled. 'Not while these novelties are available, and they always have been, dear – right down through the ages.'

Tamzin had used sex toys to pleasure herself, and was aware of the wetness soaking into her thong, her body aching to be fulfilled, left high though not dry by Alex. Inga pointing to a solid rubber dildo that represented an enormous erection, down to the details of gnarled veins and mushroom-shaped cap.

'It's sometimes used as a strap-on if one's partner fancies penetration,' she said. 'But I rate this one for solitary satisfaction.'

She picked up a vibrator, adding, 'It looks like a cock, but the top is different. See how it's shaped for clitorial enjoyment. It rotates, and is a real turn-on. Why don't you try it?'

Tamzin lay down on the yellow plush chaise-longue. Inga sat beside her, leaned across and unbuckled the front fastening of the scarlet tunic. Her thin hands and gold-varnished nails played with the exposed breasts. Then she gently sucked them, making the nipples stiffen. Need swelled within Tamzin – urgent, all-consuming. She wanted that strange, shaggy top rotating against her throbbing bud.

'You're prepared to try new things?' Inga asked in a husky whisper.'

'Oh, yes,' Tamzin's fingers closed round the pulsating pleasure weapon and kept it hovering over her bud.

'So am I. Can't wait to try Virtual Reality sex. Imagine it! But just for now, isn't this great?' She did not crowd Tamzin, letting her take her own pace, simply opening her skirt and fondling her pussy-lips as she watched.

The vibrator whirled against Tamzin's clitoris, and she held back the flushed labia with her other hand, permitting it to revolve on the sensitive tip. She knew she should take it away or her orgasm would be done and dusted, yet couldn't resist keeping it there, just to see what would happen. Her climax sprang on her unbidden, the colours in her head exploding in one single burst of dazzling light.

Inga lounged, legs wide spread, fingering her nipples, rubbing her clit with long easy strokes. She came slowly, elegantly and at length. The two women relaxed in companionable silence, letting the spasms die away, listening to the distant noises of the party.

Someone moved in the semi-darkness. Tamzin was enfolded in mighty arms, and lifted high. She found her face pressed against the smooth lapels of a dinner-jacket.

'Good evening,' he whispered and ice tingled over her skin as she recognised his voice.

'You? Here?' she could not find the words to express the emotions that flashed through her mind in rapid succession.

'Aren't you forgetting something?' His hand fastened tightly each side of her waist.

'Master,' she said, very low.

'Exactly.' He released her with such abruptness that she almost fell, and strode to the door. As it opened, the sound of music and laughter swelled. A beam of light illumined him for a fraction. He was still masked.

'No class in the morning,' Astrid said as, at long last, Tamzin prepared to stagger from Inga's bedroom where she had been part of a daisy-chain with her hostess and Lance, Maria, the aerobics instructress and a couple of men, identity unknown.

'No?' Tamzin panted, leaning against the door-jamb and surveying the scene of carnage; clothing strewn everywhere, naked limbs still locked in weird positions. They were attempting to close the gap she had left – joined via genitals and mouths.

'No.' Astrid was looking remarkably fresh, considering

the hectic sexual activity in which she had recently been embroiled. 'But be down in the stables at nine-thirty.'

Tamzin nodded uncertainly. Too much sex and not enough coffee, she decided as she found her own bed. Her head was spinning, her body sticky and, had she not been so tired, she would have taken a bath. Solitude, however, was denied her.

'Hi,' said a voice from the depths of the mattress and the jaded light of a candle showed Alex waiting for her.

'I'm tired,' she wailed, and he opened the covers and drew her in after she got rid of the tunic. 'I just want to sleep.'

'So you shall, dear girl,' he chuckled and kissed her lightly on the temple. 'I thought you might like to know that I've decided to come clean.'

'How d'you mean?' she was really too sleepy to bother, beginning to drift off, curled in his arms.

'I'll give you an in-depth interview for that ridiculously named paper of yours,' he announced magnanimously.

'That's good,' she mumbled. 'Thanks, Alex. Any strings?'

'Strings? I'm an honourable English gentleman, I'll have you know,' he said, but through the mists of pre-sleep she could feel his cock pressing against her belly.

'You might like to see to this, though, if you felt inclined.'

She supposed that she acquiesced, but was three-quarters asleep, only vaguely aware of him possessing her body. It didn't matter. He was a good friend and would make first-class copy. She was already having a conversation in her head with Mike about the layout. Front cover and centre spread. Jeff would take some super pics and Alex would leer sexily out of *Chimera*. All she needed to complete her personal triumph was for Guy Ventura to be as cooperative.

I'll see him tonight, was her last thought before she was pitched into oblivion.

'Morning, miss,' Kevlin said, with a cheeky grin. 'You're up bright and early.'

'Merely following orders,' she answered grumpily. 'I've a hangover and can't find any aspirins.'

'There's some here,' and Kevlin produced a couple from the first-aid box hanging on the rough stone wall and fetched her a glass of water.

He really was a very personable man, she decided, accepting it and downing the painkillers, quite fetching in his ragged, holey jeans. She had heard that he was

Maria's boyfriend, but judging from the maid's behaviour in Inga's bedroom, theirs must be a very open relationship.

The sun poured through the high, arrow-slit windows, its rays grainy with dust motes. Her nostrils were filled with the sweet smell of hay, and a horse poked an inquisitive head over the edge of a stall. Tamzin went over to him and he stuck his big wet nose into her hand.

'Which one shall I be riding?' she asked, turning to find Kevlin looking at her as he rubbed his hand over the outside of his fly.

'Don't you know, miss?' He grinned even wider, and moved closer. 'Haven't they told you?'

'Told me what?' Her brows winged down in a puzzled frown.

He tapped the side of his nose mysteriously. 'That's for me to know and you to find out,' he observed slyly.

It was cold in the stable, but she could feel the heat from their bodies interacting. He was a young, vigorous stud, and she liked the idea of an uncomplicated fuck with him. She glanced up at him under her lashes, and one of his strong, calloused hands touched her arm.

'How's that old headache?' he questioned softly. 'Maybe you'd like to lie down for a bit.'

'Maybe I would,' she answered, adding, 'And maybe you'd like to come with me.'

He took her to an empty stall where a bed of fresh hay was piled in one corner. Kevlin spread a horse-blanket over it, and Tamzin nestled back. She really was very sleepy, and had risen only reluctantly while Alex snored in the four-poster.

Kevlin did not mess about. He was a man with a mission, and he unsnapped his belt and the metal buttons of his jeans, releasing a cock that was of an impressive size and colour with an upward-sweeping curve. He stood in front of her stroking it, then threw himself down at her side.

Without preamble, he unzipped her quilted kagoul, stuck a hand inside and squeezed her breasts. She remembered Maria's impressive tits that looked like silicon implants and wondered if he was drawing comparison. No words were exchanged. He merely grunted his appreciation and got under her jersey. Did he know about the clitoris, or was he a slam-bam-thank-you-ma'am merchant? she mused.

Her senses were aroused by the risk of exposure and the frank eagerness of this bucolic lover. She took hold of that restless python jabbing against her thigh, and massaged the pre-emission fluid over its smooth head. Kevlin started to rub her cleft through her jeans. It was tormenting and exciting, her clit demanding harsh friction after the constant stimulation it had received last night.

She lifted her pelvis and pressed against his finger. Kevlin moved his cock in her fist, and masturbated her harder. She thought he was about to come, but he undid her jeans and found her slick-wet crease, dipping his finger in her juice and fondling her love-bud till ecstasy pierced her.

This was his cue, and her jeans were down before she knew it. He was across her, the mighty, latex-shrouded serpent thrusting between her swollen vulva. He panted and strained, braced on his hands and knees, his head thrown back. Grinding and ploughing, faster and faster, he came in a great surge.

He sank down on her, his fair curly head resting on her collar-bone. Tamzin endured his weight for a moment, then wriggled out from under him. Grabbing a handful of tissues from her bag, she wiped her pussy before adjusting her clothing.

She was leaving the stall as Inga and Lance walked under the arch and into the stable. He was in riding gear and carrying tack and she was wearing an all enveloping cloak, her hair covered by a glittering helmet.

They both smiled warmly at Tamzin. 'Time to get you ready and put you through your paces,' Inga said.

'Will someone tell me what's going on?' Tamzin asked.

'An equestrian event with a difference,' Lance replied, and went to another part of the building. When he returned he was pulling a light-weight, two-wheeled cart. 'This is called a sulky, and it's been made especially for the job.'

'What job? I've never handled horse-drawn vehicles.'

'You're not expected to, darling,' said Inga, and threw off her cloak.

Beneath it she wore a black satin basque, her bare breasts accentuated by straps passing round them and crossing over her chest. Her hairless mons formed a fascinating V between black suspenders attached to lace-topped stockings, and she had on spike-heeled red shoes. She flourished a long coachman's whip.

'In these games we have human ponies,' she explained. 'The Master wishes you to be his, and we've come early to train you to pull a sulky, obey commands, wear your harness elegantly, and recognise your driver's signals.'

Tamzin wanted to laugh, and yet as she looked at the leather restraints, her wrists and ankles seemed to have their own individual memory, responding to the idea of manacles. Her bottom stung and her clitoris jumped, and she began to wonder how it would feel to pull that delicately designed carriage.

Horses were such noble creatures. Had she not, as a small girl, sometimes galloped around, tossing her head, stamping pretend hooves? Why not try it for real? If there was any truth in the theory of reincarnation, might she not have been a wild horse with a wild mane, snorting, and pawing the ground?

Her stomach knotted and she suddenly wanted to feel a bit between her teeth, the kiss of the whip and the Master's hands controlling her movements.

Janice and Andy came in, eager to get into their roles. Janice was soon attired, her breasts projected through cut-outs, her bare buttocks swelling from under tight leather. There was a collar round her neck, and a wide belt round her waist, with metal loops attached to each side.

Andy wore a silver studded black leather choker and arm-bands, a chain linking the rings piercing his nipples and the one in his navel. A strap passed between his legs, supporting his balls and pushing his cock high, covered by a fringe. His head-dress was extravagant, adorned with metal discs and feathers and covering a splendid chestnut mane. This matched the flowing tail protruding from atop his anus.

'Well?' Inga said, her slanting eyes questioning Tamzin.

'OK. I'll give it a whirl,' she agreed, that heavy, lush feeling in her groin.

They undressed her carefully, as if she was indeed a thoroughbred filly, and then helped her into a waisted girth that covered her from lower belly to just below the ribs in front and had a corset-type back. A brow-band was fastened to her forehead, carrying three ostrich plumes for dramatic effect and she wore high heels.

A plaited leather bridle passed between her lips and teeth, and though she baulked at blinkers she found they gave her confidence. She could only see what was directly in front of her, and this made her less aware of being watched.

'I'll never remember everything,' she complained, trying to lift her feet high as a horse would. Her skin was stippled with goose-pimples due to the chilly air on naked breasts and pubes, and sheer unadulterated stage-fright.

She felt the pull of something behind her as Lance clipped the shafts in place. He took her hands and placed them there, supporting the weight which was negligible even when he mounted up. She tingled from head to foot, very aware of the filly crupper that went between her legs, its central vulval strap digging into her labia. With every movement it rubbed pleasantly, arousing her clitoris.

They took a turn round the stable. It was easier than Tamzin had imagined. 'Don't try to do anything off your own bat,' Inga shouted. 'You don't speak or use your hands, only to signal to your driver.'

'Obedience at all times,' Lance said, implementing this with a flick of the whip.

'You are allowed to lash out with your feet, rear up, neigh and make a fuss if anyone apart from your handler tries to touch you. We'll teach you the hand signals. Your trainer will see that you get water or go to the loo or whatever.'

After trotting up and down, Tamzin felt more confident. It was weird, but she was beginning to enter into the spirit of it, encouraged by her fellow ponies, Janice and Andy. Other participants were preparing themselves, though the blinkers made it impossible for her to see them. In the distance she could hear the sounds of people gathering round the exercise ring.

'Is my mare ready?' said a deep, male voice.

'She is, Master,' Inga answered.

Tamzin was aware of a presence near her head.

A hand patted her shoulder, smoothed her buttocks, adjusted a strap.

'You know what to do? How to signal?' he asked.

'Yes, Master.'

She felt him take his seat in the sulky, the weight balanced on the wheels, felt the pull on her mouth as his firm hands controlled the reins. She stood motionless between the shafts. I feel like an actress on opening night, she thought in panic. Oh, God, can I go on?

The double doors at the end of the stable were suddenly flung wide. Light poured in, and the heady uproar of an excited crowd. The reins twitched, and Tamzin tossed up her head and high-stepped out to face her audience.

Chapter Ten

As Tamzin floated down the grand staircase she admitted to herself that she was scared. This was far worse than facing the critical crowd of pony fanciers. That had been comparatively easy, once she'd got over her nerves. She had even enjoyed it, especially as her sulky had come first in one of the events.

But now she had been invited for cocktails in the bar with the Master, and he had promised to leave off his mask. Her chiffon gown billowed around her as she descended, every flounce cunningly designed by Tag. She smiled as she imagined his reaction when she told him what she had been doing.

When the games reached a riotous conclusion, she had

been led back to the stable. There the Master had fondled her breasts, moved aside the crupper and pushed his erection into her sex briefly, withdrawn it, pinned a rosette on her harness and told her she was a good little horse. Before vanishing he had asked her to meet him later. She had then been permitted to don her normal clothes and leave her equine persona behind.

Her heart beat rapidly as she reached the hall, her gown swishing over the mosaic floor as she went in the direction of the bar. Two men who stirred her to her very soul would both be present that night – the Master and Guy.

Several girls glided past her, escorted by impeccably dressed men. She recognised a tall brunette who had been a zebra in the games, and a short, plump blonde, last seen on all fours wearing the collar and lead of a dog.

And she was certain that two of the men had been pigs, wallowing in mud and being fed chocolate truffles, and another had pulled a chariot driven by the magnificently dominating Inga who had applied the whip without mercy. He had been unable to contain himself as the blows rained down, coming all over the sand.

'As my old auntie used to say,' Tamzin remarked

when she bumped into Janice, 'there's none so queer as folk.'

'*Vive la différence!*' Janice cried, in a high state of arousal, patted and petted and made much of by the racing fraternity. 'I told you Cheveral Court was unusual. Are you enjoying your stay?'

'Life will never be quite the same again.' Tamzin's eyes raked the crowded room, and fastened on the bulky figure seated at the bar. His broad back was turned towards her.

She weaved through the throng, noting the respect they accorded him, and her hackles rose at such sycophantic grovelling. Their eyes met in the mirror behind the optics, and hers slitted suspiciously.

'Good evening, Miss Lawrence,' he said, rising to his feet. 'Do you know who I am?'

She shook her head. 'I don't think so.'

His face was vaguely familiar, but she did not recall meeting him and was sure she would have remembered such a striking man. So big, dark and ugly-handsome with that aura of barely leashed power which men resent and women go mad over.

She frowned, while he raised her hand to his lips, not touching, just hovering. The sensation arrowed all the way up her arm, down her spine and into her womb. The crowd had retreated, obeying some tacit command and it was as if she was alone with the Master on a remote mountain top.

'Let me jog your memory,' he said, calmly reseating himself and ordering a martini for her. 'You did a scathing review of a film called The Edge. Do you remember it? I spoke to you on the phone and you continued to lambast my work. I saw you at a distance on two occasions and decided that you needed taming. My name is Orlando Thorne.'

Tamzin occupied the bar-stool next to him, achingly aware of his shoulder pressed close to hers and the proximity of his muscular thigh under the exquisitely tailored barathea trousers. He wore evening dress superbly, as masterful as when leather-clad.

'I remember the film, Mr Thorne. I didn't like it then and I see no reason to change my opinion,' she said levelly, though her inside churned and her nipples puckered.

'I'm not asking you to. And aren't you forgetting something? To you I'm not Mr Thorne, I'm the Master.'

'I think not.' She lifted her chin challengingly. 'That part of my education is over for the time being.'

'Is it?' His amber eyes widened and she could feel their hypnotic pull. 'Shall we put it to the test? Or are you afraid?'

He was clever, and she knew it, but allowed herself to accept his dare. Within a short time they were in his room, a spacious, splendid apartment. 'You knew I was expected at Cheveral Court?' she asked, the pieces of the puzzle slotting into place.

'Yes. Inga and Janice, Lance, too, are members of my sect.'

'And what is that? A religion? A cult?' She paced the carpet nervously, terribly conscious of the sexual energy emanating from his athletic body. Her inner thighs were wet with nectar, her clitoris responding to his maleness, her needy breasts tingling.

'Nothing so austere. A collection of people who enjoy experimenting with sensation.'

'I'll never forgive Janice for being so deceitful!' Tamzin raged. 'The lying bitch! And as for you, Mr Thorne—!'

He came closer, placed one large hand on her shoulder, the fingers performing a mantra on her bare skin. 'Don't blame her. She wanted you to share in the pleasures provided. And you've enjoyed it.'

Unable to help herself, she leaned towards him. 'I

suppose I have,' she admitted, anger dying to be replaced by desire.

His eyes burned into hers and his hand cradled her breast, thumb-pad seeking the taut tip beneath the chiffon. Tamzin gasped and her arms crept round his neck. He picked her up, and his voice held the purr of a tiger. 'You like relinquishing your will, don't you, Tamzin? Letting me be in charge.'

She could not deny it, feeling like a marionette with Orlando pulling her strings. He laid her on the bed, rolled her over and unzipped the dress, removing it and spreading it across a chair. Now she was naked apart from fragile hold-up stockings and high-heeled shoes.

He did not touch her immediately, standing by the side of the bed and admiring every part of her. 'You are so beautiful,' he murmured. 'I'd like to have you star in my next film. Will you do it? We shall be on location in Spain.'

'I can't act,' she protested, though flattered by his invitation and tempted by the venue.

'You'll learn,' he said, and fastened her wrists with silken cords to the posts each side of the headboard. Tamzin hadn't the strength to move or protest.

Her legs were spread and tied to the barley-sugar-twist

pillars at the foot. Orlando gazed at her and she was inspired by his hunger and carried away by his lust. Never had she been looked at in that way. It was as if he wanted to eat her. She drew in a sharp breath when he began to stroke her nipples, then bent and nuzzled his face in the soft, silky feathers of her pussy. She groaned as he opened her labia and found that tiny bud, sucking it strongly till she exploded into orgasm.

Then he rode her, unbuttoning and exposing his thick, hard penis. Her legs were open and tethered, forming no barrier as he eased his cock between her swollen sex-lips and inserted the head into her vagina. At first he only permitted the merest inch to penetrate her, then, gradually, worked the rest of it in until she was totally filled. Tamzin moaned her pleasure, threshing wildly till he gripped her head, held it still and plundered her mouth, his tongue as stiff and powerful as his prick.

She clenched her inner muscles, clasping them round his turgid weapon, suddenly determined to make it impossible for him to delay coming. He had thought to use her, had he? Well, it was her turn to use him.

He bucked, tried to pull out, could not summon the necessary will-power to fight the extreme pleasure she forced on him. Her mouth was open beneath his, her breasts grinding against his shirt-front, and her pussy clasped and unclasped in such regular spasms that he suddenly let go. Tamzin felt him swelling just that little bit more, and the heat as he released his seed.

He was her Master no more. Now they could meet on equal terms and they talked as they rested after coition. Though she did not actually agree to his proposal for acting, she promised to consider it. He, in turn, agreed to defend his work in an article for *Chimera*. Then she rose, put on her dress, backed up so he could zip it, tidied her hair and allowed him to return her to the party.

The first thing she heard was piano music, and little electric shocks ran up and down her back. Guy was there.

Damn him, she thought, I'm not having him ignore me!

The music salon was full, a very mixed bag indeed; some still wore pony garb, others were dressed in fantastic costumes, some had on long robes with hoods concealing their faces. A few had donned full evening dress. All were in a fret of excitement to which the rippling musical chords added an erotic counterpoint.

Tamzin, squashed at the back near the door, closed her eyes and surrendered to the sounds – Chopin, then

Liszt, and finally the atonality of Bartok. She focused on Guy, seated at the instrument, so swarthy and romantic, with his intense face and inward-turning gaze. It was as if he used the piano as foreplay.

Tamzin edged closer, till she was standing at the curved end of the black Steinway grand, looking down its highly polished length at him. When he had wrung the final resounding notes from the keys he stood up and bowed, almost contemptuously, to the enthusiastic crowd. She met his gaze, square on. His eyes blazed and his mouth clamped shut in a tight line.

Inga was hanging on his arm, and a gaggle of admirers enclosed him on each side, but he did not stop staring at Tamzin. She walked round the piano and right up to him, saying boldly, 'I want to talk to you.'

His beautiful mouth drew down in a sneer. 'I'll bet you do. What is it you want? A story for your paper?'

'That wasn't my intention when I was stranded in the snow.' Her head was high, her eyes shooting out green sparks.

He took her arm in his hard fingers and drew her into the conservatory, where the air was moist and fragrance rose from a hundred tropical blooms. He pressed her down on an ornamental ironwork seat, and sat beside her, eyes like spears as he said, 'Well, what have you to say for yourself?'

'Don't treat me like one of your besotted fans,' she exclaimed, anger rising though her pussy throbbed for him to possess it. 'You've behaved like a conceited, ignorant fool. I don't have to answer you.'

'Suit yourself,' he replied with a shrug, eyes moody. 'It was you who sought me out tonight, not the other way round.'

'All right. So I'm the editor-in-chief for *Chimera*, and proud of it. I would like to interview you, but that isn't the reason I made love with you. That was spontaneous, a need we both felt. And I wanted to see you again. I thought we had something going for us.'

He did not reply at once, flexing his long, strong fingers as if they ached from their recent use. Then he turned his handsome head and she was rendered breathless by the expression in those peat-black eyes.

'I thought so, too,' he said softly, and his accent was more marked. 'I was devastated when Inga told me about you. I felt betrayed, let down by a woman I had believed to be sincere.'

'I was sincere – I *am*,' she insisted, inching closer to him, daring to lay her hand on his broad shoulder. 'I don't

care if you never talk to *Chimera*, as long as we understand one another and continue to meet sometimes.'

She knew she should not be saying this, but the
thought of raw, physical, jouncing sex with him put her
in a frenzy. Never had a man appealed to her so much –
his romanticism, his talent, his stunning good looks fulfilling every heroic requirement.

'Can I trust you?' he said huskily, and took her hands
in his.

She nodded, unable to speak for the lump in her
throat.

Guy drew her with him as he stood up. Tamzin's
knees were shaking and she pressed her breasts to the
satin lapels of his evening jacket, and gripped his thigh
with hers, rubbing herself up and down on it. His face
blocked out the light as, with his hands at her waist, he
bent and found her mouth. His tongue, supple as a
snake, forked between her lips and tangled with her
own. She responded with fierce little jabs, moaning deep
in her throat, and his hands tightened, holding her to the
rigid line of his phallus.

She could feel it rising beneath his trousers, pressing
into her belly as he strained to get ever closer to her.
'Where can we go?' he whispered urgently.

'Fir Cottage,' she answered promptly, needing for them to be quite alone.

She fled upstairs to fetch a wrap and change into sensible boots. When she returned he was standing in the hall with a red-lined opera cloak slung over his shoulders, a white silk scarf and top hat.

They escaped without anyone noticing, as an exuberant joining of naked bodies was taking place in the swimming pool. Moonlight blasted everything blue-white, and stars sparkled frostily in an indigo sky as they covered the short distance. The cottage was a warm, blissful haven and Guy's old oak bedstead wide and solid enough for unlimited activity.

He undressed swiftly, his marvellous body stripped for her admiring eyes. Perfectly proportioned, there wasn't an inharmonious muscle, knot or sinew – just smooth, tanned skin rippling over well-developed flesh. He was lovely, and her heart sang. A beautiful man with a mighty, God-given gift for music. A man she could revere, maybe even love if she could ever bring herself to trust sufficiently.

She wriggled out of her gown and removed her stockings, wanting to be as naked as he – two pagans worshipping Pan. Lips sucking, sipping, they tasted the honeyed depths of each other's mouths. Breast to breast their nipples chafed and caressed. He released her, laid her back against the pillows, and she remained still under his searching glance over the clean lines of her, the concavity of her belly, the glossy darkness of her pussy, and the enticing cleft between.

As he leaned nearer, she bent her legs at the knee, thighs falling apart, the avenue widening, labia unfurling, her tiny, vital clitoris rising from its cowl. He sighed and she moved her hand over his stiff penis, its naked cap shining and red, already wet. She clasped it, rubbed it hard to make it even bigger. He slipped a finger into her vulva, wriggled it around, withdrew it and smoothed the moisture between her sex-lips and over the quivering bud.

He massaged it firmly. She jerked her hips and gasped. He reduced the pressure, leaving the clit-head and working his fingers round its stem, while she cried out her desire. Neatly, skilfully, he massaged each side, then flicked over it, toyed with it, while it thickened, reddened, grew, the membrane almost transparent, a gleaming gem in the depths of her treasure chest.

Tamzin's heart was thumping in unison with the pulse in her womb, waiting, anticipating, knowing he would not leave her stranded. Climax would come, as surely as day followed night, all the sweeter for this protracted play. Her eyes glazed. Her lips grew moist, matching her nether ones. Now she was climbing the highest peak. In control, she did not want it to end and placed her fingers over Guy's.

'Not quite yet,' she whispered urgently, pressing down to delay the spasm.

He smiled into her eyes, and she endured the delicious pleasure of her hand cupping his cock, gentle hand that moved slowly, examining his bare dome, tracing each ridge and prominent vein as if she was seeing with her fingertips. But she could not resist much longer. The feeling building up inside her was too intense. She wanted relief most desperately, telling herself that it did not matter – she could come and then get him to bring her off again. Whatever happened she must have it.

Guy lowered his head and wetted her pleasure point with saliva, his warm breath almost bringing her to completion. He licked her once and she moaned with pleasure, then his finger took over, trailing backwards and forwards over the lips of her sex.

'My clitoris!' she muttered, almost angrily. 'Touch it.'

'All right. Don't worry, darling.' And he carefully located the nub of erectile tissue and began the slow, stroking rhythm again.

Tamzin cried out in her extremity as hot waves poured through her, each one sharper, higher than the last. She was ascending. Oh ecstasy! Joy struck deep and she was there.

With a hand under her buttocks Guy held her off the mattress, widening her pulsating avenue and, at the moment of orgasm, sank a finger into her sex. Not his penis, and she was grateful, needing no distraction from that second of sheer bliss. As the tension relaxed, he enclosed her soaking sex with his hand and, as she lay full length, spread himself over her and eased his cock into her welcoming sheath.

She heaved against him. This was just right, this large object stretching and filling her, giving her inner muscles something on which to clench while the orgasmic ripples receded. He braced himself on straight arms, his head back, his face that of a tortured saint as his movements speeded up until at last he spent himself.

They lay together in the afterglow, he on his front and Tamzin beside him on her back, tight together shoulder to foot, with hands clasped as if to prevent escape. With her free hand she touched him carefully.

Face to one side, he squinted up at her, then changed position, saying, 'I always need a woman after I've given a recital.'

She chuckled, nudging her cheek into the bare, damp hollow of his shoulder, inhaling the fresh sweat of his efforts. 'I'd better make sure I'm always around.'

His arms tightened and his eyes expressed eagerness. 'Will you, Tamzin? Stay with me? Come on my concert tour. I need someone strong like you.'

She remained still, observing the lamplight making patterns on the low, beamed ceiling. 'I'm not sure. I have a career of my own.'

'Will you come if I promise to give you that interview?'

Oh dear, she thought. Now what am I going to do? He's quite the sexiest man I've ever met, and I could so easily sink myself in him, become his faithful shadow, organising his trips, smoothing the way, a buffer between his public, managers and agents. I have the skill to do it. But is it what I really want?

She raised herself on one elbow and brooded over him, brushing the tangled jet hair from his face and studying the perfection of those Slavic cheekbones and slanting black eyes. Such long, curling lashes and a mouth to die for.

He turned his head and licked her fingers, his arms crossing her back to pull her on to his chest, the wiry hair caressing her nipples. He was irresistible.

'I've never said this to a woman before,' he breathed in that husky, foreign voice. 'Marry me, Tamzin.'

She could feel herself drowning in the inky pools of his pupils, thrilled by this proposal. What hot-blooded woman could refuse such an offer? But even now she hesitated.

'Thank you, Guy. That's sweet of you, but I'll have to think about it.'

'You don't love me.' His lower lip drooped and his face was stormy.

'I didn't say that. This is rather a shock. I must have time to consider. Meanwhile, darling, there are so many nicer things to do than talk. Don't you agree?'

And her hand dipped down, enfolding his semi-erect prick so that it swelled and stood up, straight as a lance. Once again the magic began between them, two perfectly matched contenders on the battlefield of love, conflict escalating to a passionate crescendo.

*

'Isn't it sad to be leaving?' sighed Janice, wandering into Tamzin's bedroom next morning. 'Never mind, we'll treat ourselves to another session in a couple of months' time.'

'Will we?' Tamzin gave her a stern stare. 'There's no need to keep up the pretence. I know all about you and Orlando Thorne.'

Janice blushed to the roots of her burgundy hair. 'It wasn't only that. I really did want you to experience Cheveral Court. It hasn't been all bad, has it?'

Tamzin could never stay cross with the irrepressible Janice for long. 'Of course not,' she answered with a smile, closing the last of her suitcases and tucking Humphrey into her holdall, his head sticking out of the top. 'I've had a great time. Most enlightening.'

'And you've screwed your hero, Guy Ventura.' Janice perched on the window-seat like some gaudy morpho butterfly. 'Is he good in the sack? Tell all.'

Tamzin was disinclined to talk about the intimacies she shared with Guy. She had spent the night in his bed, and slept like a baby, waking happily to find herself still pressed to his naked body. Over breakfast he had said, 'Have you decided? Will you marry me?'

Tamzin, wearing one of his sweaters and a pair of

jeans with the legs rolled up, the waist pulled in with a belt, had considered him over the edge of her coffee cup. She didn't want to say no, nor yet commit herself irrevocably.

'I shall have to return to the office for a while, Guy, and put things in order. Maybe I can get away for the tour. Let's see how that goes, shall we? If we haven't driven each other up the wall by the end of it, then maybe we'll take the plunge.'

He had argued, taken her back to bed and done his damnedest to make her change her mind but Tamzin had remained adamant. She was looking forward to taking up the reins at *Chimera* once more, and a warm glow penetrated her inner being at the thought of seeing Mike again.

Janice rose and stretched her agile body. 'I feel so much slimmer and fitter,' she announced, and a grin lifted her damson-red lips. 'All that sexual activity as much as exercise, I suspect. My fanny feels beautifully used, so to speak. I shall miss that.'

'Not for long, I'll bet,' Tamzin opined with an answering smile, then added, 'I'm travelling to London with Guy.'

Janice gave her a knowing wink. 'Are you indeed? In

that case, I'll drive your car and take Alex. He's doing a travel programme for Channel Four, and I've said he can stay at my place.'

Arm in arm, they wandered down to the lounge. Kevlin had been detailed to fetch their luggage. Orlando was there, drinking coffee, casually attired in a dove-grey silk and wool suit. He beckoned Tamzin over, while Janice darted off in search of Alex.

'Have you come to a decision about the film?' Orlando asked, resting a hand on Tamzin's knee.

Despite herself, a shiver communicated itself to her pussy concealed beneath figure-hugging black trousers. 'Before I make up my mind, I must see what's happening with *Chimera*,' she replied, glancing at him from under her lashes.

Even now she was recalling the dark thrill of his treatment of her in the cellar, and how she had pulled him in the sulky, his pony, controlled by a bit between her teeth. She knew that one day she would long to repeat these sensations. There was a whole, fascinating, deviate world out there waiting to be discovered. She would certainly be keeping in touch with the Master.

She met Alex in the hall when searching for Inga and Lance. 'I'll see you in London,' he said, sleek-hipped in jeans and designer sweater. 'We'll set a time for my inter-view. Maybe we can discuss it over dinner?'

'I'd like that. Everyone in the office will be thrilled to hear that we are to do a feature on you. It won't be as painful as you think,' she smiled.

He slipped an arm round her waist and pulled her close. She remembered so much – Alex in the pool – Alex and herself enjoying lively, carefree sex together. Yes, she'd meet up with him in London and maybe repeat the experience.

'Why don't you come to Brazil when I go back?' he urged, lips curved in that cynical, lopsided smile. 'We could have tremendous fun. You could bring your camera and be a photo-journalist again. I know you'd like that. Sitting on your arse in an office isn't really your style, Tamzin.'

Maybe he understands me more than the others, Tamzin thought. Perhaps he's the man for me. There'd certainly never be a dull moment in Alex's company.

Lance and Inga were swimming under the stained-glass dome. They were naked, and Maria was sporting with them. Borg and Andy were lounging on the side, fingers trailing idly in the water, while Astrid swam several lengths with grim determination.

'I'm leaving soon,' Tamzin shouted above the splash of water. 'I've come to say goodbye.'

Inga mounted the steps, reaching for a towel to wrap round her elegant body. 'It's been wonderful having you, darling,' she said. 'I hope you're not angry because of our little deception.'

Tamzin shook her head. 'Not any more. I was put out in the beginning, but realise that it's been a learning experience for me. I've made my peace with Orlando, and he's going to write an article for the mag. Guy and Alex have agreed to interviews. I'll certainly come here again.'

'We'll look forward to that,' Lance chipped in, standing there naked, hands on hips, the water running off his compact body with that sizable penis nestled among crisp brown hair.

Tamzin realised that she had never quite tested it out, plenty of time for that in the future, even if she did become Mrs Guy Ventura.

'I'll bring Tag Pedra with me next time,' she promised Andy and Borg. 'You'll like him.'

Guy strode across the tiles from the direction of the conservatory, and her heart did a flip-over in her breast at the sight of him. He was so impressive in his black overcoat with the astrakhan collar, and a wide-brimmed black felt hat set at an angle on his long hair.

'Are you ready, Tamzin?' he asked in that authoritative voice.

She tucked her hand into the crook of his elbow, and with a final wave, walked out with him. Kevlin had just finished stowing their luggage in the boot and she stood on tiptoe to kiss his unshaven cheek. He grinned at her in that endearingly boyish way of his.

'Goodbye, miss,' he said. 'Safe journey. The snow's melting so you'll be all right.'

It was indeed a lovely day, the sun sparkling on the frost-covered walls and hedges, the snow slushy under the wheels as Guy's sports car glided out through the gates of the manor.

'Yours is a beautiful country,' he remarked, his hands resting on the wheel. They fascinated her, able to ring melody from the piano or caress her to climax. 'In this weather it reminds me of my home. I'm looking forward to taking you there. Our first child will be born on my father's demesne.'

Steady on, she thought. Aren't you jumping the gun a bit? Whoever said anything about children? At the same time it was comforting to hear someone else planning her future when she had been so used to organising everything for herself. But there was a possibility he might be too controlling and possessive. She wasn't sure about that.

They stopped to have lunch in an inn filled with old-world charm, and Guy was in raptures about the horse-brasses and roaring log fire in the hearth. He insisted they occupied a settle drawn close and ate roast beef and Yorkshire pudding. And all the time the tension was building between them so that when they finally reached her house, they started throwing off their clothes in the hall, giving her no time even to read the pile of mail her daily had laid on the table.

The bedroom was warm, the whole apartment smelling sweetly of fragrance. Her bed had been spread with clean sheets, and she luxuriated in being home, accompanied by a man she had never expected to screw in a hundred years.

He was lying by her now, and she could not resist bending over him to take the head of his cock in her mouth, sucking it expertly. He lifted her up and she felt herself melting, on the verge of losing her self-control. His mouth was warm and moist, but his kiss became hard, forcing his tongue between her teeth as if he would draw every breath from her body.

She felt her nipples hardening, aching for the touch of his mouth, his teeth, his hands. The liquid was pooling between her thighs. He held her firmly, rolling her on to her side, and his hands spread her legs apart. His head came down, hair falling over his face and she felt him tonguing her, searching for her clitoris.

He found it, licking gently, and knowing his impetuosity, she was delighted by that delicate touch, voluptuous pleasure swelling her lower lips. She luxuriated in the sensual bathing of his tongue. He probed her vulva with his fingers, finding her slick and wet, exploring the tight, slippery channel. He stroked her, using the same exquisite sensitivity and controlled passion as he did on the concert platform, fingers flexible and expert.

She slithered away from him, persuaded him on to his back and mounted him. His erect tool slid into her, and she rocked slightly, feeling it jab against the neck of her womb. He reached up and squeezed her breasts, teasing the rosy nipples into harder points. Tamzin gritted her teeth and tried to find the much needed friction on her clitoris, rubbing it against the wiry mass of his dense thicket.

He bucked beneath her, held her hips firmly and said huskily, 'Slow down or I shall come.'

She did not want to stop, fancied sending him over the edge before he was ready, demonstrating her power. Instead she lifted herself away from the hard shaft inside her and sat astride his face. He thrust out his tongue and ran it over her aching bud, bringing her to a swift climax.

Then she was flung on her back, and his hard cock was pounding into her, almost hurting her with the force of it, driving in, pulling out, intent on his own sensations. His movements became frenzied as he climaxed in long jerks.

Soaked in their mingled sweat and juices, Tamzin sprawled beside him, too languid to move a muscle. She could hear faint noises drifting in with the pale sunshine poking through the damask drapes – the rumble and roar of London traffic. It was good to be home.

The phone burred, and she reached out a lazy hand to lift the receiver. 'Hello, Tamzin. I'm ringing to ask you to come for a meal at my place tonight,' said Orlando, in that deep, tigerish voice.

'Sorry,' she murmured, aware that Guy was stirring, pressed against her, his cock-head nudging her side. 'I'm awfully tired. I'll ring you from the office tomorrow.'

No sooner had she put down the receiver than it rang

again. This time it was Mike. 'Welcome home,' he said, and she could imagine his sculpted face and sharp eyes. 'What about dinner? Are you free?'

'Totally wrecked, darling. I know it may sound strange, but Cheveral Court was exhausting. I'll see you at HQ in the morning. How is everything there?'

'Fine.'

'Good. Bye.'

The next call was from Alex. 'Hi. I'm at Janice's. When d'you want me for the interview?'

Tamzin named a time and hung up. Guy snuggled against her, more than half asleep. It gave her a warm, contented, cat-like feeling to have him there and to know he wanted her to belong to him, making a public commitment, but even so Tamzin lay for a long while thinking about her options.

Eventually, she got up and made a cup of tea, strolling back into the bedroom carrying it. Dressing-gown wrapped around her she considered the large man sleeping in her bed and felt that wobbly, pink blancmange sensation inside her. She lit a cigarette to steady herself.

Was ever a girl so spoilt for choice? Guy wanted to marry her. Orlando had offered her a film part. Alex needed her as his comrade on jungle treks. Mike? Ah,

Mike – she could practice on him all the SM tricks she had learned from the Master. Besides which there were her female lovers, those lovely, tender companions who lavished on her all the refined and sensual delights of Lesbos.

Tamzin stubbed out her cigarette, shrugged off her robe and eased back the duvet, sliding in beside Guy. There was no need for her to make up her mind just yet. She could enjoy them all, and her reputation would be enhanced by the interviews she had been promised by some of the most fascinating men on the circuit.

Particularly the one in her bed, and she slipped her arms round Guy and nuzzled into his neck, her hands beginning their familiar magic on his sleeping body. He moved, responded, and just for the moment she forgot everything but him.